A Most Unpleasant Picture

A Most Unpleasant Picture

Judith Alguire

Doug Whiteway, Editor

Signature
EDITIONS

Cover design by Doowah Design.
Photo of Judith Alguire by Taylor Studios, Kingston.

This book was printed on Ancient Forest Friendly paper.
Printed and bound in Canada by Hignell Printing Inc.

We acknowledge the support of the Canada Council for the Arts and the Manitoba Arts Council for our publishing program.

Library and Archives Canada Cataloguing in Publication

Alguire, Judith, author
        A most unpleasant picture / Judith Alguire.

Issued in print and electronic formats.
ISBN 978-1-927426-95-1 (paperback).--ISBN 978-1-927426-96-8 (epub)

        I. Title.

PS8551.L477M675 2016   C813'.54   C2016-904956-6
                                            C2016-904957-4

Signature Editions
P.O. Box 206, RPO Corydon, Winnipeg, Manitoba, R3M 3S7
www.signature-editions.com

To my kid sister, Carrie,
who has put up with me—most of the time—for sixty years

Chapter One

Several years before

Luella Pryce, a wealthy older lady and art collector, although not much of a connoisseur, is speaking to her friend Leonard Anderson about a proposed acquisition.

"Are you sure those examples of Cartwright will be a good acquisition, Leonard?"

He gave her a grave look. "If you don't buy them, Luella, I'm certain someone will snap them up."

She wavered. "Oh, dear, we can't have that."

Leonard waited patiently.

"You say it would be quite a coup to acquire these."

He controlled the impulse to scream. "All I can tell you, Luella, is that in years to come, as these are compared to his later works, they will stand in very good stead." He paused. "And the pencil sketches are included."

"Oh, I don't like those at all. They look like something a four-year-old did. If we get the oils, you can have the drawings."

He smiled. "Thank you, Luella."

She frowned at the paintings. "They seem a little primitive. They don't have that finished look of some of his later works."

He seized the moment. "And that is why you want these. Cartwright painted these in the full bloom of his creativity. Then he became popular." He shook his head, gave her a sad look. "I can't tell you what popularity does to the creative process."

She flicked him a glance that said he should.

"Some artists start painting what they think the public wants. They no longer paint for that most important audience of one."

Leonard waited for her to say *one what?*, gritting his teeth to control his tedium. He was fond of Luella. The old lady had been generous to him in so many ways. His main problem was usually gently spurning her coquetry, giving her the impression women just weren't his cup of tea, something she seemed to accept and not mind at all. It did put a crimp in his romantic life. But then art was his main passion. He satisfied his other needs discreetly. She usually accepted his judgments about paintings — at least about the investment value — without question. The problem here was that the pieces were small, barely ten by ten inches. Luella tended toward the large. He sometimes thought she chose painting like pieces of cake, something else she was rather fond of. Mostly she liked him and liked having him around. Her arm candy, she liked to call him.

He leaned forward, pointed over her shoulder. "Look at the fearlessness of the brush strokes. These are the work of an artist pouring his heart onto the canvas." He straightened. "Frankly, I find much of his later work…studied."

That was the magic word. She knew how he hated anything "studied." She nodded, gave him a sweet smile over her shoulder. "You know what's best, Leonard."

He smiled back, nodded diffidently. "It's my vocation, Luella."

"You're so smitten with them, Leonard, I'm surprised you didn't try to acquire them for yourself."

He raised his brows. "That would hardly be ethical, Luella. I was acting as your agent." Not to mention, he thought, that I expect you'll will the entire collection to me by and by.

She patted him on the arm, letting her hand linger. "The price is rather high."

"Not as high as it will be later."

"I guess that's true of everything."

He waited. Luella could be ridiculously cheap about things. Her house was full of treasures, yet she refused to get a proper alarm system, relying on an aged poodle that spent its days in a doghouse on the front lawn to raise the alarm. Her dogs were usually deaf. The house, although elegant, was dusty and ill kempt. She refused to have household staff, apart from an elderly cleaning lady who came in once a week, and a cook who prepared a week's worth of meals and delivered them frozen. She smoked like a chimney, something that made him cringe when he thought of her art collection. She was mostly interested in her clubs, lawn bowling, lawn tennis, croquet, which she played with malice, her patronage of the local art gallery, and her women's reading group, which she loved to preside over, boring everyone by reciting Tennyson badly.

"You will make sure they are properly authenticated," she said.

"Of course." As always, he did a second examination.

"Will they require cleaning?"

"They are in excellent condition," he said.

They would need cleaning many times over the years, he knew, if she continued to cover them with tar from her unfiltered Pall Malls. The thought made him wince. Although her collection was good, he had never developed an emotional attachment to most of the works. But these, the Cartwrights, were exquisite. They tugged at his artistic heart in a way no other painting had done in a very long time. The vibrancy of the colours, the finely controlled impetuosity of the brush strokes. It was as if the painter were driving a team of spirited horses along a narrow cliff road and barely managing to control them. What a shame Cartwright had lost that.

"You should consider getting a proper alarm system," he said finally.

She gave him an indulgent look. "Pepi will look after that."

Pepi, the latest poodle, was so old all of his teeth had fallen out. Leonard thought the only weapon at the dog's disposal was the foul-smelling gas he passed with disturbing regularity.

"Besides," Luella continued, "who could possibly sell my paintings on the island without everybody knowing about it?" She lowered her voice. "I practically own the chief of police."

The chief of police is easily owned, he thought.

"So that's it," she said. "Shall we stop at the club for a drink to celebrate?"

It wasn't a question but an edict. Another thing Luella was rather fond of was her liquor.

"And how is that nephew of yours? What's his name? Tigan? Timson?"

"Tibor," he responded. "Tibor is fine."

"You're doing a good job with him, Leonard."

"Thank you," he said. He wasn't doing anything with him, really, apart from providing him with a stimulating environment. But, at least, he was there. Tibor hadn't been left in the care of strangers while his parents gadded about, more interested in their society friends.

"It's not easy taking in an orphan," she said. "Especially one whose parents have died so violently. Airplane accident, wasn't it? Engine failure?"

"So they say," he murmured.

The Pleasant Inn, around the same time

Trevor Rudley headed toward the front door with a tub of mortar. Margaret accosted him as he passed the front desk.

"Rudley, where are you going with that?"

"To repair the base of the urn," he said.

"Shouldn't you get a professional to do that?" she asked.

"Nonsense. It's a simple do-it-yourself job."

If he does it himself, it will be far from simple, she thought.

"Why don't you get Mr. MacAvoy in?"

He crossed his eyes. "Margaret, he's the one who backed his truck into it in the first place."

"He didn't mean to."

"But he did." He ran a distracted hand through his hair. "He's as much of a nuisance as that brother of his. How could one family produce a catastrophic handyman and an irritating laundryman?"

"I don't know, Rudley." She paused. "I think we should consider getting a full-time repairman around here."

"Nonsense, Margaret, why would we need one of those? I can repair that urn to last a millennium." With that he went on out the door.

She watched him go. I believe he's getting a bald spot at the back of his head, she mused.

A few years later

Leonard locked himself into his studio and stared at the paintings in front of him. The subterfuge had started with his desire to keep a solicitous eye on the Cartwrights and ensure they remained in good condition. Then he decided the fate of the paintings would be best served if they remained with him. To what harm? Luella wouldn't know one painting from another. She was drinking more and her vision was getting worse. Not to mention the fact that, once Luella had acquired something, she paid little attention to it. That's how it started, at least. But, as he studied the paintings over and over, he came to the conclusion that the best way to ensure the safety of those vibrant colours and fluid lines was to copy them. He set out surreptitiously. He had always envied painters. He had entered art school with the dream of becoming one of the great masters, but the comments he had received from his mentors hinted — rather strongly — that his work was stiff and derivative. That it showed no creativity. They put it in a nicer way, of course: "Leonard, we believe you would derive more satisfaction and serve the art world better if you were to become a critic, an appraiser, a restorer." Anything, it seemed, but a creator.

He had followed their advice as a young man because he believed it to be true. He studied extensively and, over time, built a solid reputation as a critic, restorer and appraiser. For a long time, this life satisfied him. He got to hobnob with people with money and influence, and, in some way, could feel superior to the creators themselves. That changed when he began to spend extensive time with the Cartwrights, when he decided to protect them. After considerable trial and error making copies, he knew he had done it. He smiled as he studied his reproductions. They were equal to the best of the Cartwrights, those small, beautiful pieces that had sprung from the painter's freest and most heartfelt period. He had become Charles Cartwright.

He therefore felt no shame when he simply kept the originals and returned his copies to Luella. She barely looked at them except to say: "Wonderful job, Leonard." He suspected she would have said that if he had sprayed a mixture of bug juice and coonshit over them.

He stored the originals in a safe in his office. The combination he kept in his head. Tibor had grown into a rather cold, sullen, secretive young man and he did not trust him.

Leonard thought he was somewhat to blame for Tibor's lack of emotional development. He had attempted to cultivate his intellectual side without making an effort to probe deeper into Tibor's soul. He considered this in a theoretical way as he couldn't recall his parents probing his soul. He had to credit Sylvia, his long-time mistress, for nurturing his emotional side. He had no idea how to do the same for Tibor, especially as he grew older. One thing he had discerned about the young man was that he was like a shark in a sea of chum when he perceived weakness. Therefore, he tried to remain warm and interested and friendly without giving Tibor too much insight into his thoughts. Tibor had just one friend, a handsome but rather insecure young man named Bobby Frankes. Frankes had an abysmal education and he was poor. He had emigrated from England to St. Napoli in the British Virgin Islands when he was still a child to live with his grandfather who died when Frankes was fourteen. He was a good number two to Tibor.

None of this caused Leonard too many sleepless nights. Tibor would eventually strike out on his own, he believed, and, in the end, the situation with the Cartwrights would be resolved. Luella had hinted on many occasions that, on her demise, her art collection would be willed to him. Problem solved. He did not think she could last much longer given her lousy health habits. Not that he wished her ill. He was fond of her. But her death would tie up loose ends.

Margaret Rudley shook her head at the argument coming from down the hall. Rudley and the latest repair person were now engaged in a dispute about the upkeep of the baseboards. After another flurry of unpleasantries, Margaret heard a heavy tool hit what she hoped was the floor, and the latest repair person storm out. After a few minutes, Rudley appeared.

"Damn man," Rudley said. "He couldn't cut a board straight if his life depended on it."

"So you've fired him too."

"I did not fire him, Margaret. He quit." He set his jaw. "The man does not have the capacity for intellectual discussion."

Margaret shook her head. What Rudley needed was someone who would listen to what he had to say, then go about doing the job the way it should be done. She knew this worked. She had used this approach for years. She thought of the young man who worked at the feed store, how he was always smiling, never seemed phased by anything. Perhaps…

Although Leonard continued his routine — winter in St. Napoli, autumn in Europe, spring in England (he really did buy into the Browning thing), and, rarely in later years, summers in Canada — the Cartwrights were never far from his mind. He lived well, spent unwisely, and indulged Tibor financially to make up for a lack of emotional attention. Tibor did poorly in school once he reached his teenage years. His teachers described him as unmotivated; his tutors described him as sensitive and introspective, which Leonard took to mean cold and truculent. None of this bothered Leonard much. He was not emotionally invested in Tibor's success and knew that, with the money he had tucked away, he could guarantee his nephew at least a respectable living. He did not begrudge doing so. Tibor was generally well behaved and not too difficult to be around, probably because he knew what a will was and how easily it could be revoked.

There was someone in his life now, too, who brought him cheer and touched his emotional chords as no one had in a long time. Sylvia's daughter, Cerise. She had been ten years old when he first met her. A charming child, bright as a new penny, inquisitive. Also a bit of a charlatan. He often mused, fondly, that she would make a first-rate con artist. When Cerise was fifteen, Sylvia married a wealthy man who vacationed in St. Napoli and returned to Italy with him. He missed her; he missed Cerise more. Cerise had been sullen about moving to Italy. He was, therefore, not surprised when she showed up at his door a year later to announce she had had it with the villa outside of Florence — something to do with all of the old nuns at the religious school her parents had chosen for her — and was moving in with him. He contacted her mother in Italy and found she was quite comfortable with the arrangement, provided Cerise spent her summer vacations in Florence. Her mother agreed to send a stipend monthly to cover her expenses and stipulated that, when she turned eighteen, she would be on her own, unless she agreed to come home. And so, without the slightest effort on his own, he liked to say, he had acquired a family

In the meantime, he courted Luella assiduously. She was quite old now, deafer, drinking and smoking more. Her cats had died, something that did not bode well for the general condition of her house since rodents were now free to roam. More than one housekeeper had given up trying to keep things respectable and instead settled for a biweekly shovelling out. Luella did continue with her clubs, though. She was president of most of them, after all.

Then came the day. Leonard had gone to Luella's for tea as he often did afternoons, making his way up the hill from his house, a short five-minute walk away. They were sipping something called Madagascar Bomb and nibbling on lemon biscuits when Luella dropped another bomb.

"I've been thinking about the art collection lately," she said. "And I've come to a decision I think will please you."

He smiled. She was about to tell him she was donating the entire collection to him.

"I saw my lawyer this morning," she went on, "and I'm delighted to say I am donating the entire collection to the Luella Pryce Memorial Gallery."

He gaped at her.

"Well, it isn't the Luella Pryce Memorial Gallery now," she said, "but it will be by the time the paintings are ensconced. For now it will be the Luella Pryce Gallery, which I will fund. Building will begin as soon as we review the architect's plans."

Of course it would. Luella was the main patron and sat on the board of directors.

It was only his good breeding and silver tongue that saved him. "Why, Luella," he said, taking her hand, brushing his lips over the silky thin skin, "what a splendid plan. Not surprising, of course, given your record of generosity and leadership to this community."

She smiled. "I knew you would approve." She raised a finger. "Now, I haven't forgot you, of course, dear Leonard."

His ears pricked up.

"I have instructed that you are to be recognized on the plaque as the genius who assembled the collection."

"That's very gracious of you, Luella. I, of course, was merely a humble agent," he said modestly, all the time thinking that if he hadn't been the agent the collection would have been atrocious.

He sat smiling, occasionally sipping at his tea, while she went on about her plans for the gallery, the curtains, the floor coverings, the furnishings, his mind a muddle. When Luella finally shuffled off, he knew what would happen. The paintings would be taken to the gallery, which would call upon the services of its own curator and probably an expert on contract. And he knew that expert, because of his close relationship to Luella, would not be him.

After tea, he went home, went into his studio, locked the door, and ruminated. There was a simple solution, of course — in his opinion this sort of situation could always be solved by simple means. Unfortunately, the solution, although simple, was disagreeable. He could, for example, talk Luella into having him clean the Cartwrights again, then simply return the originals to her. The problem with this was twofold: he would lose them; she would destroy them, if only through lack of appreciation.

He moped about this for almost two weeks, all the time keeping a solicitous ear out for any hint of Luella's declining health. Finally, he decided he had just one option: Wait until Luella left the house, then steal the copies.

Stealing them shouldn't be too difficult, he thought, given Luella's nonexistent security system and her habit of going out and leaving the door unlocked, or, at least, a window open. And if he were caught, he could simply say he was concerned about Luella and decided to enter the house to check on her condition. This idea let him get one night of reasonably restful sleep. On waking, the idea seemed flawed. If he simply stole them, Luella would have the police onto it, and, as Luella suggested, she owned the chief of police. They would go over the entire island with a fine-tooth comb. The paintings would be a topic of intense interest to everyone from true-crime television producers to Interpol for decades, perhaps forever. He would probably be under intense scrutiny, if only because of his intimate history with Luella and the works in question. At least Cartwright had died a few years ago, of old age — as opposed to an exotic suicide fuelled by self-doubt, which would have increased the value of his work substantially — so he wouldn't be around for media interviews. There was only one solution: Luella's copies would have to be destroyed.

He sat back, sipping on his glass of wine. Destroying the copies would solve all of his problems. He would have the originals he so loved and no one would go looking for them. Now, how would he destroy them? Hurricane season was always a possibility, but the outcome would be uncertain. He set his jaw, swallowed painfully, a habit he had picked up after hearing Luella's plans for the gallery. He knew what had to be done. Luella's house, including the entire collection, would have to be burnt beyond recognition.

He told himself he wouldn't be doing anything wrong. Many of Luella's paintings, in spite of his advice, were not remarkable. She had a habit of fixating on the subject of the works instead of the execution. And he would have the most remarkable — the Cartwrights — saved in his own keeping. The idea of setting fire to Luella's house left him cold, however. He wasn't the criminal type; he would probably commit some sort of fatal error. He needed an accomplice. Someone who had the correct mindset, an amoral soul, someone who owed him one and would continue to owe him one.

Tibor was on the veranda with a sandwich and a glass of ale when Leonard approached, eating in his robotic way. He was whip-thin and already had a receding hairline, which Leonard often thought was the result of constant malicious plotting. Tibor never seemed to enjoy his food. Leonard wasn't entirely sure what he did enjoy. Leisure perhaps. One thing Leonard was sure of was that Tibor had no intention of working in a conventional way for a day in his life.

"Tibor," he began, "I have a proposition for you."

Tibor took a sip of ale, then set the glass aside.

"It'll be worth your while, of course," Leonard continued. When Tibor didn't respond, he added, "You have a good life, Tibor, not much is asked of you."

"I guess," Tibor responded indifferently.

"You're an adult now. Most guardians would expect that you would have pursued an education with the idea of finding a career and eventually supporting yourself. You haven't been pushed in that direction."

Tibor gave him a sullen look.

"I'm a different sort of man," Leonard continued, beginning to feel a little nervous at the enormity of his request. "I don't place any moral value in work and I wouldn't see you any differently if you chose to while away your time collecting lint." He didn't add that, as far as he could tell, all Tibor was doing was whiling away his time and would never make anything of himself.

Tibor nodded.

"I need you to set fire to Luella's house," Leonard said. *There, he'd said it.* His throat constricted.

Tibor's expression didn't change.

"It's for the best," Leonard continued idiotically. "The house is a public health hazard, dirty and full of debris. We'll wait for an evening Luella is assured to be out. The only thing that will suffer is the rats."

Tibor stared at him, forehead creased. "Why not just call in a cleaning crew or an exterminator?"

Leonard brushed the suggestion aside. "Luella wouldn't allow that."

"So what? When she dies, somebody'll shovel the place out."

"She's ruining the paintings," Leonard said without thinking.

Tibor looked at him as if he were insane. "So you want me to burn them instead."

Leonard took a deep breath. "No, that's not what I want."

"So you're going to take the paintings out first."

Leonard swallowed painfully. This was getting away from him. He stared at the wall past Tibor's shoulder. "No."

Tibor reached for his glass. "What's this really about?" he asked, peering at his uncle over the rim. "Do you get a chunk of the insurance money?"

Leonard worried his cuff button. "No."

Tibor took a long sip, then fixed Leonard with a triumphant smile. "You'd better come clean with me, Uncle Leonard, because I haven't done anything wrong, and you've tried to engage me in a criminal act."

"All right," Leonard said hoarsely. He took a few moments to compose himself, then explained his problem.

Tibor chuckled. "So you'd rather be jailed for arson than exposed as a fraud."

Leonard was silent.

"So," Tibor continued, "you made copies and sold the originals."

"No, I didn't sell the originals." Leonard regretted his words as soon as they were out of his mouth.

"But you're *going* to sell them."

"I haven't decided. It'd be a delicate transaction, you understand."

"You're going to have to," said Tibor. "And when you do, I want a big cut."

Leonard looked away. "Yes."

Tibor eyed him shrewdly. "If I'm going to stick my neck out, I want to see the paintings."

"Why?"

"How do I know you haven't already sold them?"

"I said I hadn't."

Tibor laughed. "And I should trust you since you're such an ethical man?"

Leonard got up heavily. "Come into the parlour and wait there." He went into his studio, removed the paintings from the safe and brought them to Tibor.

Tibor examined the paintings. "So the ones Luella had hanging in the dining room were the copies. The Cartwrights."

"Yes." Leonard returned the artwork to his studio, stood for a minute looking out over the garden to catch his breath, then returned to Tibor. "The way I see it," he said briskly, "is this. The job will be rather simple. The house is never completely locked and Luella is out to meetings on a regular schedule. I'll make sure to lift one of her half-smoked cigarettes from the ashtray. Simply light it and drop it into the wastepaper basket by her chair by the downstairs television. That place is so full of rubbish, it will go up like a match."

Tibor took a bite of his sandwich, chewed it slowly. "If it's that simple, why don't you do it?"

"Because I think you'd do it better," said Leonard, which was easy to say since he was telling the truth. "And I'm obliged to attend many of the events Luella does. If I don't show up, it'll seem suspicious in retrospect."

Tibor frowned.

"If worse comes to worse and you get caught," said Leonard, "you can say you were out of cigarettes and you knew Luella always had some scattered about. You went over, noticed she had a new large-screen television. You thought you'd take a look, lit a cigarette. You thought you'd put it out, but apparently there was still a spark." He smiled, pleased with his invention. "It was an accident. Why wouldn't the police believe that? What motive could you have?" He shrugged. "But you won't get caught, the investigators will think Luella dropped a cigarette into the wastepaper basket. Even she'll think she did. She's done it before and she is quite dotty."

Tibor shrugged. "And if you don't sell the paintings, what do I get?"

"You'll never have to work a day in your life and you'll inherit my estate."

"How can I trust you?"

Leonard smiled. "Because we're in this together. We'll have to trust each other."

Tibor fixed him with a long stare. "All right."

"Then it's done." He put a hand to his chest. "I think I'll lie down for a bit. I seem to have a touch of indigestion."

Leonard went into his studio, locked the door, and collapsed into his chair, exhausted. They were in this together — he and Tibor. He had a foreboding it was an arrangement he would come to regret.

Chapter Two

Leonard chose the fifteenth of April to carry out his plan. The fifteenth was the gala for the club, the place where Luella reigned and received the accolades of her subjects. He thought that Luella might have taken a cynical pleasure in the kowtowing earlier in her life. But, as the years passed, he realized she had actually come to believe in its sincerity. He regretted what had to be done because he knew the destruction of her ancestral home would be a severe blow to the old lady. But she had the money to re-establish herself. And if she had a heart attack because of the stress of the situation, then that would not be an unpleasant way to go.

He forced himself to tamp down the discomfort he felt at involving Tibor. Not that he believed he was corrupting the young man's morals. As far as he was concerned, there was nothing to corrupt. He didn't like the uncomfortable position of being subject to blackmail. But then he was already being blackmailed, albeit emotionally, by his young charge, and he had something on him too. He felt certain Tibor would not risk going to prison when keeping his mouth shut would be much more lucrative and a whole lot more pleasant.

The alternative — where Luella proudly presented her collection to the gallery and the Cartwrights were exposed as fraudulent — was simply too ghastly to contemplate.

That night, he dressed for the gala and left at his usual time. He did not usually escort Luella to these things as he liked to use the time before the event got underway to renew and reinforce his relationships with the important people in the art community and Luella was chronically late. Also, although the closeness of their relationship was well known in the community, he did not want to appear to be a complete lap dog. He realized what a good thing this arrangement was, as he wouldn't have to concoct some story to explain why she hadn't turned up on his arm.

Luella would arrive like a large steamship, breaking through the entrance and plowing into the crowd, parting it like the Red Sea. She did like the undivided attention of the assembled. Once she had made her entrance, he would, of course, hurry to her side, take her arm and guide her toward her seat at the head table before retiring to his seat off the platform. Much like a tugboat bringing a ship into harbour, he often thought. He did, however, escort her home, which pleased her because it made it look…well, as if he were taking her home.

He went over the plan with Tibor just before he left, standing in the foyer, dressed to the nines, turning his hat in his hands. "Any questions?" he added.

Tibor gave him a look that suggested he had plenty of questions that had nothing to do with the mission, then shook his head.

"She'll be gone by eight-fifteen," he finished. "If you have any doubt, take a walk through the house."

"What if she's still there?"

Leonard shrugged. "Just say you thought you heard someone scream as you were passing by and thought she might be in trouble."

Leonard left. Tibor checked his watch, then sat back. At eight-fifteen, he left the house and made his way to Luella's, creeping along the back paths. As he peered through a hole in the fence, he saw a car glide away. He checked his watch. The old lady was late getting away.

The house sat back from the road behind a tall, overgrown hedge. The portico was obscured with vines and incongruous red-and-white awnings. He glanced around to make sure he wasn't being observed, then tried the door. Locked. He tried the French window a few feet away. Unlocked. He slipped in.

The foyer was dimly lit, but the living room to the right was lit up like a Christmas tree. A television set blared out some inane game show. Tibor found the sound annoying, but decided against turning the set down. Although the noise made it almost impossible to hear other sounds, he realized if he cut the volume anyone who might happen to be in the house would notice. He entered the living room, reconnoitered briefly. The table beside the overstuffed chair contained an ashtray overflowing with butts. He also noted the decanter of spirits and its stopper lying on the floor beside the chair, with a glass drained and lying on its side.

He glanced toward the road again, saw nothing. He did a tour of the house, calling out in case the housekeeper had stayed late. The kitchen was empty. He mounted the stairs, at first carefully, then with full force, remembering what Leonard had said about his excuse for being in the house in case it wasn't empty. He glanced into each room as he passed, calling out occasionally. He stopped at what he guessed was the old lady's bedroom and looked in. The room was buried under a mountain of clothes, purses and hats, draped over chairs, hanging thick against closet doors. Leonard was right; the place would go up like a torch. A strong odour of cigarette smoke hung in the air.

He ran down the stairs, paused a moment in the dining room to glance at the fake Cartwrights. Uncle Leonard had done a good job, he thought. He shrugged, went into the living room. The wastepaper basket beside the chair was overflowing with wads of paper, old tissue and the odd apple core. He took the butt Leonard had purloined on a recent visit, slipped a disposable plastic cigarette holder over the end, took out his lighter and lit up. He inhaled deeply to make sure the cigarette had legs, then dropped it into the wastepaper basket. He waited until the refuse was flaming nicely above the rim of the basket, noting how it licked at the armchair and curled the fibres of the throw. From there, a short hop to the rugs, the dried flower arrangements, the heaps of newspapers, the curtains, the ancient flammable furniture, the paintings. He pocketed the cigarette holder and lighter and left by the back door, retracing his route home, dropping the lighter and holder down a sewer drain.

Leonard didn't notice Luella had failed to arrive right away. An art collector he considered a parvenu had cornered him and he was doing his best to be attentive. He told himself he didn't want to offend the man. He didn't mind the potential business angle — the man was rich after all — but he cringed inwardly about taking on another Luella with pedestrian tastes. He listened to the man, feigning interest, something he had become skilled at doing. At one point, he heard a kerfuffle over the polite murmur and delicate clinking of fine stemware and assumed a gaggle of guests had arrived simultaneously and were trying to sort out the order of entrance as dictated by their social status. But it proved to be nothing more than an accident at the coat rack in which two dowagers got their mink wraps entangled as they were removing them. He noticed one of the organizers glancing repeatedly at his watch. He checked his own. Luella was even later than usual. He supposed the organizer was concerned about delaying dinner but reluctant to proceed without Luella's presence. The organizer whispered to his assistant, who then slipped away.

The assistant went to telephone Luella and find out what was delaying her. He got a busy signal. He wondered what sort of phone call could possibly keep Luella away so long. Unless she had fallen asleep and knocked the phone off the hook. That would not surprise him. Luella was getting older and he had noticed an increased tendency for her to nod off. He decided to wait for another fifteen minutes, then send someone around to check the roadway in case her taxi had been in an accident, although he couldn't imagine any taxi driver daring to have a misfortune with her on board.

A few minutes later, a stricken-looking couple entered the hall. The man approached the organizer and whispered hoarsely, "Have you seen Miss Pryce?"

The organizer shook his head. "I assume she's been held up for some reason. We were just about to call her again."

"My wife and I just drove past on the lower road," the man said. "Her house is burning furiously."

"What?"

"It's in flames. We called the fire department. The pumpers were just getting out of the station when we arrived here."

The organizer went pale. "Oh, my."

"She's going to be very upset, isn't she?"

As it turned out, Luella was not in the least upset. Luella was as dead as a doornail. The door hung thick with clothes, which Tibor had assumed was simply an overflowing closet, was, in fact, the door of Luella's ensuite bathroom. Luella had drawn herself a nice bath with her favourite almond bubble bath and settled in with a bottle of sherry. Lulled by the hot water she had fallen asleep after the second glass. By the time the smoke alarm roused her from her groggy state it was too late. Her charred remains were discovered fused over the side of her antique cast-iron tub.

The old wooden house had gone up rather quickly. Everything, including Luella, was destroyed beyond recognition. The art community was crushed by the loss of so many great works. Most people in the community were appalled that such a thing could happen. The taxi driver was taken to task, but he pointed out that Luella was in the habit of calling a cab, and if it didn't arrive as quickly as she thought it should, calling another. The cabbie kept his job. The housekeeper who was scheduled to come in the next day opined that the place couldn't possibly be any more of a mess than usual.

As it turned out, no one had really liked Luella that much. She was extravagant with herself when she wanted to be and generous to her wealthier friends or favoured protégées, but inconsiderate and miserly with those of a lower station. The cab drivers and housekeeper were of a lower station. The fire department declared the whole affair an unfortunate accident by an older woman who had a habit of being careless with matches and cigarettes. This was not entirely a false assumption.

Leonard was stricken. Those who encountered him in the days after the incident thought him inconsolable. Poor Leonard, he and

Luella had been the closest of friends for years, they said, emphasizing the word *closest*. They also understood the anguish he felt over the loss of the art collection, most of which he had been instrumental in acquiring for Luella.

Luella left various bequests to her favourite institutions, generally those who would name a room after her or put up some sort of plaque or monument. She had no blood heirs. She left the housekeeper nothing. She left Leonard nothing. Apparently, Luella believed no one needed her money apart from the local topiary park, the library, and the art gallery — which of course got nothing. She also left a hefty sum for the study and preservation of an obscure tree frog. One wag noted that Luella had never shown the slightest use for the natural world and employed various poisons to keep it at bay and suggested she had made this bequest to show her contempt for those who thought they were more deserving of her money.

Leonard was relieved that Tibor had done his work discreetly and hadn't deviated from the plan. He was even prepared to believe that Tibor didn't know Luella was in the house. This left him, Leonard, free of suspicion. Of course, Leonard knew he would have to deal with Tibor one way or another for the rest of his life. But the rest of whose life, he would think at times and smile. He knew he didn't have it in him to do anything nefarious, but entertaining the possibility soothed his soul.

Trevor Rudley finally gave in to Margaret's petitions to give the young man at the feed store a trial, just in case Rudley might agree to take him on as a live-in. Rudley dutifully picked up the young man, whose name was Lloyd, in town and brought him out to fix a door. The damn thing, as he told Margaret, insisted upon scraping the floor in spite of his best efforts.

"Margaret" — Rudley appeared at the front desk, shaking his head — "do you think he ever bathes?"

"Oh, I'm sure he does."

"Well, I'm not," he said emphatically. "I don't know if we can have such a slovenly person around the inn."

"He's not slovenly, Rudley. His appearance is generally neat. He just doesn't bathe as often as you would like."

"He doesn't bathe as often as a billy goat would like."

"If he's good enough at fixing things, I will make sure he's properly turned out," said Margaret.

Rudley leaned over the desk. "It's not just that, Margaret. He gives me the willies. I have a feeling he just might snap and murder us in our sleep."

"Oh, I'm sure he won't, Rudley. He hasn't killed anyone that we know of, has he?"

"Not that I know of," Rudley admitted.

Lloyd appeared behind Rudley, causing him to shriek.

"You could have let me know you were behind me," he said.

"Like say *yoo hoo*?" Lloyd grinned.

"Yoo hoo would be fine. Stay here," Rudley directed. "I want to check your work."

"I'm sorry Mr. Rudley is so cranky today," said Margaret.

"Been cranky ever time I saw him," said Lloyd.

"Don't let it bother you, dear."

"Nope."

Rudley came back down the hall. "Good job," he barked. "You'll have to tell me how you did that so quickly and so well."

"Just have to know what you're doing," said Lloyd.

Rudley crossed his eyes.

"Rudley," Margaret intervened, "why don't you take Lloyd out to the boathouse and show him that part of the roof that needs fixing?"

Rudley sighed. "Come with me."

He took off down the steps, Lloyd travelling in his wake.

"You want me to fix that?"

Rudley skidded to a stop. "Fix what?"

Lloyd pointed to the urn. "That big cement planter."

"I fixed that some time ago. It'll be solid for decades."

"Looks like the mortar's getting thin." Lloyd grinned. "The whole thing could come crashing down. Just like Humpty Dumpty."

"Don't worry about that," said Rudley. "I fixed it myself. It's as solid as the Rock of Gibraltar."

Chapter Three

Leonard had always loved the Caribbean. Although he enjoyed April in England and autumn on the French Riviera with sojourns in Paris, St. Napoli was home. His parents had travelled widely, and, although they were born in Canada and carried Canadian passports, called no place home. His mother had cousins in British Columbia, although he had never met them. His father had spent his teenage years in Ottawa where his father was a civil servant. As a child and a young man, Leonard had often spent summers on an island in the Rideau system where his parents' friend Hiram had a cottage, usually in the company of servants. He had seldom had the opportunity to delve deeply into his parents' relationship to Hiram or engage them about their childhood or any other stage of their lives for that matter. They were always busy. He took their absences for granted.

He had enjoyed the cottage as a young person. Since he was Canadian himself, going to the cottage felt like going home. It was a nice place, one of the old white clapboard types with an upper veranda, not as opulent as many in the area but a good deal more charming. He liked Hiram, although he seemed rather secretive and strange. Hiram had advised him that the cottage was available to him whenever he wished to visit.

In the seven years following Luella's unfortunate death, Leonard travelled less. He spent one April in the Lake District and found it rainier than he remembered. Nor did St. Tropez charm him as it had in previous years; he found it drabber, the society less lively, louder, generally more annoying. So he spent most of his time on St. Napoli, mostly in his house, attending fewer social events. People were kind to him, believing he continued to grieve for Luella — which suited him, confirming that no one harboured suspicions about her death, even allowing him to imagine he was blameless. More and more, he came to mourn the destruction of his Cartwright reproductions, believing them to have been even better than the originals.

Days when the "children" were safely away, he would lock himself in his studio, remove the Cartwrights from the vault and attempt to recreate the grandeur of his wonderful copies, the ones that had burned with the unfortunate Luella and which now existed, he imagined, only in fragments of ash scattered wherever the winds could take them. Each time he came away disappointed — his fingers were showing signs of arthritis, the index fingers in particular, gnarled as old tree limbs. He would scrub his work out and consign the ruined canvases to the dustbin. But one summer day, he examined his newly finished work and felt the glow of triumph. He had done it. He stared at the copies juxtaposed against the originals. More beautiful, perhaps more beautiful than his original forgeries.

He removed his bifocals, hooked one wing into the corner of his mouth, let his gaze drift to the far wall. Everything was a blur. He guessed he had accomplished his feat in the nick of time. He replaced his glasses and took a closer look at the copies set on easels beside the originals. Only one thing was missing — a signature. He smiled, picked up a fine brush, dipped it into the black paint and added: C.A. Cartwright.

He put the brush down and did a little jig, then stopped as he felt some discomfort in his chest — a touch of angina for which he took the occasional GTN. Part of the diabetic profile, he supposed with chagrin. His doctor had recently diagnosed him as diabetic and had prescribed an oral medication. He took a deep breath. The angina eased. He went over to his sofa, lay down, and fell into a deep sleep.

He woke to find he was not alone in the room. Cerise was standing at the easel, her back to him, examining the works he had left uncovered to let the signature dry. He sat up with a start, his glasses falling to the floor.

She turned at the noise. "Sorry, Leonard, I didn't mean to wake you up."

He gasped, put a hand to his chest, feeling his heart racing.

"Do you need a nitro?" She glanced at his suit jacket hanging over the back of the chair.

"They're not there. They're in my coat in the hallway." He called her back as she started for the door. "No, I don't need one. You surprised me, that's all. How did you get in?"

She came to the sofa, gave him a kiss. "I picked the lock."

"Why didn't you just knock?"

"Well, I didn't know you were in here," she said. "You always keep the door locked. How would I know you were in here? You should put a sign up."

He shook his head. "You broke into my study and you're chiding me for not putting up a The Artist Is In sign?"

"Well, you should," she said. "Instead of making people feel bad about waking you up and almost giving you a heart attack." She wriggled into his lap. "Didn't you think about how I would feel if I had given you a heart attack?"

"I'm sure I would have felt worse."

"You would have been dead," she said.

He gave her a long look. "Do you know how much like your mother you are?"

She made a face.

"Your mother was one of the greatest con artists I've ever met," he said.

She smiled. "I kind of like that." She sat back to look at him. "How was she a con artist?"

He shrugged. He wasn't prepared to tell her that her mother could initiate a passionate kiss, then scold him for smearing her lipstick, leaving him feeling so guilty he would buy her a nice piece of jewellery. "She had you with another man, ran off with yet another man, and conned me into taking you," he said.

She smiled. "You wanted to take me."

"If you say so."

"I'm the sunshine of your life," she said. "If you want to think of our relationship in such a corny way."

"You are the bane of my existence. And," he added, "where did you develop your lock-picking expertise?"

She gave him an innocent look.

"Did Tibor teach you?"

She shook her head.

"Frankes?"

"No," she said, annoyed.

"Luther?" He mentioned the name of his cook-housekeeper.

"Tibor is an idiot, Frankes is a jerk, and Luther is a eunuch."

"Luther had an unfortunate childhood."

"As if I didn't," she said. When he failed to take the bait, she added, "I taught myself. I got a book from the library."

"I didn't know anyone had written such a book."

"It was a book about locks. I wanted to know the basic principles."

"So you could pick locks willy-nilly."

She frowned. "No, but when it was necessary."

He raised his brows. "And it was necessary to get into my studio."

"Well, what if you had locked yourself in — as you always do — and then had a heart attack?"

He sighed. "You are a rotten child."

She snuggled against him. "I am hardly a child."

He stirred uncomfortably. "You are still a child."

"Guido doesn't think so."

He pushed himself back and looked at her. "Is he still writing those love poems to you?"

"He's smitten with me. He's begging me to move back to Italy."

"And?" he asked, forcing himself to sound light and neutral.

"Too close to my mother," she said, "although he won't be in Italy much longer. He's moving to Montreal. Something about his father's business."

"The construction business, I imagine," he said dryly.

"So his father's a bit shady. He's a businessman. All businessmen are shady."

"If you say so."

"What about those paintings?" she asked unexpectedly.

He feigned surprise. "What about them?"

She stared across the room at the easel. "Well, you have four paintings. Two identical sets. One set looks older. Probably the original."

He shrugged, tried to appear casual. "Just some minor works I had around. I did the copies for my own interest." He wiggled his fingers. "Just to see if these still work."

She smiled. "Come on, Leonard, you taught me better than that."

"About what?" he asked innocently.

"The art business." She ran a finger over his lips. "The dark side."

And that, he thought, was a big mistake. "How would you like to go shopping?" he asked.

Her silence cost him a very expensive piece of jewellery. As he fastened the chain around her neck she said: "I think I'd like a parrot."

He sighed. "Happy birthday, sweetie."

At the Pleasant: Present Day

"Gregoire, this grocery list is getting out of hand." Rudley turned the list toward Gregoire, stabbed a finger at one of the items.

Gregoire pulled himself up to his full five feet three inches. "You cannot expect me to create fine food out of inferior ingredients."

Rudley nodded toward the dining room where Mr. and Mrs. Sawchuck were wolfing down a meal of fish and chips. "Most of our guests wouldn't know fine food from reheated squirrel's tail."

"That is all the more reason to educate their pedestrian palates."

Rudley crossed his eyes, reviewed the list. "You can have the real vanilla, but the saffron is out."

"I want the saffron, but the vanilla can go." Gregoire paused. "You will miss the superior flavour, of course, when I come to make your favourite chocolate fudge."

Rudley contemplated the taste of the impossibly rich, delicious fudge Gregoire had prepared the previous Christmas. "All right," he conceded. "But we'll have to scrimp on the quality of the cheese."

Gregoire's eyes flashed. "I need those cheeses to do honour to my sauces."

"Do them honour with an ode and Velveeta."

"I must have the proper cheeses." Gregoire removed his cap. "Otherwise I will take my culinary genius to a more reputable establishment."

"You won't find one of those in this neck of the woods!" Rudley let his head drop into his hands. Why him? There was nothing worse than losing a chef in the middle of the busiest season. One of the guests might be a food critic. The Pleasant could get a bad review; the Pleasant could lose its five-star rating. He considered this, twisting strands of hair between his hands. What if he got a good plain cook? Someone who was willing to take instruction without a thousand quibbles every time the inventory had to be reviewed. Someone who considered food preparation to be a job and not a higher calling like the priesthood or innkeeper. Then visions of Gregoire's creations tumbled through his head.

"You can have the cheeses," he said through laced fingers.

"Thank you." Gregoire turned and whisked back to the kitchen.

"I'm glad you gave in."

Rudley looked up to see Tim the waiter standing by the desk.

"Otherwise, I would have had to listen to his complaints for days on end," Tim finished and waltzed into the dining room, whistling.

Rudley shook his head. An impossible chef, an impudent waiter — he glanced out the window to where Lloyd was spreading unpasteurized sheep manure on the flower beds — and a handyman who smelled of sheep manure or vice versa. He noticed Tiffany the housekeeper trundling the laundry cart down the path, a book of poetry in her hand. A flower child who had developed the habit of finding dead bodies all over the place. He longed for the days when the only help was Melba Millotte, that scrawny old bat who generally followed his wishes, albeit with a strong touch of sarcasm, and the incompetent handymen hired on a contract basis who wrecked the place but were only around for short stays.

He sprawled across the desk, pulling once again at his hair. He was still in this posture when Margaret entered the lobby.

"It's no wonder you're going bald, Rudley," she said. "You must stop tearing at your hair."

He heaved himself up. "It's them, Margaret. The staff. Where did we get these people?"

"We found Lloyd at the feed store," she said. "The rest of them, we placed advertisements in the newspaper and hired them."

"How many applicants did you interview, Margaret?"

"We saw quite a few, Rudley."

"And these were the best you could get," he muttered.

"Now, Rudley, we have a first-rate staff and you know it." She didn't add that several other good applicants had been available but those chosen seemed to be the only ones with the capacity to put up with him.

"But why do they have to be so consistently, persistently aggravating?"

"Because they're like family, Rudley. Family is always aggravating."

He looked at her, bewildered. "Somehow that doesn't cheer me, Margaret."

"Perhaps I could pick you up something nice in the village." She gave him a peck on the cheek. "I'm off to get Aunt Pearl at the hair salon."

He watched her go, murmuring, "If you don't bring her back that would lift my spirits."

He didn't really mean that, of course. He was actually quite fond of Margaret's old auntie, in spite of her kleptomania, drinking habits, and appetite for all the older male guests — not to mention her cheating at cards.

He patted his hair down with one hand, straightened, and glanced out the window. Norman Phipps-Walker, a long-time regular guest, was out in his boat, several yards offshore, resting back on his pillow, his fishing line trailing in the water. He suspected Norman had long given up on the notion of catching fish; he wondered if he even had a lure on his line. He thought Norman simply enjoyed taking a nap, gently rocked by the waves.

Mr. Bole, another regular, stood on the shore gazing out across the lake, apparently deep in thought. Probably planning the next finger-puppet show, Rudley thought. The Easter production of *Spartacus* had been rather gruesome, especially when Mr. Bole decided to add fake blood to the production. He hoped he wouldn't be doing that again.

Tiffany came in at that moment.

"Back already?"

"I forgot the mail," she said. "Do we have anything for the Benson sisters?"

He reached under the desk. "Their copy of *Soldier of Fortune* is it, I believe."

She took the magazine, studied the figure in fatigues on the front. "I wonder why three elderly ladies want this piece of literature."

"They could be planning an attack on the tool shed," he said.

She shrugged. "They *are* getting bored."

Tiffany took the magazine and left. Rudley shook his head. The Benson sisters were ancient but showed no sign of acting their ages. They were living year-round in the Elm Pavilion now and had begun calling it their retirement home. Like the Sawchucks, they seemed timeless, never older, merely nuttier. He was not sorry they were bored. After years of trying to run an inn with dead bodies showing up and assorted emergency vehicles running around and those damn detectives, Brisbois and Creighton, poking around, he was due a year of boredom. He smiled a lopsided smile. Maybe this would be the year.

Chapter Four

Leonard was getting worried. Tibor was pressing for a bigger allowance, and when Leonard explained that the investment portfolio had
been performing poorly of late, Tibor brought up the issue of the
paintings.

"Those Cartwrights must be worth a pretty penny by now," he said.

"I suppose," said Leonard. Tibor had developed a keen interest in
the economics of the art market, especially the egregious sums paid for
paintings once the painter was dead, especially for newly discovered
older pieces.

"I imagine, as a set, they could bring a few million on the open
market," Tibor continued.

"They aren't worth a cent on the open market," said Leonard. "They
don't exist."

Tibor frowned.

"They were lost in a fire some years ago, as you may recall," said
Leonard, trying to keep his tone casual.

Tibor was silent for a moment, then said, "Then they're probably
worth more on the underground market."

"That will have to wait," Leonard murmured.

But Tibor's greed was not Leonard's only problem. Frankes had
virtually moved in, or, at least, seemed to be there every time Leonard
turned around. And Cerise, although she never pressured him or

made any threats, was proving to be more expensive than he had expected. She was indeed like her mother. Sylvia could wangle more things out of him than an anteater out of a termite hill, then leave him thinking he had come up with the idea of lavishing her with gifts all on his own. When he was younger, less encumbered, and anticipating a substantial legacy from Luella, he found this charming. The money from his investments should have provided him with a comfortable old age even without his patron's largesse. But supporting two — now, it seemed, three — adults in the manner to which they were not only accustomed but aspired to become accustomed was stretching him a bit. And what if their appetites continued to go unsatisfied? Then there was Luther. Although Luther remained innocent to the joys of acquisition, Leonard did feel a responsibility to ensure his cook-housekeeper was not taken advantage of after his demise.

If worse came to worst, there were always the Cartwrights. And although the prospect of parting with them pained him — something Tibor could never understand (Tibor understood only that selling the paintings was something that had to be approached cautiously and in good time) — if he stood on the brink of financial disaster, it would be done. He had been around the art world long enough to know how these things were accomplished although he himself had never been party to such transactions. He knew people. He hoped to put the day of reckoning off as long as possible.

Unfortunately, for Leonard that day arrived sooner than he had hoped. The investments his brokers had been so bullish about in the Asian markets suffered a catastrophic drop, and although he was not completely wiped out, his resources had dwindled to a point where he was forced to contemplate a more modest lifestyle. No more trips to the Riviera, no more flat in London, decanting to a more modest residence on St. Napoli. That is, if he could explain the economics of the situation to his difficult family members and gain their cooperation.

He broached the topic with Tibor. Tibor listened respectfully, hands folded in his lap, eyes on the carpet. When Leonard finished his belt-tightening speech, Tibor said simply: "It's time to sell the paintings."

Leonard fidgeted. "I would suggest it's still too soon."

Tibor replied calmly, "I think it's time." He sat back, gave Leonard a long look. "I saw a piece in the newspaper some time back, suggesting there was a collector in the hotel business who's pretty much addicted to Cartwrights. He's been snapping them up as if they were ice-cream sandwiches."

Leonard knew this of course. He didn't have to rely on newspaper pieces to know who was acquiring what in the art world. He wasn't sure of the taste of the hotelier, but he recognized his type: Someone who liked to acquire just for the sake of having something no one else had. He despised people like that, although, in this case, he might need them.

"There are always rumours like that floating around in the art world," he said dismissively.

Tibor gave him a hard look. "You owe me," he said, rising. He looked to be heading toward the door, but instead he turned and approached Leonard's chair. He leaned toward him and whispered in his ear, "Nobody will ever be able to prove I had anything to do with Luella getting burned to a crisp."

Leonard could feel Tibor's breath on his cheek.

"But you have the paintings, Leonard. Wouldn't that raise a lot of questions? If someone happened to call a tip line, I mean?"

It was eighty-five degrees in the islands but Leonard shivered.

Tibor patted Leonard on the shoulder, then left the room, closing the door behind him.

Leonard sat still for a long time after Tibor left. The day had come. He picked up the phone, dialled the number. "Dreyfus," he said when the man answered, "I wonder if you could join me for a drink at the club tomorrow?" After a few moments of small talk he hung up.

The die was cast.

The Pleasant Inn. 6:45 am

Trevor Rudley stood behind the front desk, bent over his morning paper, sipping at a cup of coffee, periodically nibbling at one of

Gregoire's delicious strawberry scones. He had to admit that Gregoire was a maestro in the kitchen in spite of his profligacy and tendency to be a prima donna. He was nibbling and sipping and feeling entirely merry when Tim approached the desk with a covered tray. He placed the tray in front of Rudley and removed the lid.

"Gregoire thought you might like to try his crepes Suzette."

"And what favour might Gregoire be angling for?" said Rudley, although his mouth was watering.

"Probably some secret, very expensive ingredient that he is trying to get you addicted to so you can't say no when he begins to put it on his inventory," said Tim. He glanced at his watch, then pointed to the wall clock. "Do you know what time it is?"

"What?" Rudley stared at the clock, then at his watch. "Damn." He abandoned his breakfast and bolted for the door. He had run down the steps and was searching the drive when the laundryman pulled in. Rudley ran in front of the truck, waving his arms. "Stop, you idiot!" he shouted. "Stop!"

The truck came to a halt. The laundryman got out and ambled over. "You seem to be in a state this morning, Rudley," he smiled. "That's not to say you are not usually in some sort of state."

"I wasn't expecting you so early."

"I'm right on time, Rudley."

Rudley galloped off behind the truck, searched the area behind it, then knelt and peered under it. He checked each tire, then stood up, relieved.

"Looking for your bullfrog," the laundryman observed.

"He's been here for years," Rudley hissed. "I'm not about to have him squashed under the tires of your truck."

The laundryman adjusted his glasses. "You know, Rudley, this may not be the same bullfrog. I've noticed he seems a little smaller."

"He's lost weight," Rudley rasped. "He's getting older."

"If you say so."

Rudley continued to scan the ground, then brightened. "There you are." He trotted across the lawn. The bullfrog was hopping toward the driveway. Unfortunately, Lloyd had just finished watering the plants.

The grass around the big cement planter was slick. Rudley slipped and slid into the base of the urn. The bowl toppled off the base and landed on his leg. Rudley shrieked.

The laundryman trotted over. "It's all right, Rudley, I headed him off toward the swamp." He leaned over Rudley, who lay writhing on the ground. "Did you hurt yourself?"

Leonard met Dreyfus at the club. They shared a drink, then wandered out onto the grounds.

"I understand your bank is involved in that new development on East Bay," Leonard began.

Dreyfus grinned. "Hoping to get in, Leonard? I thought you were with the antis."

Leonard shrugged. "You know how these things are."

"Everyone wants St. Napoli to remain pristine," Dreyfus said. "What can I do? I'm just a grubby capitalist."

"I'm not interested in the development," Leonard said. "I was hoping you might be able to arrange a meeting with Mr. Turner or his agent."

Dreyfus lit a cigarette. "I might. But why would he want to meet with you, Leonard? Not that you aren't perfectly charming."

"I have some Cartwright pencil sketches. I understand he's a collector."

"He is." Dreyfus gave him a sympathetic look. "Do you expect those pieces would bring much?"

Leonard didn't answer immediately. "You know how things are," he said finally.

"Yes, we're all in for a little belt-tightening," said Dreyfus. He clapped Leonard on the shoulder. "Mr. Turner will be here next week. I'm sure I can arrange an audience with his people."

Leonard left the meeting feeling uplifted. Dreyfus would make good. On his way home, he stopped by the bank, asked to be let into his safe-deposit box where he stored various documents and, occasionally, his most valuable pieces of jewelry when he travelled. He smiled.

The box was big enough for two small paintings. He walked home and had lunch with Luther. The young people were out. Probably up to no good, he thought with amusement, knowing he also had been up to no good.

The children came home around suppertime, first Tibor and Frankes, then Cerise. The grease on Frankes's tattooed arms announced he had been tinkering with the boat engine. Tibor's immaculate fingernails suggested he had been, as always, merely supervising. Cerise gave a typical response: Out nowhere, doing nothing. She was wearing a fetching sundress and smelled of cigar smoke, which meant she had been scandalizing the dowagers at the waterfront restaurant, sitting on the breakwater, smoking a big Cuban cigar, with Betty the parrot on her shoulder. She had taught Betty to call Tibor and Frankes "Tweek" and "Freak," to say "Papa Leonard" and to call her "Sweetie," which is what Leonard often called her. The young women would envy her chutzpah; the men of all ages would find her irresistible. He smiled. She was a lot like her mother.

"We're going to spend two or three months in Canada," he announced.

He could tell by their expressions they were not impressed. Saw images of freezing in the high Arctic or swatting blackflies as they slashed their way through dense brush. He let these impressions take hold for a while, taking satisfaction in their dismay, before adding, "We're going to a very nice cottage in southeastern Ontario. It belongs to a friend of mine. We can relax there and conduct business."

He saw Tibor's ears pick up when he heard the word *business*. Cerise gave him a calculating look. Frankes looked to Tibor for guidance and shrugged slightly.

"When are we leaving?" Tibor asked.

Leonard made a pretense of studying his daybook. "In two or three weeks."

"We'll get the boat ready," said Tibor.

"We won't be taking the boat," said Leonard. "We'll be flying into Ottawa."

Tibor scowled.

"It'll be easier this way," said Leonard. "I'm not sure if I want to deal with the three of you and Luther in close proximity for an ocean voyage."

"You can say that again," said Cerise.

Leonard gave her a wink.

They wandered off. Leonard sat back with a sigh, feeling somewhat reassured. No one had mutinied. Not so far.

"Rudley," Margaret chided, "you must stay quiet until the cast is set."

"And it will be six to eight weeks before your fracture is knit," said Gregoire. "And if you are not taking that long walk into my kitchen, it will probably heal even faster."

Tim tittered.

"And the doctor said you really should sit with your foot up until the swelling goes down," Margaret reminded him.

"What in hell does he know?" Rudley bellowed.

"He did study orthopedic medicine for eight years, Rudley." Margaret took an analgesic from the bottle and edged it toward his lips along with a glass of water. "Take this. You'll feel much better."

Rudley reached for the glass of whisky on the counter. "If I take them with this, I'll feel much better, much faster," he said.

"It says on the bottle not to take the pills with spirits," Margaret said.

He grimaced. "I'm in pain, Margaret."

"Said you should have let me fix that planter a long time ago," said Lloyd.

Rudley glowered. "Give me the pills."

Margaret popped them into his mouth. Before she could put the water in his hand, he grabbed the glass of whisky and downed them.

"When we have to call the ambulance to have your stomach pumped, I hope you will apologize to me, Rudley."

"If a man can't handle an ounce of whisky and a couple of aspirin, he's not much of a man."

"It was codeine, Rudley."

"Who in hell gave me codeine?"

"The doctor, Rudley. Have you ever considered reading a label?" She gave him a pat on the arm. "Now I have to go into the village for my hair appointment. Lloyd will look after you while I'm gone."

Lloyd grinned. "Won't leave your side for a minute."

Rudley looked stricken. "Where's Tiffany?"

"She's busy, Rudley. Besides, she hates seeing you in pain."

He looked mournful. "I hate seeing me in pain too, Margaret."

"I'll be back soon," she said.

Ten days later, Leonard stepped aboard a handsome yacht anchored in East Bay. He carried an attaché case. He was met by a skinny little man with deep black circles under his eyes.

"Mr. Evans?" Leonard offered his hand.

The man stared at him. "Yes." His eyes darted to the attaché case. "You have something for me?"

Leonard turned his back, placed the case on the table and took out the pencil sketches. He placed the sketches on the table and invited Evans to his side.

Evans scrutinized the sketches. "These are interesting," he said.

"Interesting?"

"Mr. Turner would be pleased to take them, of course, for a reasonable price."

Leonard named the price.

Evans frowned. "That seems high."

Leonard paused, as if in deep thought. "If you would meet my price on these, I have something else that might interest you." He opened the attaché case, took out some photographs.

Evans's eyes feasted on the photographs of the Cartwright oils. He inhaled sharply. "You have these?"

"Let's say I know where they can be had. I'm an agent," Leonard said casually. "Much like yourself."

Evans continued to stare at the paintings. "I'll need to consult with the presumptive buyer, of course, to determine his interest."

"Of course." Leonard returned the photographs to his case. "I'll be vacationing in Canada in a couple of weeks," he said. "I'd prefer to complete the transaction there." He lowered his voice. "People on St. Napoli are rather nosy and rather chatty, you understand, no matter how discreet one tries to be."

Mr. Evans nodded. "Where can I reach you?"

Leonard took out a slip of paper and wrote down the information. "I expect complete discretion, you understand."

"Of course."

They shook hands. Leonard climbed down into the motorboat awaiting him beside the yacht. He sat, head tilted back, pretending to be enjoying the breeze as the motorboat crossed the bay. Once he had disembarked, he sank down onto a park bench and began to sweat profusely. The first part of his plan was complete.

Chapter Five

Two weeks later

An unmarked car on the highway headed toward Brockton, the largest city near the Pleasant Inn. Detectives Michel Brisbois and Chester Creighton were driving to divisional headquarters. Neither man had spoken for the last mile.

Creighton broke the silence. "I wish people would stop driving into trees," he said. "It isn't good for the trees."

Brisbois didn't respond. He didn't care for Creighton's insensitivity, although he knew black humour was Creighton's way of coping with grisly scenes. Creighton liked to pretend nothing bothered him. Some day, he thought grimly, some day.

Brisbois planned to retire at the usual age; he had no plans of spending his retirement years, waking up in sweats from nightmares or sitting alone in the dark, brooding over his beer. He shifted to alleviate the stiffness in his lower back, an old injury from jumping into the lake to save his life. Mary had been talking a lot about post-traumatic stress lately. A retired police officer, an acquaintance of theirs, had recently committed suicide. The man's widow said he had been having nightmares where mutilated bodies called out to him for help. And he couldn't help. Brisbois told his wife not to worry. He acknowledged his feelings now and always talked them out with her. He had long ago realized that trying to protect Mary by keeping things from her was impossible. He thought about the accident scene they had just witnessed: dry road, good visibility, no skid marks. The car had hit the tree at a high rate of speed. Suicide by car. But why did the guy have to take his wife with him? He didn't realize he'd said this out loud until Creighton spoke.

"Maybe they'd been fighting. Maybe he was one of those guys with a lot of rage and no impulse control."

"Could be," said Brisbois.

"Maybe he'd found out she was fooling around on him."

"Hmm, well, we won't know until we get the report on the car and talk to the friends and family."

"Yeah, maybe we'll find a suicide note and that will wrap it up and make sure nothing throws a wrench into our vacations."

"I don't think that will happen."

They drove for a few minutes, then Brisbois said, "Have you decided what you're doing on your break?"

"Well, it's not the right time of year for hot places unless it's Las Vegas and I've never liked the Strip all that much." He grinned. "I mean after you've seen two thousand show girls you've seen them all."

"Without really seeing any of them," Brisbois countered.

Creighton laughed. "I haven't seen much of most of them but I have seen a lot of a few of them."

"You're a real card," said Brisbois. He couldn't fathom how a grown man with a responsible job could be as big an ass as Creighton in his personal life. Brisbois was twenty-one when he married his wife. He knew they would be married for life and that was it. Four children had followed in the succeeding years. He had always taken his marriage seriously. Marriage was a serious business. Raising children was a serious business. Both required a responsible adult to accomplish successfully. He firmly believed a man should grow up at some point. And there was Creighton still acting like a twenty-some bachelor when, in fact, he was nearing forty.

"How old are you?" he asked.

Creighton grinned. "Younger than you."

"Don't you think it's time you settled down?"

Creighton feigned surprise although they had had this conversation, in one way or another, many times over the years. "Why?"

"Marriage is good for you."

Creighton shook his head. "Marriage is good for you," he parroted. He pushed back his fedora, which gave him an older James Dean look. "God, you're gloomy today."

"I always feel gloomy when I see smashed glass and blood, not to mention body parts ground into spruce trees."

Creighton chuckled, then changed the subject. "You've got to admit the news on Rudley was worth a laugh."

The corners of Brisbois's lips turned up just a bit. They had received the news from Officer Vance when they arrived to investigate the accident. Officer Vance had had trouble keeping a straight face when he informed them that Rudley had broken his leg when he ran into an urn chasing a bullfrog across the front lawn. Margaret had called 911, Vance said, but in the excitement of the moment, failed to stay on the line long enough to specify ambulance, fire or police. The image of Rudley lying on the front lawn, cursing, while emergency vehicles screamed around him danced in Brisbois's head. He suppressed a chuckle. "I think it's inappropriate to laugh at a man's misfortune," he said.

"Vance said the funniest part was Lloyd standing there telling everybody he'd told Rudley he hadn't cemented the urn right."

"That urn's had a rough history. It got shot once, didn't it?"

"Sure did," said Creighton, pleased to see Brisbois's mood lighten. "And I think Rudley dinged it with a snow blower once and somebody backed a truck into it."

"How did the bullfrog make out?"

"Vance didn't say."

"I don't know why Rudley doesn't build that big frog its own little wildlife retreat with a fence around it. He's always in a fit about someone running over it."

"Yeah," said Creighton, "maybe a solarium to keep him cozy in winter."

"I think they burrow into the bottom of the lake."

Brisbois had known Rudley for quite a few years. Rudley could be rude, cantankerous, unreasonable, a general pain in the ass, but he figured a man who worried so much about an aging amphibian couldn't be all bad. He still couldn't understand how he had managed to persuade a sweet woman like Margaret to marry him. He turned his head to look out the window. He had never been unfaithful to Mary and never would but if he did…

He didn't realize he had been in reverie so long until Creighton spoke.

"A penny for your thoughts," said Creighton.

"Oh, just wondering what I would do on my vacation."

"I thought you were going to the cottage."

Brisbois had recently bought a cottage not far from the village of Middleton.

"Oh, I'm going to the cottage," he said, "but I might take a weekend to visit my parents in Sudbury. Maybe take the grandkids to a Blue Jays game." He turned to Creighton. "Why don't you spend some time at the cottage? It's got that nice little sleeping cabin with the bunk beds. Mary'd be glad to have you."

"Thanks," said Creighton. "That's really nice of you to ask."

"I mean it."

Creighton grinned. "I think bunk beds might put a crimp in my plans. Mary probably wouldn't be keen on that."

"Probably not."

"The idea of a cottage sounds good, though," Creighton said. "Maybe I'll rent one of those little efficiency units just outside Middleton."

"Suit yourself," said Brisbois. "We'll have to have you for supper a few times though."

"Sounds good," said Creighton. He sat back and listened while Brisbois went on about the herb garden he had planted at the cottage and how he used the plants in his cooking. It was good to get his partner's mind off the besmirched spruce trees.

The days before Leonard and his entourage left St. Napoli were largely uneventful as far as Leonard was concerned — contacting Hiram's agent, booking the flight, arranging for Betty's transportation. Betty was too tall to fit into an under-the-seat cage and hence required her own seat. Tibor groused that buying a seat for a parrot was a waste of money. Cerise countered that buying a seat for Tibor was a bigger waste. The two conducted a proxy war by teaching the parrot insults aimed at one another: Tweek is a twit, Frankes is a freak, Sweetie stinks. Tibor hated Betty, but Leonard thought he hated Cerise more. Sibling rivalry, he thought. He had no doubt that Tibor thought he favoured Cerise. So Tibor sulked, Cerise smirked. Frankes went with the flow. Luther went about his business, cheerful as always, apparently unfazed by the fractured family dynamic.

If Tibor hated Betty, Leonard did not mind her. As long as she didn't disgrace herself on him, he was willing to let her be.

So here they were on the island on Wood Lake just east of the village of Middleton. They had taken a flight to Ottawa and hired a car to the village. Hiram's agent met them at the dock in an ample boat, ferried them to the island, then went on his way.

Bringing the paintings had not been a problem. First, no one was looking for them. He simply wrapped them in birthday paper and wrote a card to Hiram: *Happy birthday, Hiram. I hope I'm not being too immodest making you a gift of my humble work. As they say, it's the thought that counts.* He wasn't overly concerned about the authorities, reasoning, if queried, he would simply say they were reproductions he had made for a friend who was fond of the artist but couldn't afford originals. Still, he was grateful when they cleared customs.

The deteriorating relationship between Cerise and the boys was a bit grating. On St. Napoli they had been able to avoid each other if they chose to. At the cottage this was difficult. Tibor was suspicious of Cerise's motives and suspected she was always up to something, plotting some new way to separate Leonard from his money, mainly, Leonard guessed, because he, Tibor, was up to something himself.

Leonard smiled. He was up to something as well. He had been preparing the ground the last few days on St. Napoli, nodding off during meals, smiling with a befuddled expression. He caught the young people looking at him curiously. Like many older people he had exhibited certain changes of late — trouble finding words was one that disturbed him the most, although he gathered it was somewhat normal, and in his case, partly the result of anxiety. But he sensed the children were becoming increasingly fractious and he thought he might buy a little peace and a little leeway by feigning a bit of dementia. Also, being viewed as dotty would come in handy if, as they say, the shit hit the fan.

"Maybe he had a heart attack," said Frankes. "My grandfather got confused after he had a heart attack."

The boys were talking outside his room, thinking he was asleep.

"No, he didn't have a heart attack," Tibor countered. "Haven't you noticed? He was acting dippy before we left. He wasn't that sharp before."

Leonard smiled. There were times when it was convenient to appear ignorant.

Cerise was the only one who seemed concerned.

"What's going on, Leonard?" she asked when they were alone.

He smiled. "Mustard, I guess."

She looked at him incredulously.

"Mustard goes on the hot dog," he said and smiled. "Maybe some relish."

She frowned, looked around to make sure the boys were out of earshot. "What are you up to, Leonard?"

"About six feet," he said.

She gave him a suspicious look. "Don't try to con me, Leonard."

He gave her a confused look, then winked.

Rudley sat in a chair behind the front desk, his leg up on a hassock topped with two firm pillows. He was feeling very hard done by. In this position he was not lord of the manor. People had to look over the desk to see him, as the Phipps-Walkers were doing now.

"How are you doing today, Rudley?" Geraldine asked.

Rudley stared up at her. He had never seen her from this vantage point. She loomed over him, a substantial woman dressed as if she were going on safari, her large bosom propping up a pair of binoculars.

Norman, her husband, hovered at her shoulder. Even he, although about half as big as his wife, seemed more imposing. With those buckteeth, Rudley thought, Norman looked like an enormous rat about to bite into a piece of cheese.

"Fine, Geraldine," he said, lowering his newspaper. "I've never been happier."

"It's a shame they had to change your cast so soon," Geraldine said. "I'm sure that will set you back."

"These things happen," said Rudley gloomily.

"They had to get the toothbrush out," said Lloyd, who was waiting his turn for Rudley's attention.

"Aha," said Geraldine, triumphant, "you were trying to scratch an itch. You should never use anything you can't guarantee you can pull out."

"The doctor said that, too," said Lloyd.

"You can leave," said Rudley.

"Can do," said Lloyd, "but got to tell you first there's a man out there who said I was to bring you a message."

"Yes, yes."

"He's got a tent on the lawn and he says that's his."

"What's his?"

"The lawn," Lloyd said.

"Well, I never," Rudley fumed. "What kind of idiot is he?"

"Says his name's Chief Longbow," said Lloyd. "Says the whole place is his, but he don't want to be greedy."

"Damn," said Rudley.

Chapter Six

"Where are you going, Rudley?" Margaret grabbed his arm as he struggled up on his crutches.

"Out, Margaret."

"You'll get your cast dirty."

"I'm sure it's dry by now." He beckoned to Lloyd. "You come with me."

"Yes'm."

"I'm going out to speak to this interloper and find out why he's laid claim to our property."

"Why don't you let me deal with that?"

"Because you'd end up ceding the whole place to him, Margaret. You're a generous woman." He paused. "We'll probably find out this man's just some loon who thinks you've booked him into a tent on the front lawn."

Margaret shook her head but let them go.

Rudley headed for the steps and would have fallen down them on his head if Lloyd hadn't grabbed his arm.

"You got to go slow until you know what you're doing," said Lloyd.

"Just stand by," said Rudley. He set off at a ridiculous pace across the lawn with Lloyd striding alongside him.

They arrived at the lower lawn adjacent the boathouse. A pup tent had been erected and a man was busy laying a circle of stones for a fire pit. He stood as they approached, a tall reed of a man with a cracked leather face and grey-green eyes. His long grey hair was braided under a battered grey felt hat. He wore a brown leather jacket, a blue plaid shirt and blue jeans. His feet were bound in splayed moccasins. He would have looked like any ordinary eccentric apart from the necklace of bear claws and the three grey and white feathers shoved into his hatband.

"Trevor Rudley," Rudley barked. "Owner and proprietor of this place."

The man grinned, displaying a set of yellowed teeth. "Chief Longbow," he replied. "Proprietor and owner of this place." He motioned to the area around the tent. "Didn't that young yokel tell you?" He indicated Lloyd.

"Now see here," Rudley spluttered.

"I'd invite you in," the chief said, "but as you can see, there isn't a lot of room in my tent."

Rudley surveyed the scene with rising bile. "I assure you, you are misinformed. You have pitched your tent on Pleasant property. I have the deed."

The man nodded amiably, took him by the elbow and eased him back a foot. "That's what they all say."

Rudley opened his mouth. No words came out.

"Now," said the man, "I don't want to be pushy. I have no plans to occupy any land beyond"— he glanced around —"ten feet on either side of my tent and the land the tent is pitched on, with water access, of course, and rights to the boathouse. I'm willing to let you use it. I know you need a place to put your canoes and motorboats in the winter months."

Rudley found his voice. "I can show you my deed."

The man smiled, shook his head. "What are deeds but empty words on paper? Kind of useless you know. As I said, I don't mean to be pushy. I'm agreeable to letting you remain on the land, conduct your business." He thought for a moment. "I could trade you for my rights to a piece of land on the DEW line." He shrugged. "It's contaminated with mercury and such but that won't matter for your purposes, will it? It's not as if you're farming or living off the land."

Rudley could only stare in disbelief.

The chief put a hand on Rudley's shoulder. "Don't worry, Mr. Rudley, I won't turf you out. Not for a while, at least. Landlord-tenant law being what it is." He paused, then added, "I haven't got my camp set up yet. I was wondering if I could get a cup of coffee from you."

Rudley gaped at him.

The man clapped him on the shoulder. "Much appreciated, of course. And maybe a couple of pieces of toast."

Rudley's ears turned red. He turned and poled back to the inn, cursing.

Margaret was at the desk, sorting the mail. Norman and Geraldine Phipps-Walker lingered nearby.

"You will not believe this, Margaret," he said once he could get a civil word out. "This man — Chief Longbow, he calls himself — has made claims on the Pleasant. He says he won't make us vacate, at least not right away, then has the audacity to ask for toast and coffee."

"Oh, I think we could do better than that, Rudley. Gregoire has some nice scones."

"Margaret, the man is implying we're on land not transferred by treaty."

She put a hand to her mouth. "Oh, Rudley, you don't suppose we're occupying sacred ground."

Rudley crossed his eyes. "Believe me, Margaret, there's nothing sacred about this place."

Norman grinned. "As you are probably aware, Rudley, the entire continent was his at one point. He probably thinks coffee and toast isn't too much in recompense."

"He's hinting he plans to turf us out at some point," Rudley barked.

Norman's expression sobered. "Do you think he'll allow us to fish the lake?"

Rudley crossed his eyes. "I don't know, Norman. We didn't get that far into the negotiations."

"You should sort that out," said Norman.

"Your regular guests will want to know," Geraldine chimed in. She paused and looked wistful. "You know, Rudley, before Europeans came, the sky was dark with passenger pigeons. That must have been beautiful."

"Unless you happened to be under them," Rudley grumbled.

"Keep us updated," Norman urged.

He and Geraldine went on into the dining room.

"What a damn mess," said Rudley.

"Sit down and put your leg up," Margaret urged. "We'll call Alan and have him look into the legalities. In the meantime, let's give Mr. Longbow a decent breakfast."

"Chief Longbow," Rudley said, deflated. He screamed as his leg slid off the hassock.

"Are you in pain?" Lloyd asked.

Rudley glared at him. "No, I'm practising for Music Hall." He let his crutches fall to the floor. They clattered against the desk and dropped. "Of course I'm in pain. Help me get my leg back up."

Lloyd took Rudley's leg and plopped it back onto the hassock, causing Rudley to scream again.

"Practising for Music Hall?" Lloyd asked hopefully.

"Go!" Rudley bellowed. "Now!"

When Lloyd left, he picked up one of the crutches and used it to snare the pack of cigarettes from the shelf under his desk. He took out one and lit up. Why did every summer have to start with some disaster? He and Margaret had been operating the inn for almost thirty years and it was the same damn thing every year: People coming here for the purpose of being murdered, flocking to his beautiful lakeside property to drown themselves in the lake, hang themselves from ski lifts, poison themselves with their own pills, not to mention the non-lethal accidents with powerboats, water skis, and toboggans. Not only was all that a nuisance, but it also involved having the police, the paramedics, and an assortment of nosy people around.

He took a deep drag from his cigarette. Now he had Chief Longbow showing up to make a land claim. He laughed mirthlessly. And Margaret was suggesting Alan, their half-assed lawyer, as a solution. He knew Alan. He was a gentle, well-meaning man who did a decent job with real estate, could write up a will and do the usual small-town things. Alan could spend the next twenty years trying to sort out the chief's claims, consult every law book in his office, and still not arrive at a solution. In fact, it could be worse. He could imagine Alan appearing one day, smiling with pride to say: "Rudley, I think I've found the problem. Your very distant ancestor Harmonious Rudley, a member of the King's Army and United Empire Loyalist, was granted this land. He didn't care for it so he granted it to an army buddy, the first Chief Longbow, and moved with his family to Galt, Ontario." Alan would close his law book with finality and say, "That explains the whole misunderstanding." Rudley clenched his teeth so hard he almost bit the cigarette filter in two. Why him? What did he do to deserve this?

"Mrs. Rudley will be disappointed to find you smoking."

He looked up to see Tiffany regarding him with reproach.

"I don't give a damn," he said.

"Feed Betty, feed Betty."

Leonard waved away the parrot, who was staring greedily at his morning fruit cup. "This is mine," he said. "I'm sure you have had or will have your own."

"Dirty bird," Betty squawked.

"Now, you know I'm not a dirty bird," he said.

She cocked her head, gave him an appraising look. "Dirty bird."

"Sweetie taught you that to say to Tweek and Freak," he said, making sure the boys weren't within earshot.

"Sweetie's a bitch."

Leonard shook his head. The boys were fighting back. They were adults. Why couldn't they behave themselves? He sighed. Adults acting like children. Tibor was miffed that the cottage didn't have a bigger motorboat. He and Frankes had found a set of hunting knives and were busy ruining the bark on a nice birch with target practice. Tibor was bothering him every day about the arrival of the art appraiser. How were they going to know he was legitimate? How could he be sure the appraiser wouldn't try to cheat them? Tibor's pestering gave Leonard a headache and drove him to use his dementia ploy to the point that even he wasn't sure if he were still *compos mentis.*

"Got to go, got to go."

"Yes," said Leonard absently to the parrot, "you've got to go."

"Got to go," Betty muttered. "Sweetie's got to go."

Leonard froze. "Did the boys say that?" he whispered, realizing how foolish it was to expect an answer. He took a piece of melon from his bowl and held it out to her.

She took it happily, then said, "Dirty bird."

Chapter Seven

By the sixth day, Leonard and his entourage had run out of good movies and fresh food — or at least what the children thought were good movies — and Tibor decided he and Frankes were going into the village. Leonard wasn't keen on this. Tibor had shaved his head out of sheer boredom and looked like one of the minor villains from an early James Bond flick.

"Where are you going?" he asked as Tibor grabbed his jacket.

Tibor looked at him with exasperation. "We're going into the village."

"What for?"

"To get lettuce, Leonard," Tibor growled. "I told you that."

"I think our friend might come today."

Tibor, his hand on the doorknob, turned back abruptly.

"Isn't someone coming to see us?" Leonard asked innocently. "I thought someone was coming to see us."

Tibor whispered something to Frankes. Frankes left. Tibor took off his jacket and sat down.

"Are you sure it's today?"

Leonard frowned. "I think so." He went over to the daybook. He spent a few minutes thumbing through the pages, then turned, triumphant. "Yes, today."

Tibor wasn't sure if Leonard had got the day right or not. For the past few days he had noticed changes in Leonard's mental state.

Sometimes he seemed quite befuddled; other times he seemed to grab memory out of thin air. This confounded Tibor but not Frankes.

"That's the way my grandpa was," he'd told Tibor. "You'd think he didn't know anything. He couldn't remember what he just ate, but then he'd remember some little thing you didn't think he'd even heard."

"Really?"

"Yeah, his girlfriend used to say it was because he had all this stuff in his head and it just spilled out, so it stood to reason that, every now and then, something made sense."

This made Tibor feel more confident that Leonard could be amenable to direction, and, at some point, controlled completely. He wasn't worried about Frankes. Frankes would tag after him and accept whatever crumbs came his way. Cerise was the problem, a conviction he was working to plant firmly in Leonard's diminishing brain.

"Do you want a drink?" he asked Leonard.

"A martini might go quite well," Leonard replied. "Dry with two pearl onions."

"I don't think we have any pearl onions."

"A single olive then. Do you think it's late enough in the day?"

"Sure," said Tibor. It was ten o'clock in the morning, a little early, Tibor thought, but that wasn't of concern. He wanted Leonard in a mellow mood. He made the drink, got himself a glass of ginger ale and sat down in the chair opposite him.

Leonard sampled the martini. "Nice," he said.

"I don't think you should trust her," he said.

"Trust who?" Leonard asked.

"Cerise." Tibor leaned toward his uncle. "I think she's up to something."

Leonard chuckled and patted his arm. "Of course she's up to something. She's a woman. You really should learn more about women, Tibor."

Tibor's eyes darkened. "It doesn't have anything to do with her being a woman, Leonard. I wouldn't trust her if she were a man."

Leonard looked at him blankly. "Who?"

"Cerise" — Tibor slammed his glass down — "pay attention, Leonard."

Leonard sat up straight, gave him a mock salute. "Aye, aye."

"She's up to something."

"Almost five feet," said Leonard.

"I think she sees this transaction as a chance at a big payday for her, Leonard. She'll probably try to wheedle you out of your money."

"Of course she will," Leonard said amiably. He leaned toward Tibor, whispered conspiratorially. "She's like her mother that way."

"I'm just saying we should be alert," Tibor persisted.

"I promise you," he whispered again, regarding Tibor solemnly, "I'll be alert."

Tibor tried to smile beneficently. The chances of Leonard being alert were slipping away every day. He was glad they were out of St. Napoli. What if he started babbling at the club? Sooner or later, someone would put two and two together. He hoped Frankes was right. The old man had had some kind of heart attack. Maybe if he let nature take its course… But Leonard was talking again:

"I'd like another of those martinis, Tibor."

"Sure." Tibor rose and went to the bar. He mixed the drink and was adding the olive when Leonard said: "Don't worry, Tibor, you're treated generously in my will."

Tibor set the drink in front of him.

"I'm leaving you my second-best bed." Leonard laughed uproariously.

If Tibor had been more familiar with William Shakespeare and had a sense of humour, he might have laughed too. He didn't, so he forced a smile.

"Guess I gotcha," said Leonard, continuing to chuckle to himself.

Or maybe nature could be helped along, thought Tibor.

Rudley was thumping around in the cupboard behind the desk, trying to forget about Chief Longbow, who had made himself quite at home in his little encampment. He now had a Coleman stove and an outdoor shower and Margaret had invited him to use the facilities in the inn. Rudley had to agree this was a better arrangement than a porta-potty or a camp toilet, which he was sure would completely destroy the ambiance of the Pleasant. He loved Margaret, thought she was a great girl, but did she have to be so damn kind, so accommodating, to everyone? He had complained about this to his father once, only to have his father retort that the girl had committed the ultimate charitable act in marrying him. Given that his father was not a man given to capricious wit, Rudley had rather resented the remark. Margaret had married him because he was charming, levelheaded, sensible, and the best dancer west of London, England. He would have done a little two-step behind the desk if he hadn't been carting around this damn cast. The thing had dried, although his foray down the lawn had added bits of dog hair, grass, spruce needles, and a few unfortunate spiders to the collage.

He was in the closet now searching for any papers that might challenge the chief's claim to the inn. Alan was making very little progress. The lawyer had contacted a classmate, an Algonquin woman. She had made some inquiries, but, to date, said she was having no luck tracking the individual who called himself Chief Longbow. She guessed he was not an official chief, although there was a possibility one of his ancestors might have been. Alan asked her if there was any record of the ownership of the land on which the Pleasant sat ever having belonged to the Algonquins. She had just raised her brows, Alan reported with a chuckle.

Rudley was relieved to hear from his brother, Alex, who had an interest in the family genealogy, that there was no record of any United Empire Loyalist Rudley ever residing in the area of the Pleasant Inn. Alex suggested, with a chortle, that the Rudley clan might have been run out of New York State on a rail and were, in fact, not Loyalists or Late Loyalists but common criminals. Rudley knew Alex was joking, but he was relieved to know no ancestor of his had given his land grant to the Chief's ancestors in a fit of benevolence. That, he thought, was the kind of thing Margaret would do.

He was ruminating about the downside of Margaret's compassion when someone gave the bell at the desk a sharp rap. He would have fallen over if he hadn't managed to catch hold of the cupboard door. He was cursing and hanging on for dear life when someone grabbed him from behind.

"We're sorry, Mr. Rudley. We didn't realize you were in a cast."

He looked over his shoulder to see Miss Miller waving to him from the desk. Mr. Simpson helped him to his chair, propped his leg up on the hassock, then collected his crutches.

"We didn't know you'd been injured," Miss Miller said. "We've been in Australia."

Rudley knew that. Mr. Simpson had taken a sabbatical at the University of Queensland. Miss Miller had amused herself by roaming the outback.

"Was it a motor accident?" Simpson asked.

Rudley shook his head. "I slipped on the lawn." He wasn't about to elaborate, knowing that Norman or Tim or Lloyd would fill them in at the earliest opportunity. He started to get up to sign them in, but Miss Miller waved him off.

"Don't worry, Mr. Rudley, we can check ourselves in. Mrs. Rudley will have booked us into our usual room."

"I'm sure she has."

"Perhaps the broken leg will be your last bit of bad luck for the season." Simpson gave him a hopeful smile.

"I could stand an uneventful summer," said Rudley, "although I don't see why I had to sacrifice my leg for it."

"I noticed someone has pitched a tent on the lawn," said Miss Miller. "Do you have children booked in?"

Rudley shook his head. "Nothing that dire, Miss Miller. Just a Chief Longbow claiming the lawn for his nation."

Miss Miller and Mr. Simpson looked at one another.

"Jolly good then," said Simpson. "Things are as usual."

Miss Miller and Mr. Simpson went on up to their room. Rudley sat back, his expression lugubrious.

Miss Miller and Mr. Simpson had been coming to the inn for several years now. They had, in fact, been married right there on the lawn, not far from where the chief had pitched his tent. Miss Miller was bright and sarcastic and confident. Mr. Simpson was sweet and kind and putty in her hands. Miss Miller was not in the slightest deterred by the Pleasant's reputation as murder central. In fact, she found the intrigue right up her alley and had been instrumental in solving several of the crimes. A blessing, he thought, since those two idiot detectives, Brisbois and Creighton, were so inept. Like the rest of the regulars, Miss Miller and Mr. Simpson felt entirely at home at the Pleasant. In fact, he thought, they all acted as if they were major shareholders. He was distracted from his ruminations by Tim's coming out of the dining room and heading toward the veranda with a trolley laden with food.

"Where are you going with that?" he bellowed.

"It's for the Benson sisters," Tim replied.

"Oh," said Rudley, deflated. "I thought you were trucking that down to the chief."

"Don't worry about the chief," said Tim. "The sisters are having him for brunch." He gave Rudley a cheeky look and whipped out the door, whistling.

Rudley watched Tim's head bob as he descended the steps. He hated being stuck behind this damn desk, barely able to see over the top, with Margaret or Lloyd or Tiffany or any one of several guests coming by and chiding him the moment they saw him standing. Sitting made him feel small and inconsequential and totally out of control.

"Yoo hoo, where are you, Rudley?"

He craned his neck to see Aunt Pearl tottering into the lobby.

"I'm here," he shouted.

"Oh." She came to the desk and looked over. "I was just having a chat with Chief Longbow. He's a charming man. So handsome."

He studied her face, noting the extra bit of rouge and the liberal amount of her favourite lipstick, Scarlet Temptress. "I see you're trying to get your clutches on him."

"He is a charming man," she said again.

"I hate to tell you this, Pearl, but you may have some competition from the Benson sisters. They're having him to brunch."

She smirked. "Oh, Rudley, I have so much more to offer than crumpets."

Aunt Pearl headed toward the kitchen. Rudley considered the situation. The chief, he concluded, won't know what hit him.

Tibor was sitting at the table, glancing occasionally at Leonard, who had fallen asleep in his chair. He was about to get Luther to make him an omelet when he heard a motor outside. He went to the window and watched as a boat drew alongside the pier. A man stepped out, tied the boat and reached into it for a bag.

And who should be strolling down the dock at that very moment? Tibor gritted his teeth. "Cerise," he hissed.

Chapter Eight

"What's the matter?" Leonard asked as Tibor stepped back from the window, cursing.

"We've got a visitor."

Leonard smiled. "Well, I guess we should be hospitable, Luther," he called over his shoulder. "Would you put together a tray?" he asked when Luther appeared. "We have someone for elevenses."

Luther nodded. Elevenses meant a selection of small sandwiches, fruits and, of course, petit fours and assorted pastries. Leonard was well schooled in the customs of St. Napoli.

"I don't know what that's for," Tibor sniffed. "This is a business transaction. And not a civilized one at that."

"A gentleman is a gentleman even if he's up to his neck in it," Leonard murmured. He affected confusion. "Who did you say we had invited?"

Tibor flicked his uncle an exasperated glance. Was he about to go on one of his walkabouts? He took three quick steps to Leonard's side, knelt down and said, "This is not the time to go queer on me, Leonard. This man is here to seal the deal on the Cartwrights."

Leonard feigned surprise. "Oh," he said, "I didn't know." He winked. "I'll try to behave."

"And is that damn parrot locked up? We don't need her in here shitting in the watercress."

"Mind your language, Tweek," Leonard said solemnly.

Tibor gritted his teeth in disgust but the door was opening. Cerise entered, a slight man with dark circles under his eyes in tow. The man was wearing khakis and a windbreaker over a sport shirt. He carried a backpack over his shoulder. He introduced himself to Tibor as William Evans, then turned his attention to Leonard.

"Mr. Anderson," he said to Leonard, "I believe we have some business to conduct."

"Indeed," said Leonard, "but perhaps we could have some refreshments first."

Evans nodded and took a seat as Luther wheeled in a tea trolley topped with a pitcher of lemonade. He poured two glasses. Leonard took one of them and raised it. "To business."

Evans smiled.

Tibor cursed inwardly as he hurried to find a glass of his own.

Rudley was at the desk, balancing himself on one crutch while he worked a plastic ruler down the side of his cast. He hadn't tried such a manoeuvre since the toothbrush incident, but the itching was driving him crazy. Margaret would be appalled if she saw him, but what could he do? His guests needed not only his undivided attention but also his customary unfailing good humour and grace. As he concentrated on gripping the slippery ruler between his middle and index fingers so he could stretch and get to the desired spot, he wondered why these boobs couldn't design a cast with a little brush built right in or, at least, allow enough room to get a hand down when necessary. That's the problem with the health care system, he ruminated, no spirit for adventure and innovation. He had barely reached the spot when Lloyd appeared without warning — as he was wont to do — and startled him.

"Damn," said Rudley as the ruler slid from his fingers. He lost his balance and lurched forward on to the desk.

"I guess I was supposed to say yoo hoo," said Lloyd.

"Now you've done it," said Rudley, red-faced. "Now you'll have to help me get this ruler out of here."

"Is it the metal one?"

"No, it isn't," Rudley growled.

" 'Cause if it was the metal one, I could scoot a little magnet down on a string and fetch it back."

"It's the plastic one."

"I could put something hot down and melt it and it would catch on," said Lloyd.

Rudley bit down hard on his lip to keep himself from hitting Lloyd with a crutch. "You aren't putting anything hot down my cast," he seethed. "Now what in hell do you want?"

"The chief wants to talk to you."

"Tell the chief to drag his ass up here if he wants to talk to me."

"Can't do. Says you need to come there seeing as how he's had a vision and doesn't want it to get away."

Rudley crossed his eyes.

They finished their lunch.

"Could I interest you in a liqueur and perhaps a fine cigar?" Leonard asked.

Evans gave him a short smile. "No, thank you." He checked his watch. "I'd really like to get down to business."

"Oh," said Leonard. He put on a befuddled expression, aware of Tibor cringing as he added, "What business?"

The visitor stared. "The paintings."

"Oh, yes," Leonard said amiably. "I'm always happy to talk about the paintings." He put a hand on the arm of his chair to rise.

"I'll get them," said Tibor. He left, returning with the suitcase.

"Perhaps you'd like to see them at my desk," Leonard suggested. "The light's good there. We'll wait here," he added, as Tibor seemed ready to hover over the man.

Cerise drifted over to the window overlooking the back lawn. Tibor stood at the far wall, hands behind his back, his eyes glued on the appraiser bent over the desk. Leonard sipped at the remains of his tea, smiling, gazing myopically at the far wall. For a time all that could be heard was the light tinkle of china as Luther cleaned up the kitchen.

Evans straightened, paused, then bent again and moved his magnifying glass over the paintings. Finally, he turned back to them. He tucked the magnifying glass back into its case, put his case into his bag and zipped it up. His face wore a perplexed expression.

"These paintings are reproductions," he said.

Cerise snickered.

The muscles in Tibor's face tightened. "What are you trying to get away with?"

Evans shrugged. "I'm not trying to get away with anything. I came here to recommend the purchase of some early Cartwrights. These are reproductions. Good ones but still reproductions."

"Reproductions?" Leonard asked innocently.

"It's the signature," Evans said. "I've studied Cartwright extensively. "The bar on the first *t* in his signature is always off centre." He shrugged and continued, "I suppose you could get a few dollars for these at a garage sale," adding with a sniff, "We'll probably be seeing them someday on *Antiques Roadshow* where the experts would point out that very same thing."

Tibor took a step toward Evans, controlling himself with difficulty. "I don't know what kind of scam this is," he rasped.

"I don't know how this could happen," Leonard murmured.

"My client will be disappointed," Evans said, lifting his backpack over this shoulder, "but at least he won't be the victim of fraud."

Tibor stared after him as he returned to his boat.

Leonard called toward the kitchen. "Luther, *Luther*. Do we have any more tea?" he asked when Luther appeared in the doorway. "Perhaps some more of those little cakes?"

Luther smiled and ducked back into the kitchen. Leonard noted Cerise had disappeared.

Tibor bounded across the room and hovered over Leonard. "What in hell happened? You're the one who authenticated them in the first place."

Leonard looked at him, puzzled.

"Listen to me," Tibor commanded. "I know you've been a little squirrelly lately, but you remember what went on with the Cartwrights. You bought them for Luella."

"Yes, I did."

"And you verified they were the Cartwrights."

"Yes."

"And now they're not."

Leonard put a hand on his forehead.

Luther came out of the kitchen with a plate of desserts. Tibor grabbed the plate, plunked it down on the table behind him, and shooed Luther away.

"I don't know," Leonard said. "Maybe they were the wrong ones."

"We know they were the wrong ones," Tibor said, gesturing impatiently at the paintings.

"I must have returned the wrong ones to Luella."

Tibor's forehead crimped.

"My copies were good," Leonard insisted. "They were every bit as good as the originals. I had studied the Cartwrights so painstakingly. I knew every brushstroke, every nuance of colour. I knew that man's soul better than I knew my own." His mouth fell open. "I must have given Luella the originals."

"You had me burn down Luella's house with the *originals* in it?"

"I could have. I don't know," Leonard dithered. "Mine were incredibly good," he protested. "I must have made a mistake." He paused. "Or maybe the ones I authenticated for Luella were also reproductions."

"You were the expert, Leonard," Tibor rasped. "You had to know what you had."

"You would think so, wouldn't you? Would you pass me those cakes, please?"

Tibor grabbed the plate and thrust it toward him. It landed in Leonard's lap, but, fortunately, right side up. Leonard selected a petit four, bit into it and smiled with pleasure. Luther certainly knew how to cook.

Tibor was down at the dock when Frankes finally returned from Middleton.

"What kept you so long?" Tibor demanded.

"I got the stuff," Frankes responded petulantly. "I just wanted to look around a bit. We've been holed up here for a week."

"So you got lost in the big city."

"It wasn't very big. Just a main street and a dock. But it was better than hanging around here."

Tibor was prepared to harangue him further, but decided it wasn't worth it. "Doesn't matter," he muttered.

Frankes hauled the bags out of the boat. "I got beer."

"Good, good," said Tibor without interest.

"Did that guy come yet?" Frankes asked. "About the paintings?"

"Yeah," Tibor snapped. "He did. He said they were fakes and he wouldn't give us anything."

Frankes eyes widened. "You're kidding."

"No."

Frankes narrowed his eyes. "Are you trying to pull one on me? You're just saying this so I don't get my share."

"Nobody's getting anything." Tibor grabbed one of the bags as it started to slip from Frankes's arm.

"How do I know that?"

"Because the goddamned things are still here. He wouldn't take them because they weren't any good."

He listened as Frankes cursed, though he didn't know why the man cared. It wasn't as if Frankes's share was going to be very much.

Tibor's thoughts coursed. Maybe, given the state of his mind, Leonard had brought the wrong ones. Maybe he had made copies. He'd done that before, after all. Maybe he'd never had the originals. He thought of Cerise's little smirk as she had turned away. Maybe the real ones were still on St. Napoli. Maybe Cerise had filched them. Maybe she had made her own deal with the buyer when she'd had that little conversation with him down at the dock. Maybe she and Leonard were pulling a trick on him so he wouldn't get his share. Cerise always could wrap Leonard around her little finger. Tibor gritted his teeth. Nobody was going to cheat him.

Rudley made his way to the pup tent on his crutches, his arms pump-ing furiously. Lloyd loped along beside him, telling him to slow down or he would fall and break his cast.

"Mrs. Rudley will be real mad," Lloyd persisted.

"Mr. Rudley is even madder," Rudley grumbled.

The chief was sitting outside his tent, cross-legged, smoking something and gazing dreamily into the lake. Rudley drew to a halt in front of him, leaned forward, gripping the crutches so tightly his knuckles turned white.

"You wanted to talk to me?"

The chief smiled. "Yes."

"Lloyd said you had a vision."

"Well, sort of."

"Did it come from what you're smoking?"

The chief regarded him with surprise. "No, this is just a little pot." He took a toke. "I wasn't talking about a supernatural vision, Mr. Rudley. More of a vision of the future. It seemed to me we could share this land. In the meantime, I would like the boathouse. And later on, when the weather turns colder" — he paused, eyes twinkling — "I've been looking around a bit in my spare time. I noticed you have a nice little place up on the hill that would do quite well."

"The High Birches."

The chief shrugged. "If that's what you've traditionally called it. By the names these cottages have, I really have to say you don't know your trees."

Chapter Nine

"Now, Mr. Rudley" — the emergency room physician looked at him, shaking his head — "I believe we cautioned you about putting things down your cast."

"It was itchy," Rudley grumbled.

"You were advised to seek medical advice if you were having problems."

"The last advice I got was that I would have to put up with it."

"Nurse Hammerstone tends to be a stoic," the doctor murmured. "Now, I want you to lie still while I remove the cast. As before, this device is designed to cut hard objects only. It will stop when it contacts flesh." He added briskly, "Just let me know if you feel any discomfort."

"You won't need to worry about that," said Margaret, who was quite fed up with her husband.

The doctor picked up the cast cutter. "When exactly did he do this?"

"This morning," said Margaret.

"That's good," the doctor murmured. "At least the object won't have had time to create too deep an ulcer."

"Thankfully," said Margaret.

"You'd think he could find something with a longer handle than a toothbrush or a ruler," said the doctor.

"Stop talking about him as if he weren't here," said Rudley.

The doctor cut the cast in two neat lines. "Now, Mr. Rudley, after I remove the ruler, I'll have the nurse clean up the edges of the cast and secure the two pieces with a tensor bandage. That way, if you're careful, you can remove the top part to scratch whatever you want to with whatever you want to."

"What would you recommend, doctor?" Margaret asked.

The doctor put down the cast cutter. "How about one of those hedgehog boot scrapers?"

"Well, I never," Rudley spluttered.

"I think the doctor is fed up with you too," said Margaret.

The next two days were uneventful on Hiram's island. Tibor and Frankes prowled around the property, watched movies or sat in the solarium, Frankes bored, but otherwise contented, Tibor quietly brooding, constantly smoothing his incipient moustache.

"You're going to discourage that thing's growth if you keep rubbing it," Frankes remarked.

"Shut up," said Tibor.

"You're in a lousy mood."

"I'm trying to think," Tibor shot back. "Do you know what that is?"

Frankes shrugged.

Tibor had decided to share with Frankes only on a need-to-know basis — that is, if he needed his help or, at least, needed him to keep quiet. He wasn't worried about Leonard; the old man had so many senior moments it was easy to convince him he was being forgetful or that he had misunderstood something. Cerise worried him. She should have been more upset about the way the deal had fallen through. She might have just decided she could separate Leonard from the rest of his money by charm alone. Maybe she could. Leonard showed a hell of a lot more affection for her than he ever had for him. Not that he cared so much, except it afforded her more influence.

That night, as he lay in bed obsessing about the paintings, Tibor became convinced that Leonard had simply brought the wrong ones. The more he thought, the more confident he became that this was the case. The question was, where were the real McCoys and did Cerise know? He was hoping to get some clues from Leonard, but the old man seemed steadfast in his explanation that he had either destroyed the originals or made an error in his original authentication. He was sure the Cartwrights were on St. Napoli.

It was almost three and he was still awake. His thoughts turned to what would happen to him once Leonard's money ran out. He'd never had a real job in his life, apart from answering the old man's beck and call. And that was unfair. It seemed to him he had been working for the old man for years — looking after the boat, working on things around the house. He was good with his hands but he got bored.

He was totting up the value of his work when he heard the front door open, jingling a strip of sleigh bells someone had mounted on the top rail. He got up, crept to his window and looked down. At first he saw nothing, then he noticed a beam of light bobbing away into the night. He dressed quickly, grabbed his knife, then stole across the hall and shook Frankes awake.

"Bugger off," Frankes mumbled.

"Somebody just left the house." Tibor switched on the bedside lamp and tilted the light directly into Frankes's eyes.

Frankes squinted. "Yeah?"

"Get dressed," Tibor barked, tossing clothes at him. "Cerise just snuck out. I think she's up to something."

"What time is it?" Frankes managed to get his legs over the side of the bed.

"You don't need to know," Tibor rasped. "Bring your knife."

Frankes did as told and followed Tibor down the stairs. Tibor grabbed the flashlight from the stand near the door.

"She was headed for the dock," said Tibor, staring out over the water.

"There's a light out there," said Frankes.

Tibor headed toward the boathouse. "Come on."

They ran down the incline to the boathouse. Tibor shone a light around. "I think she took the rubber dinghy," he said.

"She wouldn't have got far. It doesn't have a motor."

"OK." Tibor got into the motorboat. "We'll just pull up alongside and find out where she's going at three in the morning."

"Maybe she couldn't sleep," said Frankes.

"We'll see," said Tibor.

They pulled out, moved slowly away from the dock, gradually picking up speed as they moved further from the cottage.

"There she is," said Frankes. He pointed out toward the centre of the lake. "I just saw the light."

Tibor shook his head. "I don't know what she's doing that far out."

"She's a pretty good swimmer."

"On a strange lake in the middle of the night?"

"She probably took a life jacket."

Tibor snorted. "Have you ever known Cerise to do anything sensible?"

"Guess not."

"OK," said Tibor, "we'll pass her, do a little run around the dinghy, see what's up."

Cerise stopped rowing as they approached.

Tibor killed the motor, shone the flashlight on Cerise. "What are you doing?" he yelled. "Sleep-rowing?"

She rested the oars across her knees. "What's it to you?"

"What're you up to?" He let the boat drift up to the dinghy. He reached over and grabbed the oarlock.

"Wouldn't you like to know?" she said.

Before he could react, she swung an oar at him. It hit him hard in the upper arm, causing him to gasp and curse. "That's the way you want it?"

"Suits me fine," she said.

He took the knife from his ankle holster, jabbed it into the side of the boat and ripped a three-foot hole. He yanked the blade down, deflating the bottom compartment. "Go around," he shouted at Frankes. "Get the other side." He grabbed the oar as she swung it toward him again and pulled it on board. As Frankes manoeuvred the boat around the shrinking dinghy, he tore open the remaining compartment.

"Let's get out of here," he barked at Frankes.

"What about her?"

"She's trying to kill us, you idiot." Tibor scrambled aft, pushed Frankes aside and opened up the motor. "Let's go," he yelled.

They headed back to the cottage.

Chapter Ten

Creighton parked his car in the lot in Middleton and wandered down to the dock. He looked around, then approached the man at the bait shop. "Do you rent fishing rods?"

The man shook his head. "Sorry, just live bait here. There's Howard's on Main Street." He paused as Creighton looked uncertain. "Lose your gear?"

Creighton shook his head. "I don't fish much. I thought I'd just rent some stuff."

"What're you fishing for?"

Creighton laughed. "How in hell should I know? I grew up in Toronto. The most I've done is go fishing in the creek with my nieces and nephews. We hook whatever's there."

The man shrugged. "Yeah, you don't really need to know much for that kind of fishing. Mainly how to get a worm on the hook."

Creighton laughed. "The kids usually do that. It's kind of messy." He looked around. "Maybe I'll just get a coffee for now."

"Sorry I can't help you," the man said. He gave Creighton an appraising look. "Snazzy outfit."

Creighton tipped his hat and wandered off down the dock.

A couple of kids were fishing off the end of a houseboat moored at the dock. Creighton stopped to watch a six-year-old send the lure thirty feet with a flick of the wrist. He glanced at his watch. Six o'clock.

What in hell was he doing up at six o'clock? Because Brisbois told him that was when the fish were biting. He yawned and reflected that Brisbois's descriptions of the joys of fishing were grossly exaggerated. He decided to get a packed lunch on Main Street, then have a long nap in the rented boat he had anchored at the dock. He'd just throw a line in the water and hope for the best. But first he needed a rod. He walked back to where the kids were busy filling up their basket with perch.

"Do you think I could rent your fishing rod for a while?" he asked.

The boy tightened his grip on the rod. The girl studied him with calculation. "How much?"

"Ten bucks?"

She screwed up her face. "How do I know you'll bring it back?"

He gave her a salute. "Scout's honour."

She hesitated. "What if you break it?"

"I'll buy you a new one." He smiled. "Believe me, it'll be used as little as possible."

"Don't forget," she said. "This boat's the *Intrepid*. We'll be here all day."

He took the rod. The child reluctantly included an extra lure. It wasn't until he had got his lunch and was arranging his gear in the little motorboat that he discovered the rod had a purple reel covered with Hello Kitty stickers.

Tibor managed to doze off for an hour before the sun splitting the blinds woke him. He fumbled on the bedside table for his watch, then realized it was still on his wrist. Almost seven. He crawled out of bed, took a quick shower and dressed.

He had told Frankes to shut up about Cerise, justifying sinking her boat by saying she had tried to kill him. She had, too. Of course, swinging the oar might be construed as self-defence. He took a deep breath. This was nothing new. He and Cerise had been beating up on each other since they were young. It was no-holds-barred from her and he didn't see why he should feel guilty about not ceding her any quarter. He knew what she was doing. She thought the Cartwrights were still on St. Napoli and she was trying to beat him to them. Well, he'd put the kibosh on that — for now, at least. Even if she hadn't drowned, she would have to regroup considerably to get back to St. Napoli before he did.

But how to explain Cerise's absence to Leonard? He decided the best thing to do would be to appear ignorant. Leonard would ask where she was, and after looking around the island, he and Frankes would report that they hadn't found her, though the rubber dinghy was missing. They would then suggest to Leonard that Cerise was up to no good, that she had somehow sequestered the paintings in a safe place and was, even now, on her way to them. Or she had made a deal with Evans. Had she sold him the paintings and was making off with her money, which she had secreted in a safe-deposit box somewhere?

He had slowed her down at least and in that he felt entirely justified.

Leonard was not up when he arrived downstairs. Luther was not yet in the kitchen. He imagined Frankes would sleep until noon, not having to worry about thinking. He was passing the solarium when a squawk made him jump.

"Tweek is a twit. Frankes is a freak."

"God damn." Tibor went into the solarium and flung open the door of the cage. He tried to grab the bird by the throat but she eluded him. He was chasing her around the cottage when Luther came into the kitchen. He opened the door and went out onto the back porch with a basket of waste for the composter. Betty flew straight through the open door and disappeared into the foliage. Luther, oblivious, returned to the kitchen, surprised to see Tibor, who stamped off into the breakfast nook. Luther followed him and hovered nearby.

"French toast," Tibor grumbled. "Maple syrup, bacon, coffee."

Luther nodded and returned to the kitchen.

A few minutes later, Leonard appeared, shuffling out of his main-floor room. He was dressed nattily in a light grey suit, a white shirt and blue tie. He had no socks on and was wearing slippers on the wrong feet. He smiled when he saw Tibor.

"Have you seen the paper?"

Tibor picked up the *Globe* Frankes had purchased in town the day before and handed it to Leonard, who scanned the front page, apparently unaware he had read it the day before. And the day before that. At least, Tibor thought, amusing him was cheap.

Leonard carried the newspaper to the table and sat down. "That smells good," he said as Luther appeared with Tibor's breakfast. Luther set the tray in front of Leonard, then looked to Tibor.

"I'll have the same," Tibor barked.

Creighton lowered himself into the motorboat. Although he had little appreciation for fishing, he did like boats, especially those with a motor. In fact, exclusively those with a motor. He supposed most men preferred vehicles with motors. Brisbois, he thought, would have something to say about the psychology of that! He waited until he had cleared the basin, then opened the motor to full throttle, which wasn't all that gratifying, given the limitations of his little eggbeater.

As the breeze ruffled his hair, he realized Brisbois was right. This was better than the hassle of airports and six-lane traffic. He felt footloose and fancy-free. Nothing compelled him at home since Louise had died. His landlady had suggested he get a new goldfish, saying the sight of Louise's empty bowl brought a lump to her throat when she went in to check on his apartment during his absences. She even suggested he try a kitten. He imagined the landlady enjoyed the extra excuse to interact with him that a pet afforded. He kind of missed her too, and their conversations about Louise and everyday things.

He glanced at the fishing rod and wondered, in light of Louise's death, if he should even think about catching a fish. He knew what Brisbois would say: Louise was the only woman he had ever committed to.

He grinned. Brisbois was worse than his mother when it came to pushing him toward marriage. In fact, his mother had given up inquiring about his prospects some years before. He had suggested to his sister Carol that their mother had concluded that there wasn't a woman good enough for her son. Carol had responded that their mother had finally decided there wasn't a woman bad enough.

He had to admit Carol was right — he wasn't good marriage material. He was used to living by himself and seldom did anything for himself. He ate out a lot, had a cleaning service in every couple of weeks, took his clothes to the laundry. Domesticity wasn't his strong point. As Carol pointed out, not only would he not feel guilty about having his wife do everything, he wouldn't even notice what she had done. He wasn't even used to doing traditional male things. He'd always lived in an apartment so he didn't do yard work. If anything broke around the apartment, his landlady fixed it — she was, for instance, a virtuoso with a monkey wrench. He took his car to the mechanic. Brisbois, meanwhile, talked about gardening and making dinner. He got the feeling Brisbois liked being at home, liked taking part in the general work around the house. Brisbois even knew what to do with kids. Creighton didn't have a clue. Although he was the oldest in the family, he had never paid much attention to what his mother did with his siblings. He was the man of the house, going to school, hanging out in pool halls, playing baseball and softball.

He considered all of this as he turned up the lake, looking for one of those dark, cool places or piles of rock or reed banks where Brisbois had assured him fish liked to hang out. He supposed he'd make a decent father. Why wouldn't he? He'd had ample opportunity to observe his brother-in-law, Gary, who didn't do anything special other than just be there. That was the rub, wasn't it? Being there. That's what seemed to bug Brisbois; there were times he, Brisbois, wasn't there. He shrugged. Another good reason to remain a bachelor.

"Where's Cerise this morning?" Leonard looked from the clock to Tibor and to Frankes, who had finally made an appearance, unshaven and glassy-eyed.

"She wasn't around when I got up," Tibor responded. "Maybe she's still sleeping."

"Perhaps someone should check," said Leonard.

Tibor got up from the table and went down the hall. He looked into Cerise's room, which was directly across from Leonard's. "She's not there," he said on his return. He took a sip of coffee and added casually. "The parrot isn't here either. Maybe they both flew the coop."

"Flew the coop," Leonard repeated, frowning.

"Yeah," Tibor murmured. "I thought she was up to something."

"Who's up to something?"

"Cerise," Tibor persisted.

"Oh," said Leonard, then grinned. "About four-eleven."

Tibor rolled his eyes.

Creighton slowed the boat to a putt-putt when he spotted the weeping willows leaning over the rocky bank. "I think this is what we're looking for," he told a seagull that had landed near his boat. He dropped anchor and tossed out his line. The seagull watched him for a few minutes before flying away, wheeling above him briefly before taking off down the lake.

"I guess he didn't think I was much of a bet," he said. He sat back and let the line drag in the water. He had to admit that fishing was relaxing. Boring was more like it. Still, the scenery was nice. Finally, he pulled his line in and lay back, tipping his hat over his eyes. He chuckled to himself. This was what Norman Phipps-Walker called fishing.

He was enjoying his nap when he thought he heard something. He opened his eyes, lazily scanned the lake, perking up at the sight of a large bird splashing in the middle of the lake. Too big to be one bird, he thought, perhaps a gaggle of loons having a meeting. He narrowed his eyes, wishing he'd brought binoculars. Maybe it was a pair of otters or muskrats. Or did you only find those on the river? Maybe it was a dog, perhaps from a cottage just around the bend. His eyes widened as he realized it was a swimmer who, nearing his boat, vanished into the water then resurfaced a moment later a foot away.

"Sorry to scare you. I was just scoping you out."

He stared at the red-haired, brown-eyed elf who hung by her forearms to the side of his boat. When he didn't respond, she said, "Hey, I've swum a long way. Mind if I come aboard?"

Chapter Eleven

"How are you this morning, Mr. Rudley?" Simpson entered the lobby with Albert on a leash. His hair was windblown, his cheeks flushed.

"I see Albert's had you chasing squirrels," Rudley said.

"He is rather full of vinegar."

"Did you lose Miss Miller?"

"She stopped to talk to Chief Longbow. She thinks his story might make an interesting piece for the papers."

Rudley crossed his eyes. "The man's clearly deranged."

"He is quite eccentric. But he wouldn't be the first eccentric to grace these premises."

Rudley struggled up onto his crutches. "He'd be the first to lay claim to my land, although" — he winced as the arm of the crutch bit into him — "the Benson sisters seem to have laid claim to the Elm Pavilion. The only saving grace is that they don't have anything in writing, and they're older than the planet."

"I imagine that you'd miss them if they weren't here."

"I have to say they do keep me feeling young," Rudley conceded. He winced again. "These things are killing my armpits."

Simpson cleared his throat. "If you don't mind me saying, Mr. Rudley, you aren't supposed to take all of your weight on your axillae." He paused. "Didn't they teach you how to use those at the hospital?"

"I think they just wanted him to leave," said Margaret, who arrived with Tim on the tail end of the conversation. "Especially since everything they told him previously seemed to have gone in one ear and out the other."

"Which requires there be nothing in between," Tim murmured.

"Now, Rudley," Margaret said as her husband fumed, "Tim is just trying to introduce some levity into the situation."

"I don't see any levity in me being imprisoned behind this desk with this damn cast and everyone looking down on me and making jokes about my predicament."

Margaret circled the desk and put an arm around him. "We're sorry, Rudley, but you have to admit you've been a beast about this whole situation. Not only are you suffering, but you've made everyone else suffer." She tidied the papers on his desk. "I think you should take some time to relax, perhaps sit out on the veranda and enjoy the view."

"And we would enjoy the view," Tim muttered, "of you sitting out on the veranda."

"I heard that," said Rudley.

"Now," said Margaret, "Gregoire is making you something special for lunch." She gave Rudley a pat on the arm and left with Tim in tow.

"It's demeaning," Rudley complained to Simpson, "to have everyone ignoring your wishes and doing whatever they please."

Simpson regarded him sympathetically as he turned to leave. "In my experience, Mr. Rudley, life is much easier when you learn to go with the flow, as they say."

Abandoning his crutches, Rudley leaned over the desk, supporting himself on his elbows, and tried to enjoy his paper. The idea of sitting for more than five minutes repelled him. The idea of sitting on the veranda especially repelled him. The view from the veranda these days would be sure to repel him. There was his pristine lakefront, his unsurpassable wildlife retreat and, in the middle of it all, Chief Longbow who had set up housekeeping in earnest. He had added a clothesline strung between two pine trees and a lawn chair with a table and umbrella, courtesy of Margaret. "The next thing I know, he'll have added a carport and bought himself a Lamborghini," he told Albert, who had collapsed on the rug in front of the desk and was wriggling about, happily transferring whatever stench he had picked up from rolling in the dead fish down on the bank.

Rudley thought his conduct exemplary, given his circumstances. He didn't think his behaviour was any different than usual and felt abused by suggestions it was otherwise. "What these ninnies don't understand," he said to Albert, "is that an innkeeper cannot be perpetually sunny. Being an innkeeper demands being authoritative, of steely determination, and sometimes being impatient when things are not going according to plan."

Albert frisked in behind the desk and stood on his hind legs to lick Rudley's hand.

"At least you understand," Rudley said, grabbing his crutches and backing up to his chair. He eased himself down, feeling defeated.

Miss Miller entered at that moment. "How are we today, Mr. Rudley?"

"We are fine," he muttered.

She fetched a chair, came around the desk, and sat down beside him. "I know it's hard to live in a cast," she said. "Especially with everyone telling you what you should and shouldn't do."

He nodded, surveying her with hound-dog eyes.

"When Edward was in his leg cast, I treated him as if he were fully able," she said.

"As I recall, you had him driving you all over the place, thumping through the forest, rowing you miles around the lake."

"And he was the better for it." She smiled. "I had a long talk with Chief Longbow. He's a rather charismatic man."

"He's a damn annoying man," Rudley grumbled.

"I wonder if he has amnesia," she mused. "He seems to have arrived here without much of a history. The history he recounts, I'm not sure if it's his."

"He's probably been in jail for the past ten years," Rudley said.

"I think he's a bit of a mystic. He has mesmerizing eyes."

"I think he's a hobo taking advantage of my good humour." He sat back. "His story doesn't check out," he continued. "None of the people our lawyer contacted have any memory of him or can connect him to any tribe."

"What do the police say?"

The mention of the police made his pupils dilate. "I'll put up with him for the next ten years rather than having those flatfeet mucking around here."

She smiled. "Speaking of the police, how is Detective Brisbois?"

"Well?" The brown eyes probed Creighton's. "Aren't you going to invite me aboard?"

He reached down to grip her arm, tangling his wristwatch in her necklace, which broke and fell into the boat at his feet.

"Now look what you've done," she said, aggrieved.

He picked up the necklace and glanced at the inscription. Happy Birthday, Sweetie.

She plopped her small frame down in the aft seat. "It was a gift from an old friend. Sherry Brown," she said, offering her hand.

"Chester Creighton."

She laughed. "Chester? What a weird name."

"My mother was a big fan of *Gunsmoke.*"

"Sorry?"

"Never mind," he said. "What brings you out here?"

"My boat sank," she said cheerfully, then sighed. "I have had the worst day. I just don't seem to be able to get things together. Know what I mean?"

He raised his brows.

"I was supposed to meet my new boss at his boat, but I missed the train. I got on the wrong bus. I would have sent an e-mail but I didn't have an address. So I hitched a ride —"

"You shouldn't hitch rides."

"It's all right. I carry Mace." She reached into her pocket. "Damn, it must have fallen out when I went into the water."

He rolled his eyes.

"I knew he lived on a lake somewhere around here so the truck driver said I should ask at the dock, but they'd never heard of a Mr.

Bartok and had no idea who he might be since I didn't know the name of his boat. I guess he's not the only one around here with a big boat."

"If you didn't know where he lived, what were you doing out here?"

"I thought if I rented a boat I could motor around until I found his boat."

"But you said you didn't know the name of his boat."

She frowned. "I thought if I actually saw the boat I might recognize the name."

"So, once upon a time, you knew the name."

Her expression turned peevish. "He told me but I forgot because he said it would be at the pier. I knew I would remember the name of the boat when I saw it."

Creighton raised his brows.

"I try not to remember anything more than I have to," she continued, "because I don't like to clutter my mind with extraneous details."

"Extraneous details?"

"And then my boat sprung a leak and sank. It was like the *Titanic* all over again." She peered at his fishing rod. "Cute stickers."

"It's a rental." He covered the stickers with his hand. "So?"

"So? What?"

"You're sitting here drenched, your boat's sunk to the bottom — like the *Titanic*." He shrugged. "You can't stay here forever."

She glanced at the near bank. "Now that I'm rested up, I guess I can swim that little distance."

He laughed and put a hand on her wrist as she started to rise. "Hold your horses. I'm just asking where you want to go. I can drop you off in town. You can make whatever phone calls you need to make from there."

"I'd like to try Mr. Bartok again."

He raised on eyebrow. "If you have his phone number, why didn't you call him from the dock?"

"I must have written the number down wrong. When I tried it I got one of those 'this number is no longer in service' things."

"I suppose," he said with some exasperation, pointing to the water, "that the number is down there."

"No, it's in my pocket." She dug into the pocket of her shorts and came up with a piece of soggy paper. She frowned. "Can you read this?"

Creighton took the piece of paper, squinted. "All I can make out here is a *1* or it could be a *7*. This looks like pencil."

"I didn't have a pen. How was I supposed to know I was going to fall into the water?" She took the paper back, tore it into pieces and tossed them into the lake.

"That's pollution. I could fine you for that."

"You're an environmental superhero?"

"Something like that." He peered at her. "Do you have enough money to get home?"

She turned out her pockets, shrugged. "I suppose I could go to the real estate office in town and see if anyone called Bartok has a place around here."

"Now you're thinking," he said. She seemed scatterbrained, but he had to admit she was cute. Young but not a kid. A bit of an airhead, but a damn good swimmer. "What do you do when you're not sinking boats?"

"This and that. I was supposed to work as a housekeeper for Mr. Bartok." She bit her lip. "At least I think his name was Bartok."

"You think?" he said, incredulous.

"I really haven't decided what I want to do permanently. Or if I want to do anything permanently." She reached over and lifted the brim of his hat. "So, what do you do when you're not fishing with Hello Kitty?"

He smiled. "I'm in sales."

"You don't look like a salesman."

"Sorry," he said amiably.

She studied him critically. "I think you're a cop."

"Why would you think that?"

"Well, you're dressed like Indiana Jones, which you think is cool. Except it's not cool unless you're wandering around Kathmandu or Cairo in the thirties and forties."

"So you're trying to tell me cops don't have any style."

"Most of them don't. Neither do the military. Oh, they look fine in uniform, but in civilian clothes, mostly they look crappy."

"If you say so."

She frowned. "I hurt your feelings, didn't I?"

"No, well, maybe a little."

"I'm sorry. I'll make it up to you."

He smiled.

"You can take me to lunch," she said. "And you can get my necklace fixed. Since you broke it."

"The guy who had it inscribed didn't know you very well, did he?"

Leonard glanced at his watch, then squinted at the wall clock. "Is that thing right?"

"I think so," said Tibor, who didn't care.

"I don't understand why Cerise isn't back yet. Where did you say she went?"

"I don't know. Maybe she went back to St. Napoli."

"Oh." Leonard paused, then said, perplexed, "What for?"

"Maybe she got bored? I don't know, Leonard. Why do you think she would go back to the islands?"

"Maybe she had a date."

"Or," said Tibor, "maybe she thinks there's something valuable there, maybe something she could fence."

Leonard wrinkled his brow. "I don't know what that could be."

"Maybe something in your collection."

"My stamp collection?"

"Your art collection," said Tibor, struggling to keep his tone even. "Maybe the Cartwrights?"

Leonard considered this, then leaned toward Tibor. "Didn't we burn those?" he whispered.

Chapter Twelve

She folded her arms over her knees. "So are you going to take me to lunch?"

Creighton raised his brows. "Since I'm the life saver, don't you think you should be buying me lunch?"

"Remember?" She turned out her pockets once again, gave him a scathing look. "You didn't have to save me, you know. I would have made it to shore." She glanced toward the bank. "It isn't that far."

"Guess not." He waved toward the bank. "Be my guest."

"And you did break my necklace."

"Oh, yeah." He reached behind him, brought forth the picnic basket. "Want to share my lunch?" He opened the basket.

Her eyes examined the contents.

"Ham sandwiches, dill pickles?"

She looked forlorn. "I'm a vegetarian."

"I'm glad I didn't catch any fish." He sorted through the basket. "Okay, I'll eat the sandwiches. You can have the dills and carrot sticks. You can have the apple, but I get the Twinkies — just in case they contain animal matter."

"I'm an ovo-lacto vegetarian," she said. "We'll split the apple and the Twinkies."

"Fine with me."

He tucked into his sandwich, watched her surreptitiously as she ate. She was sitting in his boat with nothing to her name but a T-shirt and cutoffs, showing every intention of calling the shots. "Hey, slow down," he said as she hiccoughed.

"I'm just wound up," she said. "I always gulp my food when I'm wound up." She finished the carrots, chewing more slowly. "You have to admit I have lots of reasons to be wound up. I sank my boat, missed my ride, missed my train. I don't have any money left and I don't know where my job is."

He pushed his hat back, gave her a big smile. "Look on the bright side."

She gave him a dubious look.

"Things can't get any worse." He shrugged and broke open the Twinkies.

After breakfast Tibor beckoned to Frankes. They headed out the door and down to the dock.

"Do you think she drowned?" Frankes said.

"I don't know," said Tibor.

"They'll find her floating."

"Not right away."

"They always come up eventually. Then we'll have the cops around asking questions."

"We'll just have to keep our mouths shut then." Tibor shot Frankes a steely look.

Frankes held up his hands. "I'm not saying anything."

"It'll take a while before the body comes up."

"They'll see her ID and track her back to us."

"Her ID will be at the bottom of the lake with everything else." Tibor stared across the lake. "If they find any of her ID, we'll just stick to our story: She left and took everything with her. We'll need to get rid of her stuff."

"Burn it?"

"No. Leonard might wonder why we had a bonfire going. The best thing to do would be to put it into a garbage bag, take it into town, and dump it into a dumpster or a garbage can. You can do that, I imagine."

"Yeah, I can do that."

"What if the cops come here?"

"They won't come here until they find a body," Tibor said, trying to keep his voice even. "And they won't be able to link her to us until they can identify her. And even if they do identify her, we can just say we didn't know she was missing, that we thought she left to go back to the islands."

Frankes knit his brows and nodded to indicate he had memorized the story line.

"If it makes you feel better, we can take the boat around the lake for a few days, pretend we're fishing. See if we spot anything, see if there's any police activity in the area."

"What about the old man? We can't count on him to go along with our story."

When Tibor didn't respond, Frankes persisted, "I mean, what if they come here and ask the old man about Cerise? He's so loopy, he might just say something incriminating."

Big word for you, Tibor thought. "Well, we'll just have to prep him. We'll keep to the story that she left without saying anything. And then, if the police finally identify her and come nosing around, we'll feed them the same story and express shock and sadness that she met an unfortunate end."

Frankes grinned. "Yeah, that sounds as if it might work."

"Good. So practise acting shocked and sad." Tibor paused in thought. "We'll clear out her room, then tell Leonard that when we checked on her because she was gone so long that we found her stuff missing, including her passport and plane ticket. We'll tell him we assume she was headed back to St. Napoli."

"Okay…so when do we start working on the old man?"

"Let me deal with that. You just follow my lead."

"Why don't we just go back to St. Napoli?"

"We'll have to get the old man softened up first," Tibor said. "He'll probably act up if we move too fast."

"What about the paintings?"

"Now that we've got rid of our little problem — slowed her down, at least — we can afford to take our time. The one thing I know is, if we don't play it right with the old man, he could cause a big problem."

"Like spilling the beans to the wrong people?"

"I think you've got it, Frankes."

"I'm not stupid."

"Of course not," Tibor said. Not too stupid, he thought, but just stupid enough.

Creighton balled up the waxed paper and tossed it into the basket, then picked up the container of dill pickles. It was empty. "For a little girl, you sure eat a lot of pickles," he said.

"You took the Twinkie."

"You ate the whole apple." He closed the lid of the basket and stowed it under the seat. "So what do I do with you now?"

She shrugged.

"I guess I could ask at the police station if they know a Mr. Bartok in these parts."

"What if they don't know?"

"Then you'll have to phone home for money or find another job."

"I don't have anybody to phone home to," she said.

"You don't sound too broken up about that."

"It's not as if it happened yesterday."

Creighton felt guilty for his insensitivity. "You should be able to get something to do."

"I don't exactly have the right clothes for an interview."

"If you apply for a job at one of the hotels, they won't be too fussy. Just tell them what happened. They'll probably advance you enough for a uniform."

She folded her arms over her chest. "Did anyone ever tell you you were a cheapskate?"

"What?"

"Here I am with absolutely nothing and you don't offer me enough for a room and a set of clothes. And you wouldn't even give me your Twinkie." She paused at his startled expression. "I found you out, didn't I? Coming out here pretending you're Indiana Jones with delusions of rescue."

"It's just a hat."

"And the jacket and the khakis."

He heaved a sigh. "OK, so I happen to resemble Indiana Jones. Purely by accident, you understand." He pointed a finger to silence her as she opened her mouth. "So you figure I set out here in a boat dressed like Indiana Jones and waited around for some sassy little brat to sink her boat." He hauled up anchor, rowed the boat a few feet away from the shoals and yanked the cord for the motor.

She flicked him an uncertain glance. "Where are we going?"

"I'm going to take you into Middleton — that's the nearest town — and introduce you to social services, bid you adieu, and get on with my vacation — such as it is."

She held out her hand. "Lend me a twenty. I'll pay you back in a week."

He shook his head. "I knew I should have gone to Myrtle Beach."

"Isn't it kind of hot at this time of year?"

He let the motor idle and rested his chin on his hand. "I knew I should have gone anywhere else."

"Make it forty."

Betty was sitting in a tree a half-mile from the cottage when she saw the big boat. She tilted her head to one side. She had been flitting through the woods and hadn't found anything to eat that suited her champagne tastes. A large bird that swooped near her had also frightened her. She huddled close to the tree trunk under the canopy. Finally the raptor went on its way.

The forest and raptors she was unfamiliar with, but the big boat was like old home week. She took a look around and flew to intercept it.

"Mary's coming to the cottage tonight," Brisbois said to Creighton over the phone. "I caught some nice trout today. I'll put them on the grill. Make a salad. Chill a nice bottle of wine."

"Sounds great," Creighton said, "but I've got a little problem."

"Oh?"

"Yeah"— Creighton tucked the phone into his shoulder, glanced around the corner —"I've got this girl…"

"Which bar did you meet her in?"

"I resent that," said Creighton. He took another look around, returned to the phone. "I met her on the lake. Actually, I fished her out of the lake."

"Did you rescue her or catch her on your line?"

"Actually she swam up to my boat. She'd sunk hers."

"Good story so far."

"As it turns out, she lost everything when the boat went under, although I don't think she had much to begin with."

Brisbois hesitated. "Why don't you bring her along to dinner."

"I'll have to ask." Creighton glanced around the pillar. "She's trying on clothes. All she had was a T-shirt and shorts when I met her. And, I suppose, underwear."

"You suppose," said Brisbois dryly. "So she lost everything she owned with the boat."

"Apparently. She was on her way to a job with some old guy in these parts. She was supposed to meet his yacht at the dock, but she missed the train."

"Bring her to dinner. We can drop her off at her job later."

"She doesn't know where it is. She rented a boat. She thought she could just troll around every lake in the province until she spotted a yacht."

There was a long pause. "You're sure she didn't escape from…you know where."

"A local institution?"

"Yes."

"She's perfectly sane."

"How old is this girl?"

"It's hard to say," Creighton said. "Maybe early to mid-twenties. She's a bit of an elf."

"An elf?"

Creighton hesitated. "Something like that. She kind of sparkles."

"Sparkles?"

"Sparkles."

Brisbois considered this for a moment. "Are you sure you weren't drinking out there?"

"Nothing stronger than coffee." Creighton filled Brisbois in on the rest of the story.

"So you got her a hotel room and lent her some money," Brisbois concluded. "And she'll pay you back once she gets settled."

Creighton winced at Brisbois's tone. "I did save a lot of money by not going to Vegas."

"Yup," said Brisbois. "Well, if you'd like to bring her to dinner, Mary'd be happy to have the extra guest. She gets bored with us — for some reason."

"She's vegetarian. Ovo-lacto something."

"I'll make her an omelet."

Creighton hung up and returned to his seat by the dressing room. Presently, Cerise came out in a blue sundress.

"Do you like this?" she asked.

"Do you?"

"Yes, but you're paying for it."

He looked at the price tag. "I like the yellow one better."

"All right," she said.

"A friend of mine has invited us to dinner."

"Where?"

"He and his wife have a cottage on the next lake. They're an older couple."

"Older than you?"

"Way older than me." He looked at her feet. "Did you see any shoes you like?"

"I just want a pair of runners."

"Runners with a sundress?"

She gave him a tired look. "As if you're one to give fashion advice."

The proprietor of the houseboat did not immediately notice Betty. When she flew down from the roof to the voices below, she was met by a rush of fur and a large set of fangs. She squawked and flew up.

"What in hell's wrong with you, Attila?" a man shouted.

Attila continued to snarl and lunge. Betty managed to escape back to the top. Attila scrambled after her, challenging her from a few feet away.

The man's wife went to see what was bothering Attila. She caught a flash of feathers as Betty made her escape.

"Raymond, Raymond!" she shouted. "Attila was after some kind of cockatiel."

"A what?"

"Maybe a budgie or something."

"Elise, what would a budgie be doing out here?"

"I don't know. It was a very bright bird."

"Maybe one of those painted buntings," he said. "We've seen those around before."

"I suppose it could have been. It seemed bigger."

"Everything seems bigger on the water, Elise."

"I think that's closer, Raymond."

"Bigger, closer, clearer, whatever," he muttered.

While Elise and Raymond were sorting out these truisms, Betty hopscotched her way to shore on a little series of islands.

It was almost dusk when she reached her destination, guided by what proved to be a well-stocked bird feeder. After she had eaten her fill, she settled into the limbs of a thick spruce, tucked her head under her wing and slept.

Chapter Thirteen

Rudley left Lloyd in charge of the front desk and hobbled down the back stairs to the basement and out onto the bench just below the back porch. He glanced right and left, then removed a package of cigarettes from his pocket, stuck one into his mouth and lit up. He puffed away happily, feeling the tension drain from his shoulders, enjoying the light breeze and the sight of birds flitting tree to tree, secure in the knowledge that Margaret had gone down to the Oaks to paint a splash of daisies that had taken her fancy. He knew, too, if he washed his hands and chewed a stick of gum, she would never know he had been indulging — or at least she'd be able to reasonably pretend she didn't know.

He finished the first, stubbed it out, then thought, why not have another? After all, it would be more efficient than going back to the desk, waiting until he found someone else to cover it, and hobbling all the way downstairs again. Besides, not stressing his injury would be more prudent from a medical point of view. Margaret would have to appreciate that. He inhaled deeply, smiled.

"Dirty bird."

He flinched, surprised by the hoarse voice behind him. He turned, but saw nothing. He took another drag.

"Dirty bird, dirty bird."

Rudley seethed. Obviously, someone was playing a trick on him. Tim, he guessed, probably in the pantry, lurking below the window that looked out onto the back porch, popping up when his back was turned. "On time I'm paying for," he said loud enough for Tim to hear. He waited for a response. When none came, he called out, "Pretty poor imitation of a parrot, too, I must say." Still no answer. "I know you're there," he shouted.

"Stupid, stupid. Tweek and Freak."

Rudley dropped his cigarette, thumped up the back steps, and stuck his head in the pantry window. No one. He caught a glimpse of Gregoire passing by into the kitchen, but he appeared to be alone. He thumped back to where he had left the cigarette and ground it into the ground with the tip of his crutch, then, with difficulty, retrieved the butt.

"Ouch." He put his hand to his crown. Something had snagged a strand of his hair. He turned, incensed. "Damn it to hell."

"Stupid, stupid. Leonard's stupid."

Rudley looked up and found himself staring into the inquisitive eyes of a large parrot.

"Dirty bird."

As Rudley watched agape, the bird climbed up the trellis, inched along the porch roof, and disappeared around the corner. He seized his crutches and hobbled around the side of the house, squinting into the sunlight along the roof and muttering obscenities under his breath.

"Is there a problem with the roof?"

Rudley turned awkwardly to see James Bole watching him with perplexity.

"The roof is fine," Rudley rasped. "I'm looking for a bird."

Mr. Bole smiled. "I didn't realize you'd taken up birdwatching, Rudley." He tapped Rudley's crutch lightly with his walking stick. "Good for you. You need a hobby." Before Rudley could reply, Mr. Bole continued down the path toward the Sycamore.

Rudley was lurking furtively in the bushes when the Phipps-Walkers came into view, binoculars and cameras slung around their necks.

"Rudley," Norman greeted him with a bucktoothed smile, "good to see you out enjoying this fine morning."

"I'm not enjoying the weather, Norman," he replied irritably, "I'm looking for a bird."

"You've come to the right place," Geraldine trilled.

"There are lots of birds around of all types, in case you haven't noticed," Norman said.

"Norman and I got some wonderful shots of a bevy of quail," said Geraldine. "Usually they're deeper in the forest, but we came across these just behind the High Birches." She thrust her camera toward Rudley. "Take a look."

Rudley glanced at the pictures. "Yes, yes, very nice, but the bird I'm looking for is a big one with a hooked beak. A parrot."

"Oh," said Norman. "I imagine some sort of hawk."

"I'm acquainted with hawks," said Rudley, peering into the spruces, "and this was not a hawk."

Geraldine was thumbing through her photos blissfully. "There are quite a variety of hawks, Rudley. This may have been one you're not familiar with."

"We have an unabridged copy of *Birds of North America* in our room," said Norman. "We'd be glad to bring it down and go over it with you."

"The damn thing spoke to me!"

Norman and Geraldine looked at Rudley, then exchanged glances.

"Perhaps it was a mockingbird," said Norman.

"It was *not* a mockingbird."

"What did it say?" Geraldine asked.

"It called me a dirty bird."

"Perhaps it's someone's pet that got out," Geraldine suggested.

"Apparently one that knows you well." Norman grinned.

Rudley crossed his eyes.

"Don't worry, Rudley. Norman and I will keep a sharp eye out. Not many birds can elude us."

"If I were a bird around here, I'd feel as if I were in a perpetual peep show," Rudley muttered.

"We should try to find it," said Geraldine. "If it's a pet, it will be at risk."

"People shouldn't imprison birds in the first place," said Norman.

"It really isn't nice," said Geraldine.

"That damn bird took a chunk out of my head," Rudley complained.

Geraldine patted Rudley's crown. "She was probably collecting material for a nest."

Frankes slipped into town with the excuse of getting fresh greens and deposited the garbage bags containing Cerise's belongings in a bin at the back of a restaurant. They had been able to ascertain that she had taken a few clothes, her jewellery, and all of her papers. Tibor was waiting for him on the porch when he returned.

"You're sure no one saw you."

"The place was like a tomb," said Frankes. He opened his bag to show Tibor an assortment of candy and licorice. "Want some?"

Tibor took a bag of jelly beans. "You forgot the lettuce."

"I think we've got a refrigerator full."

"Well, if the old man asks, say the stuff didn't look good, and you decided to wait until they got the fresh stuff in."

Leonard was in the breakfast nook, watching Luther serve up his lunch. He glanced up as Tibor and Frankes entered. "Did you find Cerise?"

Tibor's jaw twitched. "No."

Leonard tried to keep his expression neutral. "I don't understand why she left that way," he said. "Without telling anyone."

"She's been part of the family for a long time," he continued when Tibor didn't respond. "Why wouldn't she say goodbye?"

"Maybe she did," Tibor said, suddenly inspired.

Leonard looked at him sharply.

"You've had some problems remembering things," said Tibor hesitantly, as if he were reluctant to acknowledge this unfortunate fact.

"I think I would have remembered Cerise saying goodbye," Leonard murmured.

Before Tibor could respond, Frankes stepped forward holding out the bag of sweets. "I got the licorice you wanted."

Leonard frowned, then said, "Thank you."

"The red kind. Nibs, the ones you like," Frankes added. He handed the bag to Leonard.

Leonard studied the contents. "Actually, I like the Dutch variety better," he said, smiling, "but this is my second favourite."

Frankes nodded. Tibor turned to leave but not before poking Frankes in the back to signal he was to follow — which Frankes did reluctantly.

"What was that all about?" Tibor demanded once they were out of earshot.

"You said we were supposed to make him think he had a memory problem."

"Yes, except he's never eaten licorice in his life."

"I got him thinking he has," said Frankes.

Tibor stuffed his hands into his pockets. "I think we have to be careful about how we gaslight him. It's one thing to suggest he didn't remember something that happened recently. It's another thing to suggest he liked something he never ate."

Frankes shrugged. "You could talk my grandfather into thinking there was a polar bear on the front lawn," he said.

"It's not the same thing. From now on, follow my lead."

Leonard opened the bag and popped a piece of licorice into his mouth. Not bad, he thought. He was quite sure he had never been particularly fond of the confection, however. He wasn't sure if Frankes was making fun of him or if he were honestly mistaken about his fondness for it. Perhaps he had confused him with his grandfather, a man Frankes mentioned from time to time. He was troubled about Cerise's abrupt departure. He didn't want to believe that she would leave without saying goodbye. He had no doubt she was up to something. Exactly what, he wasn't sure. Perhaps she *had* returned to St. Napoli, expecting to find the Cartwrights in his studio. She was unpredictable, much like her mother — full of surprises. He liked that in Sylvia. He smiled. He was capable of the odd surprise himself.

Margaret was at the desk with Rudley, sorting through the invoices and confirming bookings. Rudley smelled strongly of Doublemint gum, which suggested he had been smoking again. She decided to let it pass until his cast was off and life was back to normal. As much as she deplored his behaviour since he had broken his leg, she realized he found his immobility extremely frustrating. Three more weeks, she thought. Three more weeks. As Gregoire had suggested when she mentioned this earlier, it might prove to be the longest three weeks of their lives.

And now he was on about a parrot that had spoken to him in a disrespectful manner and had had the audacity to peck him on the head. She had examined the wound and found it not terribly significant.

"It's humiliating," he had said, "to be attacked by a parrot."

"Well," she'd responded, "if anyone asks just say you were wounded at the Battle of Dorking."

He was about to retort when the door opened and Chester Creighton entered with a young woman.

"Detective Creighton," Margaret greeted him while Rudley rolled his eyes.

"Detective?" Cerise grabbed Creighton's arm. "You didn't tell me you were a detective."

"And you didn't tell me you were the world's worst back-seat driver," Creighton countered.

"That's not the same."

"Margaret, Rudley," Creighton continued, gesturing to his companion, "this is Sherry Brown. You might say I ran into her on the lake."

"He was asleep in his boat with a Hello Kitty fishing rod," said Cerise. She held out her hand to Rudley. "Pleased to meet you both."

"Likewise," said Rudley.

Margaret smiled. "It's lovely to meet you. Why don't you come into the dining room and have a nice cup of tea. And Gregoire has made some delicious fruit tarts."

"Are you here on business?" Rudley asked the detective.

"I'm on vacation."

"I would think you could have gone further away," Rudley muttered.

"I'm renting a place near Middleton," Creighton said.

"Anything to ruin my life," said Rudley.

"Be nice, Rudley," Margaret whispered.

"Actually, we came here for another reason," Creighton said. "Sherry's in kind of a pickle. She's new to the area. She tipped her boat on the lake and lost all of her money, ID, credit cards, and so forth. So until she can get things sorted out, she needs a place to stay and maybe some sort of job."

"Your friend is welcome to stay in the bunkhouse," said Margaret. "There's an extra room always, but it'll be a problem hiring her if she's lost all of her papers."

"What kind of work can you do?" Rudley asked gruffly.

"Almost anything."

"Why don't you say she's a friend you're putting up and she's just helping out," Creighton suggested. "To show her immense and eternal gratitude." He gave Cerise a meaningful glance. "And she would be extremely grateful for your help."

Cerise smiled. "I would be extremely grateful."

"And when she gets her papers, you can put her to work in earnest," Creighton added.

"With Rudley laid up, we could use a little extra help," Margaret said, moving from behind the desk to take Cerise's arm. "Come with me. I'll have Gregoire make you a snack."

Creighton leaned over the desk. "Thanks, Rudley. I appreciate you taking her on. She's driving me nuts."

"You know how Margaret is about stray cats," he said.

"I was sorry to hear about your leg."

"So it's spread all the way to regional headquarters."

"Vance filled us in."

"Vance," Rudley scowled. "The man had trouble keeping a straight face when he arrived to find me on the ground in pain." A smile twitched along his lips. "So that young woman is driving you nuts?"

"She is."

Rudley's smile broadened. "That's the best thing I've heard in days."

Chapter Fourteen

Gregoire had been in the kitchen since four-thirty, as was his custom. He liked having the Pleasant to himself for an hour or so in the morning. No Tim cracking wise and snatching ingredients, no Lloyd traipsing in dirt, no Rudley bellowing, no Aunt Pearl looking to top up her vodka with a drop of orange juice. He washed the ingredients for his omelets and fruit cups thoroughly, set them aside in bowls, and nodded with satisfaction. There was nothing more beautiful, in his opinion, than the robust palette of his cuisine. He inhaled with satisfaction and began to hum a strain from *Carmen*. He was conducting opera and whipping up eggs for his popovers when he became aware of someone watching him. He turned to see Cerise leaning against the doorjamb.

"It's nice to see someone so happy in the morning," she said.

He returned to his popovers. "It is the best time of the day."

"Before the old man gets up," she said.

"It is usually more peaceful before Mr. Rudley is up," he conceded. "But then, of course, everyone else is up soon after so it seems like he is responsible for all of the kerfuffle."

She came up beside him and peered into the bowl. "Aren't you going to put any cinnamon in?"

He gritted his teeth at this sacrilege. "One does not put cinnamon into popovers. Their charm depends on the simplicity of a few fine ingredients prepared just so."

"I put cinnamon in everything," she said. She opened a cupboard door. "Where do you keep your spices?"

Under lock and key from this time on, he thought. "They are in the middle cupboard," he said, "but" — he raised his spatula — "in this kitchen no one touches anything without my consent and under my direction."

She made a face. "You're quite the tyrant, aren't you?"

He narrowed his eyes. "In this place, yes." He drew himself up to his full height. "I am the head chef."

"I could be the sous-chef."

"I do not have a sous-chef. Except perhaps Mrs. Rudley. But that is because she is sensitive to my requirements and does everything exactly as I wish."

"I could do everything exactly as you wish."

"I somehow do not believe that."

She shrugged. "So you got me."

"Besides, you cannot help me here because you are not cleared to handle food. You should not be touching anything in here."

She put her hands behind her back. "There! I'm very good at taking directions when I want to."

He shook his head.

"I'm bored," she said. "All these silly rules."

"They are to keep everyone from dying around us. Although," he added, pouring the popover batter into the muffin tins, "they are not always successful."

"So I can't do anything for you, like whip up a batch of sunflower-seed muffins."

"Not in my kitchen. You can do anything you want in the oven in the bunkhouse."

She slumped down onto a stool. "Tell me about Chester."

"Detective Creighton?" He turned to her, surprised by the sudden change in topic.

She nodded.

"Detective Creighton is a very nice man," he said, sliding the muffin tins into the oven.

"Now that's boring."

"Detective Creighton is a ladies' man," he said.

She snorted. "You've got to be kidding. What ladies are you talking about? The blue-hair set?"

"He is not that old."

"But the way he dresses."

"He turns out very well for work."

"He's a cop. A uniform is a uniform."

"He is a detective. He wears just normal clothes."

"And he's a personal friend of everybody around here."

Gregoire cracked the eggs for a second batch of popovers. "He is here a lot."

"To investigate things?"

"Mostly to investigate murders."

"Oh."

"That means he is here a lot," Gregoire added.

"And he's a bachelor?"

"He is that."

"He is fairly good-looking," she mused. "Although not as much as he thinks." She watched as Gregoire whipped his batter. "Does he bring a lot of girls around here?"

He hesitated. "No," he replied, putting the batter aside and wiping his brow. "According to Officer Owens, mostly he just picks them up in bars."

She bristled. "Then why would he think he could go out with me? I'm not the kind of woman men meet in bars."

He threw up his hands in surrender. "I do not know anything about the kind of women men meet in bars. I would just say the ladies like Detective Creighton and he likes them."

"There's that word again," she grumbled. "Detective. Boring."

"Believe me, once you have spent any time around here, you will know there is nothing boring about it."

"Is he any good?" she asked.

"I would not know that," he said primly.

"I mean as a detective, you goof."

Gregoire had never been called a goof before and was momentarily taken aback. "That is hard to say. Most of the crimes around here are solved by Miss Miller."

"That little woman with the thick glasses," she chortled. "She looks like a librarian."

"She *is* a librarian, but I would not underestimate her."

"So Detective Creighton is a mediocre cop and a womanizer."

"I did not exactly say that." He glanced at her. "If you want something useful to do, go down to the garden and get some shallots."

"Where will I find them?"

"Find Lloyd and tell him he is to help you find the shallots. Except say fancy onions or he will not know what you mean."

"Lloyd," she said, wrinkling her nose. "Does he always smell?"

"Yes." Gregoire waved her away.

He was glad when she was gone. "She does not," he muttered to himself, "beat around the bushes."

Lloyd was working at the side of the house when Cerise found him.

"Gregoire wants you to show me where you keep the fancy onions," she said.

Lloyd grinned. "In the refrigerator."

"He said they were in the garden."

"OK." Lloyd put the rake aside and headed toward the garden with Cerise in tow.

"That's a big garden," she said.

"Big as we need." Lloyd took her down a row. "There's the onions and there's the fancy onions. " He selected a dozen shallots. "This should do him for now."

"They're kind of muddy."

"You got to rinse all the dirt off under the tap there by the house. Then they can go into the kitchen. Gregoire doesn't like dirt in the kitchen."

"Go figure."

"On account it's against the law."

"What does he think's going to happen? Is Detective Creighton going to arrest him?"

"Did once. On account he thought Gregoire killed somebody. But he was wrong."

"So Detective Creighton isn't too bright, I guess."

Lloyd grinned. "Mr. Rudley says he's a boob and a flatfoot."

"Really."

"But Mrs. Rudley said it wasn't nice to say that."

"It's not."

"And Tiffany thinks he's like a detective in the movies on account he wears a felt hat and a raincoat and likes to look good. And Mr. Rudley says it's too bad he just looks good."

"What do you think?"

"He looks good, I guess. Can't tell if he's smart."

"Why not?"

"Just because he's smart doesn't mean he acts smart. Mr. Rudley says he wouldn't know a clue if one bit him on the behind."

"That bad."

"Mostly he goes around after Detective Brisbois and helps him, except Mr. Rudley says Detective Brisbois couldn't find a clue if one fell into his coffee."

"So Mr. Rudley doesn't like him."

"Mr. Rudley don't like the police around, seeing as how they disturb his peace." Lloyd walked Cerise to the water tap and turned it on. "There you go."

"So all of these crimes around here go unsolved."

Lloyd grinned. "Miss Miller solves most of them. And Mr. Rudley says she doesn't disturb things as much."

Cerise held the shallots under the water. "I got to tell you, this is a very strange place."

"That's what Detective Brisbois always says." Lloyd turned the tap off. "That's good enough. Shouldn't waste the water. It comes from the well."

Cerise didn't understand about the water shortage with a lake out front, nor did she particularly care. What was clear was that nobody around here was very bright. Except perhaps Miss Miller. She would have to be careful around Miss Miller. Manipulating women was not her forte. Once she had some resources — acquired one way or another — she would proceed with her previous plan.

Lloyd picked up his rake and finished smoothing over the flowerbed at the side of the house. He figured Gregoire had sent Cerise to get the shallots because he wanted to get rid of her. Gregoire didn't like too many people around him early in the morning. He said he got enough of them once the guests came in for breakfast. Plus he had to put up with Tim, who came before seven, so Lloyd guessed Tim was as hard to put up with as all of the guests. And Cerise was really hard to put up with because she asked a lot of questions, most of them nosy ones. He figured she was sweet on Detective Creighton and that was why she was asking all of the questions. Lloyd figured a lot of girls were sweet on Detective Creighton, and Tiffany was always comparing him to actors in the movies. Lloyd didn't know if Detective Creighton looked good or not to most people. He thought people he liked looked good, although Rudley was going bald, and Norman had teeth like a beaver, and the Benson sisters had a lot of wrinkles, and Mrs. Millotte had a skinny behind.

He liked them all and was always glad to see them so he guessed that meant they were good-looking. He figured he looked good to most people because someone was always saying that it was good to see him, sometimes because they needed to move furniture or have something fixed, but sometimes just because they were glad he was around. Rudley was always shooing him away, but that was because Rudley thought he looked best when he was doing something somewhere else. Gregoire was always making him take off his boots and wash his hands, but he let him sit in the kitchen and eat. And Tim, although he liked to tease him, always made sure he got some of whatever was being cooked in the kitchen. And Tiffany was always kind to him. So he knew they thought he looked good to see. And he knew for sure Mrs. Rudley thought he was good-looking because she called him sweet and liked having him around.

So, he decided, if people liked him, they liked the way he looked. He thought most people looked good, but the only things he thought really beautiful were the animals and plants he met around the inn. Albert was nice-looking and had a big smile and Blanche the cat was beautiful. The deer were the most beautiful. He was thinking of all of their attributes when he saw something he thought anyone would think was good to look at.

He watched it with fascination as it hopped along the edge of the house toward him. He held out his arm and the big bird happily scrambled toward him and perched on it.

"Feed Betty, feed Betty," it rasped.

Chapter Fifteen

Rudley was at the front desk when Lloyd entered. Lloyd was grinning.

"What are you smirking about?" Rudley demanded.

"Saw that bird you was looking for," said Lloyd. "You was right. He was this big" — he held out his hands to show Rudley — "and with a big hooked beak and bright feathers. And he talked to me just the way you said."

Rudley's eyes widened. "What did it say?"

"Asked me to feed him" — Lloyd paused — "except maybe he's a girl. Said his name was Betty."

"Betty," Rudley growled. "It seems a rather sedate name for such a vicious bird."

"Wasn't vicious. Came to sit on my arm and took the food I gave her just so. Then she picked around my head, but she didn't bite."

"Probably looking for lice," Rudley muttered.

"Don't have lice. Mrs. Rudley said so."

Rudley shrugged. "Margaret does know her nits." He grabbed his crutches and stood up. "She bit me."

"That's 'cause you probably scared her by yelling."

"I didn't yell until she yanked my hair out." Rudley started for the door. "Where did you put her?"

"Didn't put her anywhere. After I gave her the food she went back up into a tree."

Rudley turned back. "Damn. You should have got her and locked her up."

"Don't know if she wanted to get locked up."

"She can't stay out there. She'll be eaten by a hawk." Besides, he thought to himself, I'd love to prove to these naysayers that I know a parrot when I see one. "She belongs to somebody," Rudley continued out loud. "They'll want her back for some damn reason and she would probably be happier at home."

"Couldn't be too happy if she left," said Lloyd.

"She probably got out by mistake, got turned around and couldn't find her way home. Like Margaret when she gets onto a strange back road."

Lloyd knew that Mrs. Rudley sometimes said she was late because she decided to take a strange back road and got lost. He thought Mrs. Rudley had a good sense of direction and that sometimes she stayed away because she didn't want to come home, at least until she got over being mad at Mr. Rudley. He didn't say so because Mr. Rudley always got mad and yelled when he made that suggestion. "I think she'll just stay in that tree until she gets hungry again. Then she'll call me."

Rudley crossed his eyes. "It must be wonderful to have such good relationships with birds."

"Yes'm."

"I want you to show me where she is."

"You got to promise not to yell."

"I won't yell."

"And don't move too quick toward her."

Rudley glared. "How in hell am I going to move quickly on these damn things?"

"OK." Lloyd set out down the front steps, Rudley thumping behind him.

"Luther indicated we're short of greens," Leonard told Tibor.

"Frankes said the refrigerator is full of them."

"Luther says they're getting a bit gunky." Leonard smiled.

Tibor shook his head. How in hell could Luther say anything? The man was mute. Leonard had always said Luther had been traumatized as a child, and, as a result, wouldn't speak. There was, apparently, no anatomical reason. Sometimes Luther made noises that sounded like laughs or chuckles. Sometimes, they were inappropriate. Tibor thought he merely mimicked things he heard — much like Betty. He seemed to be able to perform a severely limited set of tasks. He could cook. He could clean up properly. He could dress himself and attend to his personal hygiene. Tibor couldn't see that Luther had learned a single new thing since he'd first met him.

Tibor gave in. "I'll send Frankes into town," he said.

He found Frankes on the veranda, leafing through a magazine. It galled him that Frankes could be so contented doing nothing.

"We need some stuff in town," he said tersely. "The lettuce is going bad."

Frankes got up cheerfully and held his hand out. Tibor reached into his pocket and handed him some money and a list. "Don't get too much fresh stuff at once," he muttered. "It doesn't keep more than a few days."

"Gotcha."

"Just do your business, and don't draw attention to yourself."

"Gotcha."

Frankes headed down the steps. Tibor watched him go, a sour expression on his face. Frankes had recently begun to use the word *gotcha* excessively. He found this rather irritating, even a bit insouciant. Since the appraiser had delivered his opinion, he found Frankes generally less respectful.

What a mess, he thought. Frankes was being semi-mutinous while Leonard was being erratic. He resolved they would return to St. Napoli in not more than two weeks. Sooner, if he could get Leonard inclined in that direction.

Rudley was quite miffed when the parrot proved not to be where Lloyd suggested it had been. He was at the desk now with Lloyd, explaining to the Phipps-Walkers that Lloyd had indeed seen the parrot. Cerise had arrived during the conversation and was leaning against the desk looking bored.

"She was a big bird," said Lloyd. "Said her name was Betty."

"That's a nice name for a bird," said Geraldine. "Although it's probably not her real name."

"You mean she's using an alias?" said Rudley.

"No, I mean it's a name a human has given her. She probably has some other sort of identification in the avian world."

"We're quite species-centric when it comes to these things, Rudley," said Norman. "For all we know, our avian friends have symbols to identify one another as individuals that our small unimaginative brains can't comprehend."

"Speak for yourself, Norman." Rudley turned to Lloyd. "I want you to go into town and get a birdcage big enough for that parrot. We need to capture her and hand her over to the authorities."

"She won't like a cage."

"Then get whatever you need to build something fancy, something she might like."

Cerise rolled her eyes.

"I saw that," said Rudley. "Take her with you," he told Lloyd.

Cerise made a show of holding her nose.

"Go," Rudley hissed. "If you want your allowance."

Cerise reluctantly followed Lloyd.

"She's a rather spirited young woman," said Norman.

Geraldine sniffed. "I find her rude and not particularly kind. I don't see what Detective Creighton sees in her."

"Who knows what anyone sees in anyone," Norman observed. "These things are very idiosyncratic, Geraldine."

True, thought Rudley, because I don't know what either of you see in each other. Apart from this infernal birdwatching.

"Yourself excepted," Norman continued, turning to Geraldine.

She gave him a pat on the cheek, "Why, Norman, that's very sweet."

He grinned.

"Well, we're off to lunch," said Geraldine.

As Geraldine turned away, Rudley said. "Good recovery, Norman."

"You might try a bit of that sort of tact and charm with Mrs. Rudley. That way she wouldn't be so annoyed with you at times." He hurried after Geraldine, leaving Rudley spluttering.

If I tried such nonsense on Margaret, she'd be appalled, he thought. Margaret appreciates the fact that I'm straightforward, not given to empty words or gestures. She knows I think she's the most beautiful, talented woman in the world. I don't have to come up with platitudes every few minutes. She knows what I'm thinking.

Frankes got the items on Tibor's list. The list did not include several chocolate bars, but so what? He was bored and when he was bored he found a few Cadbury bars just what the doctor ordered.

He was leaving the store when his eyes spotted something so unbelievable he had to squint. He hefted the grocery bag up to cover the lower part of his face and bent his head as if checking the bag's contents.

He saw Cerise emerge from the hardware store across the street with a lanky young man and get into the passenger's side of a half-ton truck. She didn't look Frankes's way. The young man placed what seemed to be wire and a paper bag into the bed of the truck. Then he climbed into the driver's seat and started the engine. Frankes peered at the writing on the side of the truck. The something Inn. He strained to see the rest of the inscription but a car passed between himself and the truck. He waited until the truck had disappeared, then hurried down to the dock. He got into the motorboat and set off to the island. He grinned. He couldn't wait to tell Tibor the news.

Rudley was hopping mad, his anger unmitigated by the exertion of poling his way down the lawn to the deep pit Chief Longbow was busy digging.

"Now see here," he demanded. "What do you think you're doing to my lawn?"

"I thought we had agreed it was my lawn, Mr. Rudley." The chief smiled.

"We agreed to disagree," Rudley bellowed. "We've let you stay out of the kindness of my wife's heart. We never imagined you would sully this land by digging a pit in the middle of it."

"It's hardly a pit, Mr. Rudley. I simply wanted a deeper arrangement for my bonfire."

"What bonfire?"

"The one I plan to have tonight. I want to make sure there's little risk of it spreading."

"I suppose this has to do with some sort of ritual."

"No, it has to do with me feeling a little chilly at night. I'm not a spring chicken."

"Do you realize how much work we do to keep this lawn in order?"

"Quite a bit, I imagine."

"Chief Whatever," Rudley said through clenched teeth, "I will be coming down here tomorrow morning. When I arrive here, I want to find that gulley filled in and suitably prepared for sodding. Then I'm going to call the police and you have no idea how it pains me to do that. But I have had it. You have taken advantage of my good nature for the last time. You will be out of here tomorrow or else."

"Or else?"

"You don't want to think about it."

"Now, that's rather harsh, Rudley," said a voice behind him. Rudley turned to find James Bole.

"I'm a patient man," Rudley protested as Mr. Bole urged him away. "But look at what he's done to my lawn."

"Lloyd will have it looking like new the minute he can get at it."

"That man is incorrigible."

"I find him rather charming, actually. Perhaps he's trying to make a point." Mr. Bole paused. "Or he may simply enjoy giving you a hard time — since you've been so unfailingly cordial."

"Why doesn't anyone ever take my side?"

Mr. Bole patted him on the back. "You have broad shoulders, Rudley. Providence never sends more than one can bear."

"Damn Providence! Why don't I just give each of the guests a spade? They can dig the whole place up."

"That might prove to be an interesting recreation. Perhaps I could top up the event by doing a puppet show. Perhaps *All Quiet on the Western Front*. The muddy, desolate terrain, the great craters."

"I get it."

"Now, come up to the inn. Mrs. Rudley will make you a cup of tea. Tim will serve it at your desk with a scone. I hear Gregoire has made some with blueberries that are very nice."

Rudley took a step forward, lurching as one crutch came down on the end of his elastic bandage, which had come loose and was trailing on the ground.

Mr. Bole put out an arm to keep him from falling. "Hold on a minute, Rudley. We have to do up your bandage." He knelt and rewrapped the bandage. "You seem to have lost your bandage clips."

"Those damn things are always falling out," Rudley muttered.

"I'll just tie it around until we get back inside," Mr. Bole said patiently. He gave Rudley an encouraging smile. "There, everything is, as they say, hunky-dory."

"Nothing will be hunky-dory until that man is gone!"

Tibor listened to Frankes's story, the muscles in his jaw working. "Are you sure it was her?"

Frankes hesitated. "It looked like her. She got into the other side of the truck. I had to keep my head down."

"Which way did they go?"

"Straight out of town. Headed west."

"Get that map of the lake."

"What for?"

"It should have the inns marked on it. If it doesn't, then get the phone book. Bring both of them."

Frankes returned a few moments later with the items. Tibor grabbed the map and scanned it, his eyes darting over the page. "There," he said finally. "There's three inns on that side of town."

"Doesn't look too far."

"You said she was with a guy and they were getting stuff from the hardware store."

"Yeah."

"She's probably not a guest then. Maybe she latched onto that guy you saw her with. That would be her style."

"She never tried to latch onto me."

"That's because you don't have anything she wants."

Frankes laughed. "So I guess she wouldn't have anything to do with you, either."

"She's a con artist. They could have coined the word for her."

"So what are we going to do?"

Tibor folded the map and threw it at Frankes. "We'll take the boat out around those inns, see if we can spot her."

Chapter Sixteen

Brisbois and Creighton left Cerise and Mary to talk and walked along the shore at his cottage, wandered out onto the dock. Brisbois glanced back at the cottage, then lit up a cigarette.

"I guess Mary's not too crazy about that." Creighton indicated the cigarette.

"No."

"Think maybe it's time to stop?"

"It's always time to stop." Brisbois took a deep drag. "She's a little more sensitive to it because I'm on vacation so I'm around more. Usually I do most of my smoking at work."

"I'm glad I never started," said Creighton. "I can thank my mother for that."

"Among other things."

"Yeah, I would have turned out to be a bum if it weren't for that woman."

Brisbois smiled. "You really admire your mother, don't you?"

"Sure, don't you admire yours?"

Brisbois blew a series of smoke rings before replying. "Of course. But I think that's one of your problems, Creighton. Your mother spoiled you for any other woman."

Creighton shrugged. "I guess she set the standard."

"So why don't you date someone like your mother?"

"Please, I don't want to be nagged to death the rest of my life."

"All of these women you've gone out with and I think Sherry's the only one I've seen more than once."

"Is this going to be one of those 'marriage would be so good for you' conversations?" He poked Brisbois in the arm. "You're as bad as my mother."

"It's not that." He gave Creighton an assessing gaze. "I just wondered what was going on with this girl."

"Not much. Mostly dinner and shopping."

"Is she making any progress in getting together her identification papers?"

Creighton cast his eyes over the lake. "She's done all she can for now. It'll probably be another couple of weeks before much happens. She doesn't have any family who can help."

"Are the Rudleys paying her?"

"They're giving her room and board and a little spending money."

"What does she do out there?"

"She can't work in the kitchen or dining room because of public health requirements. She helps out Lloyd mostly. Tiffany a bit. Although"— he added —"Tiffany doesn't seem to like her that much."

"I'm not surprised. Tiffany's been head of her piece of the kingdom for a long time. She probably finds it hard to work with someone, especially someone as" — he paused —"as forceful as Sherry."

"Forceful? You think she's forceful?"

"A T. Rex would think she was forceful."

Creighton laughed.

"She doesn't mind telling you where to go either, I've noted."

"I guess that's part of her charm."

"What does she do for a living?"

"She's kind of a flower child," Creighton replied. "It seems she mostly likes to travel. Works her way around as a caregiver or housekeeper." He watched as Brisbois snuffed out his cigarette. "I think she had kind of a bad childhood. She hints she spent time in an orphanage. I think that's why she's so antsy and kind of scatterbrained at times."

Brisbois sighed. "I can see that." He thought of some of the kids he'd met when he was assigned to the youth division. Maybe she'd been on the street and learned to live by her wits. He'd met those sorts of girls before. He glanced at Creighton. Some of those girls could tug at your heartstrings and string you along at the same time. He hoped this wasn't the case with Creighton because, as blasé as he tried to be, he appeared to be getting seriously attached to this girl.

Gregoire came to the front desk accompanied by Tim, who was trying hard to keep a straight face. "You must do something about Betty," he told Rudley.

Rudley crossed his eyes. He was waiting for Lloyd to finish the humane trap, though Lloyd seemed to be dragging his feet. Meanwhile, the Phipps-Walkers were urging him to do something before the poor bird was eaten by a raptor, though Rudley was finding this a less disturbing idea. Betty, or whatever her avian name was, kept calling him names whenever he put his nose out the door. His suspicions were growing that some of the guests and staff — he gave Tim a suspicious look — were teaching her new ones.

"She has tried to poke a hole in the screens so she can get into the kitchen," said Gregoire. "And then she almost flew in this morning when Lloyd opened the door. I cannot have her come into the kitchen. We would have to clean it with chlorine and throw all the food out."

"That drastic?" Rudley muttered.

"Birds carry viruses."

"She called him *fat*," said Tim with a smirk. "She said as clear as a bell 'Gregoire is fat.'"

"And I have been generous with her," said Gregoire.

"He saves her the worst parts of the fruit. Things that normally go into the composter," said Tim. "That's why she's insulting him."

"Ingrate," Gregoire muttered.

Rudley held up his hands in surrender. "Enough." He lurched over the desk and bellowed, "Lloyd!"

Lloyd appeared from the drawing room. "You was calling?"

"I was calling." Rudley tottered back on his crutches. "Now, Lloyd, I want that parrot trap finished and sitting on this desk in one hour."

"Mrs. Rudley wants me to hang the pictures in the drawing room."

"I don't give a damn what Mrs. Rudley wants." Rudley took a quick look around to make sure Mrs. Rudley had not heard him. "On this desk in one hour," he repeated. "Or we'll have to fumigate the kitchen. And that," he added on a note of triumph, "means no pie."

Lloyd grinned. "You can have it in an hour."

After trolling around the lake for four days, armed with binoculars, Tibor and Frankes finally caught sight of Cerise as she crossed the lawn at the Pleasant Inn early one morning.

"So," said Tibor with satisfaction, "we know where she's staying." He flipped open one of the brochures Frankes had picked up in Middleton. He traced a finger along the map of the grounds. "That's the bunkhouse."

"So she probably isn't the only one who lives there."

"We'll go there early in the morning, hide out, and the minute we see her, we'll grab her." He nodded toward the boathouse. "That looks like the perfect place to get in without being seen and get out fast."

"But what if somebody sees us?"

"We'll just have to make sure there's nobody else around." Tibor lowered his binoculars. "If it doesn't look good the first time, we'll abort the mission and try again."

Frankes laughed. "Now we're going into space."

Tibor shot him an angry look. "Just shut up and pull in the anchor. We've got to get back before the old man freaks on us and starts trying to use the phone."

"Yeah, it was a good idea to take that out," said Frankes.

"He's getting a little too edgy."

Tibor scanned the shoreline and raised a hand. He and Frankes were fifty yards offshore, directly in line with the entrance to the Pleasant Inn's boathouse. "Cut the motor," he growled at Frankes. "We'll paddle in from here."

Frankes did as told, squinting into the darkness. "How do you know we're in the right place?"

Tibor counted to ten before he spoke. Frankes had developed cold feet once he announced that tonight was the night for Operation Cerise. He was tired of Frankes's what ifs — what if this or that happens, what if we get caught — and any number of tedious questions that showed Frankes was losing his nerve now that the mission to nab Cerise had turned from theory to reality. "Do you see that light?" he asked, pointing to a blinking red light to the right.

"Yeah."

"Well, that's the light at the end of the dock. The boathouse is approximately thirty yards to the left of the dock."

"Oh," Frankes said uncertainly. He pushed a hand into his wetsuit and gave his chest a vigorous scratch. "This thing is itchy."

"I don't know why you're wearing that," Tibor groused. He was wearing a black pullover and jeans himself.

"The water here's cold and slimy."

"You won't be going in the water."

"Yeah," Frankes mumbled, "but if anybody has to, it's going to be me."

Tibor picked up a paddle. "Let's do this."

They paddled toward the boathouse. The night was dark, the moon a pale shadow behind shifting clouds.

They eased the boat into the boathouse. Tibor threw out a rope, the loop finding a mooring post. Tibor hoisted himself out onto the broad apron. Frankes followed. Tibor shone the flashlight around, noting two doors, one on each side, and a small window over a storage chest. "We'll take that door," he decided, indicating the one to his left.

"Why?"

"Because it's further away from the main house," Tibor hissed.

"What time is it?" Frankes asked.

Tibor shone the flashlight on his watch. "Twenty to three." He pushed open the door and looked around, noting with satisfaction the faint glow of the decorative solar lamps along the pathway to the bunkhouse. He tucked his flashlight into his pocket and beckoned to Frankes. "Come on."

They approached the bunkhouse and crept around the side toward the front door. Tibor stopped and held up a hand. Frankes, following closely, stumbled into him.

"Careful," Tibor whispered. He eased up to the end of the wall, poked his head around, then withdrew quickly. "Damn."

"What?"

"It looks like some sort of stationary camera over the door," Tibor mumbled. "It's probably got a motion-detection light."

"Let's get out of here." Frankes turned and headed toward the boathouse. Tibor followed.

They slipped in the door of the boathouse and came to an abrupt halt. The flame from a Zippo lighter illuminated a leathery face.

"Who are you?" Frankes blurted.

"I could ask the same," said Chief Longbow. "I thought I saw somebody sneaking around," he continued as Frankes and Tibor gaped at him. He winced at the heat from the lighter, then fumbled along the wall for a light switch.

Tibor moved quickly, ramming a shoulder into the chief. The chief grabbed at him, but his fingers slid from Tibor's neck. He fell backwards, striking his head on the apron. He uttered a deep grunt and rolled into the water.

Frankes scrambled after the chief. Tibor held him back.

"He's unconscious," Frankes protested. "He's going to drown."

"Let him."

Frankes stared at Tibor in horror, then backed away. He turned toward the water, gulping as bile rose in his throat. "Let's get out of here," he whispered.

Tibor grabbed Frankes's upper arm and squeezed down hard. "Wait." He took a deep breath. "We'll wait. We saw her come out of that bunkhouse before. She'll do it again."

"It's going to get light soon."

"If anybody else comes around, we'll just say we got lost and came into the wrong boathouse."

"What about him?" Frankes gestured toward the water, his voice quavering.

Tibor shone a light into the water. The chief floated just below the surface. His hat bobbed gently on the surface. Tibor turned and scanned the boathouse, his gaze settling on a long box along the wall under the window. He walked over and opened the lid.

"What is it?" Frankes asked.

"Life preservers," Tibor snapped. "We'll stuff him in here."

"Let's just leave."

Tibor seized Frankes by the shoulders, turned him around, and shoved him toward the water. "Get in there and bring him to the side. I'll help you pull him out. Get his hat too."

Frankes hesitated, then did as told. Tibor waited as Frankes towed the body to the side, then reached down and grabbed the chief by the shirt. Together, they hauled him up onto the apron. Tibor folded the chief's arms over his chest. "Get him under the hips," he commanded Frankes.

With effort, they lifted the chief into the life-preserver box. Tibor retrieved the hat, stuffed it in beside the chief and closed the lid.

Frankes opened the lid and put a hand on the chief's wrist.

"He's dead," Tibor snapped. He pulled Frankes away from the box, lowered the lid again, then peeked out the window. "All quiet," he whispered.

For the next fifteen minutes, the boathouse was silent except for Frankes's shallow breaths.

"What time is it?" Frankes said weakly. He had sunk down against the wall, and sat with his legs pulled up against his chest, his head resting on his knees.

Tibor checked his watch. "Nearly four." He was about to tell Frankes to get a grip on himself when something caught his attention. A light had gone on in the bunkhouse. "Someone's up," he muttered.

Frankes rolled onto his knees, wincing as a nail bit into his leg. He got up unsteadily and stared over Tibor's shoulder. "Somebody heard us," he croaked. "Let's get out of here."

Tibor reached to stop Frankes but he was already in the boat, reaching to undo the rope to cast off. Tibor cursed and followed.

In the bunkhouse, Gregoire dressed for the day, unaware of the drama taking place a few yards away.

Chapter Seventeen

Rudley went to the veranda the next morning, eager to check the cage Lloyd had placed there. The minute he opened the door, he heard the scratching. I've got her, he thought triumphantly, thumping his crutches over to the cage. He groaned. Inside was a bright-eyed chipmunk that regarded him with bulging cheeks.

"What are you doing in there? I set this trap for a specific purpose. There's plenty of food around here to suit your needs. I don't even know if pineapple is part of a proper diet for a rodent like yourself." He opened the door and shooed the chipmunk away. "Off with you now."

The chipmunk scampered onto the porch railing and across the lawn into a maple. Rudley thumped down the stairs, casting an eye about for the bullfrog, which met him on his way up. "Now, you can just turn around and be on your way back to the swamp."

The bullfrog blinked at him without interest.

"As you can see," Rudley continued, "I'm somewhat compromised. You'll have to get back on your own. That should not be a problem. You always get here on your own, after all."

"Talking to the frogs again?" Tim chortled as he approached.

Rudley stumped around to face him. "I'm glad you're here."

"Well, that's different," said Tim.

"You can carry him back to the swamp."

Tim looked at the frog askance. "He has frog slime on him."

"He's a frog."

Tim reached down and gingerly picked up the bullfrog. "No funny stuff," he told the amphibian.

Rudley watched Tim head for the swamp, holding the bullfrog at arm's length. He knew Tim had nothing against the creatures; he just didn't like to get a spot of anything on his pristine white shirt. He returned to the front desk in a better mood.

Cerise was there when he arrived, writing on a piece of paper.

"Where's Margaret?"

"In the kitchen." She gave him an aggrieved look. "I'm not allowed to go into the kitchen, you know." She finished her note and stuck it on the spike.

"What was that?"

"Mr. Smith, about a reservation."

"Why in hell is anyone calling at this time of morning?"

"Maybe he's calling from where the time's later," she said. "He wanted to change his reservation."

Rudley grabbed the note and began to leaf through the reservation book. "Alvin Smith. Alvin Smith," he muttered.

"Oh, maybe some other name," she said wearily. "He just said Mr. Smith and Alvin seemed to suit him."

"Damn," said Rudley.

"He said he's booked into the Oaks for the first week in August. He wants to change it to the second week. I looked at your reservation book. There wasn't anyone booked then so I pencilled him in."

He flipped ahead to August. There it was, just as she said. "Why didn't you tell me that in the first place?" he said, aggrieved.

"It's so much fun to see you blow your stack. Anyway, now that you're here," she continued, sounding as if he had been egregiously truant, "I'm getting some breakfast. Do you want anything?"

"Coffee," he said, subdued, "and whatever Gregoire thinks is good. A scone or muffin."

After Cerise left, Rudley consigned her message to the recycle bin. "She's cheeky," he told Albert, who had padded in from the drawing room in anticipation of food. "I'm rather accustomed to that, but she has no respect whatsoever. I hope she gets her issues straightened out soon and can go back to wherever she's come from."

He paused in thought. Except she didn't seem to have come from anywhere. When he'd asked her, she'd replied that she was a citizen of the world. "What in hell does that mean?" he harrumphed to Albert.

He himself was from Galt, Ontario, and wasn't shy about saying so. The place a man is from shapes who he is, he thought with conviction. Galt was a solid town in a solid part of the world, an exemplar of the Canadian experience, and he, Trevor Rudley, was a solid man, a fine example of a Canadian.

"You came from a den dug in under a barn," he told Albert, who favoured him with a dog smile and drooled on the rug. "The people at the pound said you were as dirty as a pig and smelled like dead fish."

Cerise reappeared with a tray containing two cups of coffee, a fruit salad, and a raisin scone. A second scone was clamped between her teeth, which she removed when she placed the tray on the desk. "I hope this suits you."

"It suits me fine."

He expected her to go, but she leaned against the desk and took one of the cups as if she were ready to make herself at home.

"Don't you have anything to do?" he asked her.

"No."

He was about to suggest something when the sound of a motor announced the arrival of the laundryman. Rudley thumped to the door and threw it open. Betty flew in, landed on his head, then launched herself onto the desk. Rudley turned to see her chowing down on his fruit salad.

"Damn!" Rudley hobbled back to the desk, bellowing for Tim, Lloyd, or whoever else could hear him.

The laundryman came up the steps and entered, closing the door behind him.

"What are you doing here?" Rudley demanded as Cerise narrowed her eyes at the avian intruder.

"I've come to deliver your linens, as usual," said the laundryman. "I heard you bellowing. I assume you're concerned about your bullfrog. I did not run over him." His eyes travelled to the bird. "I see you have a parrot."

"She is not my parrot," said Rudley. "She flew in here expecting us to feed her and is generally making a nuisance of herself."

"Just one of the guests then," said the laundryman.

"If you want to do something useful, keep your ears open in case someone is looking for their parrot."

"I will, of course, do that. But have you considered contacting the pound?"

"Now, there's an original idea," Rudley grumped. "The pound doesn't have the facilities for her. They've suggested a wildlife refuge several thousand miles away."

"Sweetie, Sweetie," the parrot chirped. She flew suddenly to Cerise's shoulder, leaned down and speared a raisin from her scone.

"She seems to like you," the laundryman observed.

"She wants my scone," said Cerise. "Besides, I'm the only one who hasn't been trying to trap her and put her in a box."

"Mr. Rudley has always been a master of the subtle approach," the laundryman tittered. "By the way, I noticed that pit on your lawn is getting rather large."

Rudley gripped the hand rests of his crutches so hard his knuckles turned white. "And that's something that's going to stop right now!" He abandoned his breakfast and thumped off down the front steps.

"He's a very dynamic man," the laundryman said to Cerise.

Rudley made his way to the chief's camp, pausing to stare at the gaping hole in his lawn. He next noticed that, although it was well past sunrise, the chief's fire pit was cold, the coffee pot absent. He went around to the front of the tent and called to him. Receiving no answer, he tried again. He bent forward on his crutches as far as he dared and tried to see past the tent flap.

"Guess he isn't up."

"Damn." Rudley jerked back in alarm, noting Lloyd at his shoulder. "What in hell are you doing here?"

Lloyd grinned. "Was looking to tell you I'm going into town. You said to look for you when I went because there was something you wanted from the feed store."

Rudley searched his mind but found it blank. "How in hell should I know what I want?" he barked. "I don't want anything." He peered into the tent again, cupping his hands around his mouth, shouting, "Chief, I need to talk to you." He paused. "I refuse to be ignored. I know you're in there." He considered the chief's boundary line and took a step forward. "I want you to know I'm crossing the line."

"Mrs. Rudley says you did that a long time ago," Lloyd noted.

"Grass seed," said Rudley, suddenly remembering. "We need grass seed." He took a step closer to the tent. "Chief, I'm coming ahead." He turned to Lloyd. "Be on your way now."

"I'm going to take the boat on account I can't find the truck keys."

Rudley thought about the last place he'd thrown them, recalling the metallic sound as they slid through a heat register. "All right." He made a shooing motion toward Lloyd. "Off with you now."

After Lloyd had gone, Rudley cleared his throat. "Now, Chief, I don't wish to be unpleasant, but we must resolve this issue for once and for all. I'm sure if you consult the area maps you will find that the piece of land you have pitched your tent on is the only one that could remotely be in contention and only because there was a crease in the paper when it was copied for the office. That certainly doesn't include the boathouse or the other lands to which you have recently laid claim. As I've made clear, I respect your right to contest what you believe is yours, but we need the boathouse, and even if we were to give you the run of the place, we need it from time to time. I cannot pretend to address the issue of your original dispossession from this land. But I paid the Mafia — albeit once or twice removed — for this property. Surely we can work out something, man to man."

"The Chief ain't in there," a voice behind Rudley announced.

Rudley started. Lloyd again. "Where in hell is he?"

"He's in the boathouse."

"So he's gone ahead and moved in."

"Don't know."

"What did he have to say for himself?"

"Nothing. He's in the life-preserver box."

Rudley gave him a quizzical look. "What's he doing in there? Didn't you tell him those things are the property of the Pleasant?"

"Didn't tell him anything. On account he's dead."

"Nonsense." Rudley took off, poling vigorously toward the boathouse, Lloyd loping behind him. He thumped into the boathouse and stopped. "Where is he?"

"In the box."

"The lid's down."

"Closed it after I opened it. You like it kept closed so the rats don't get in."

Rudley cast Lloyd an aggrieved look, then flung the lid open. "Damn." He looked down at the chief's strangely pale face. "He can't be dead."

"Dead as a doornail,' said Lloyd.

"Damn," Rudley repeated. "What the hell." He gave Lloyd an accusing look. "Why are you finding dead bodies? Isn't that Tiffany's job?"

"Tiffany's taking around the laundry."

"Well, he can't be dead. He probably got cold in his tent and came in here to keep warm." He shook the chief, recoiled. "God damn it, he's as stiff as a board."

"On account he's dead as a doornail."

"Damn," said Rudley yet again.

"Guess," Lloyd said, "we've got to preserve the scene."

Rudley stood on the lawn outside the police tape, waiting impatiently for Detective Sherlock, who had ordered him to remain there, to return. He was about to complain to Officer Owens, who stood just inside the tape, when Sherlock returned.

"So you're Trevor Rudley," said the dapper young man. He was perfectly groomed with a slender moustache. He wore a blue blazer, grey slacks, white shirt, and club tie, gleaming black oxfords and a black fedora set at a conservative angle.

Rudley glared at the detective. "Didn't I just tell you that?"

"Just murmuring to myself." The man reviewed his notes. "To recap…you found the deceased, whom you identify as Chief Longbow, in the boathouse in a box of life preservers."

"I didn't find him anywhere. Lloyd, our handyman, found him."

"And he summoned you."

"He came to tell me that Chief Longbow was in the boathouse because I had been looking for him at his campsite."

"Why was the handyman looking for him?"

Rudley counted to ten. "Lloyd wasn't looking for him. He discovered him when he went to take the boat out."

"And he told you he was deceased."

"Eventually. I didn't believe him."

"Oh, is he in the habit of telling you someone is dead when they are not?"

"No, I simply don't like to hear that sort of news. Then I opened the lid —"

"That would be the lid on the chest of life preservers."

"Yes."

"But he didn't run up to you and say the chief's in the boathouse and he's dead."

"Not immediately."

"That seems strange."

"It doesn't seem strange at all," Rudley protested. "We're talking about Lloyd. Besides…" He started to say that finding dead bodies at the Pleasant was nothing to write home about. Instead he asked, "Where's Brisbois?"

"I'm the detective on this case."

"I take it Brisbois refused to come this time." He stopped as the detective gave him a long look. "We've always had Brisbois and Creighton. It seems inconsiderate to send someone we have to break in."

The detective started to say something, changed his mind. "If you've got a problem with that, take it to the brass." He reached into his breast pocket, removed a silver cardholder, and handed it to Rudley.

"John Sherlock," Rudley murmured, adding, "I suppose you're finished with me."

"You suppose right. For now."

Rudley cleared his throat. "Surely, you don't believe this is a homicide. Surely it has to be death from natural causes."

"If you think it's natural for someone to die in a box of life preservers with the lid down."

"Perhaps he got tired of sleeping on the ground. He was not a young man."

"Did you ever consider giving him a cot?"

Rudley bristled. "We gave him everything but the kitchen sink. My wife is a generous woman. She'd give anyone the shirt off my back."

Sherlock allowed himself a quick smile. "The man's dead. He'll be autopsied. Perhaps we're dealing with an unexpected death through natural causes and nothing more. But in the meantime, we'll be poking around, asking questions, the usual. Keep your guests where they are and make your staff available."

"All right, all right." Rudley waved his arms in frustration. "We know the drill."

Sherlock gave him a knowing smirk. "So I've heard."

Sherlock left Rudley spluttering and strode over to where Lloyd was waiting for him on a bench on the lower lawn. He introduced himself formally, showed his badge, then sat down beside him.

"Full name?" he asked, pen poised.

"Lloyd Brawly."

"Middle name?"

Lloyd grinned. "Don't think so."

Sherlock paused, slightly taken aback, then forged ahead. "You were the person who found the man known as Chief Longbow in the boathouse."

"Yes'm."

"And where was he when you found him?"

"In the box of life-preservers. Dead as a doornail."

"And how did you know he was dead?"

"Didn't have any pulse. Wasn't breathing. Kind of cold and stiff. Just lying on his back as nice as you please with his arms folded over his chest."

Sherlock checked his notes. "Lid up or down?"

"Was down until I lifted it. Then I put it down again on account Mr. Rudley don't like it left up." Lloyd grinned. "Says it lets the rats get in."

"And what were you doing in the boathouse?"

"Went to get a boat to get the groceries."

"And that's your usual practice? To take a boat to get groceries?"

"Mostly take the truck but Mr. Rudley lost the keys."

Sherlock made a few notes, then pressed on. "So what made you look in the life-preserver box?"

"'Cause I was going in the boat. It's the law."

"Commendable," Sherlock muttered. "So," he said, "how well did you know the chief?"

"Not much."

"Did you like him?"

"Nothing not to like."

"Did Mr. Rudley like him?"

"Didn't like him digging up the lawn but never said he didn't like him. Let him pitch his tent on the lawn and gave him stuff."

Sherlock flipped back through his notes, reviewing what Officer Owens had told him about this odd situation. He decided to shift tactics. "So how did you sleep last night?" he asked pleasantly.

"On my cot in the tool shed just like always. In my shorts."

Sherlock's brow creased. "I mean, did you sleep all night? Did you wake up during the night?"

"Woke up around five."

"Why so early?"

"Things to do."

"Things?"

"First I have to get out of bed. Then I have to feed the chipmunks."

"So around five you got up and went out to feed the chipmunks."

"Nope. They came in."

Sherlock rubbed his forehead. "The chipmunks come in?"

Lloyd grinned. "Yup. Right down the tree onto the roof and in through the transom."

"What about the skunks and raccoons?" Sherlock said sarcastically. "Do they come in?"

"The raccoons are too fat to get in and the skunks don't climb so well."

Sherlock sighed. "All right. What did you do next?"

"Got dressed and went to get breakfast. Apple muffin and milk on account the pancakes weren't ready. The grill has to be hot so a drop of water scoots."

"Take the chipmunks with you?"

"Nope. On account Gregoire won't let them into the kitchen."

Sherlock rolled his eyes. "And who is Gregoire?"

"The cook."

Sherlock decided to try a different approach. "You like Mr. Rudley?"

"Yes'm."

"Chief Longbow was ruining Mr. Rudley's lawn. That must have made you mad."

"Nope."

"Really? I'd be mad if someone did that to someone I liked."

"Never get mad. It's hard on your digestion and makes your blood pressure zoom way up. Mr. Rudley is always mad and Mrs. Rudley says he's going to have a heart attack and a stroke."

"So nothing makes you mad."

"Maybe if somebody hurt Blanche or Albert."

Sherlock made a note. "And who are they?"

"Our cat and our dog."

Sherlock sat back, gave Lloyd a long appraising look. "What would you say if I said I thought you killed Chief Longbow?"

Lloyd grinned. "Would say you was wrong."

"Would it make you mad?"

"Nope, but would make Mrs. Rudley mad if you said I did something I didn't do."

Sherlock sat in silence for a minute, trying to decide if Lloyd were incredibly stupid or incredibly smart. "So when you found Chief

Longbow and you decided he was dead, you ran and told Mr. Rudley right away."

"Didn't run. Walked fast."

"So you walked fast and said to Mr. Rudley 'The chief is dead.'"

"Not all at once."

"Why not?"

"Sometimes it's better to tell him things in little bits. He gets mad when you tell him somebody's dead."

Sherlock nodded wearily. "And then he would have a stroke or an upset stomach." He folded his notebook. "Have you ever had your fingerprints taken? Has anybody ever swabbed your mouth?"

"Yup, on account Detective Brisbois had all that done and on most everybody who ever came here."

Sherlock smiled. "I guess that's one thing I won't have to do."

Sherlock let Lloyd go, sat back and stared into the canopy. Interviewing that guy was like pulling teeth, he thought. He drew a hand along his jaw. His own teeth.

Chapter Eighteen

After Sherlock released him with the usual admonishments, Rudley returned to the inn. He had elbowed the front door aside when Margaret came up the back stairs from the basement. The phone was ringing.

"Rudley"—she stopped at the top of the stairs—"what is going on? I was down in the basement, looking up some of the old receipts and the phone was ringing off the hook. I took calls from the butcher, the baker, and the candlestick maker."

"Well, at least no one barged into the office to arrest you."

She shook her head, uncomprehending.

"The chief is dead." He slumped against the doorjamb. "Dead as a doornail."

She put a hand to her mouth. "Oh, Rudley!"

"Lloyd found him in the life-preserver box," he said gloomily. "Dead as a doornail."

She came to him, put her arms around him. "Rudley, I'm so sorry."

"You couldn't possibly be sorrier than I am, Margaret. I've just spent twenty minutes being grilled — most disrespectfully — by some young whippersnapper called Sherlock."

"Sherlock?"

"Yes, natty young ass, no personality, no sense of how things are done around here."

"Where's Detective Brisbois?"

"Apparently, he's not available. Perhaps he's still on vacation."

"Perhaps he's tired of coming here," she said with a sigh. "Or perhaps they thought at the office we were all becoming too familiar."

He grabbed the phone. "Well, I'm going to call the station and find out where he is. I'm not putting up with this idiot."

She moved the phone away from him. "Rudley, I don't think you can put in an order for the police officer of your choice. It's not as if it's takeaway."

"He doesn't need to be here anyway," Rudley grumbled. "No one killed the old bugger. I think he just climbed into the box and had a heart attack."

"Rudley, why would he crawl into a box in the boathouse to have a heart attack?"

He shook his head. "How should I know, Margaret?" He sagged forward on his crutches. "Perhaps he thought it would be warmer in there. Or softer."

"It wasn't particularly chilly last night. He had a ground sheet in his tent and a sleeping bag. I think that would be more comfortable than a box of lumpy life preservers."

"Perhaps he had a heart attack, became disoriented and ended up in the boathouse."

She considered this. "I suppose that could happen, Rudley. But it's more likely someone put him in there."

He sighed, thumped in behind the desk. "Couldn't you be on my side on this, Margaret?"

"It's not a matter of being on your side. If the poor man's been murdered, we can't hide our heads in the sand."

"Damn." He collapsed forward onto his desk, elbows digging into the wood, head between his forearms. "I never thought that was an appealing place to stick one's head, but if someone gave me a pail of it right now..."

She patted his arm.

"I don't know how you missed all of this, Margaret. Ambulances. Sirens. Police cars."

"I was rather distracted with the phone ringing, Rudley. Besides, it's not that easy to hear anything from the boathouse when you're in the basement. If they had come across the front of the inn, I'm sure I would have noticed."

He lifted his head, tufts of hair sticking out in all directions. She patted it down with one hand. "You must stop pulling at your hair, Rudley. I'm sure that's why you're going bald."

He stared across the lobby, his expression doleful. "I'm going bald, Margaret, because of all the nonsense that takes place around here."

She sighed. "I'm afraid it's all an inconvenience for us, Rudley. For Chief Longbow, it's a tragedy. The poor man is dead."

He nodded reluctantly. "I know. He was not a bad man, even likeable in a way. But in many ways he was damn irritating, and why did he have to die here?"

"Everyone else seems to, Rudley, whether they want to or not." She brightened. "On the positive side, statistically, it does tend to make every other place safer."

"Somehow that doesn't make me feel better."

"Did the police have any idea of who he might be?"

"No," he said, distracted. "I imagine they'll be able to figure that out eventually."

"It seems strange that he would come here alone to make a land claim. Why wouldn't he bring members of his tribe with him for support?"

He crossed his eyes. "Margaret, if I had a chance to get away from my tribe, I would take it."

The silence was broken by a knock at the door.

"Come in," Rudley bellowed. Receiving no answer, he hobbled across the lobby and flung the door open.

Detective Sherlock stood on the veranda, hat in hands.

"You don't have to knock," Rudley snapped. "This is an inn, for god's sakes."

"Merely trying to be courteous."

"I don't know why," Rudley grumbled. "No one else does."

Sherlock glanced at Margaret. "And she is?"

"She's my wife, Margaret," Rudley replied.

Sherlock nodded and addressed her: "And where have you been?"

"I've been here. I've been in the basement most recently. I didn't realize anything had happened until Rudley told me."

"And what did he tell you?"

"He told me that Chief Longbow had been found dead in the box of life preservers in the boathouse."

"And when did you last see Chief Longbow?"

"I saw him last evening, about six, when I took a plate of food and a thermos of coffee to him."

Sherlock made a note. "And this was a regular habit? Taking food to the deceased?"

"I don't think he had much with him. And it did keep him from setting fire to the tent." She paused. "He didn't seem very good at managing his campfire. He had a nasty burn on his arm. I don't think his vision was the best." She smiled. "Detective, could I get you a cup of coffee?"

"No, thank you," he responded, absorbed in his notes. "Do you know if he was taking any medications?"

"I don't know. Apart from his vision, he seemed in reasonable condition."

"Did he say anything about his family, associates?"

"He said he was a member of the Algonquin nation," Margaret said.

"That's like saying his name was Smith."

"Now see here," said Rudley. "There's no reason to insult my wife. She's from England. How is she supposed to know anything about our Canadian tribes?"

"I wouldn't think Longbow would be a common name," said Margaret.

"Did he have any visitors?"

"Not that I know of."

"According to your husband, he laid claim to a patch of land when he arrived and then expanded that claim to include the area up to and including the boathouse."

"That's true."

"And your husband was happy with that?"

"Of course he wasn't, Detective."

"And he wanted him away?"

"He was willing to let him stay undisturbed when he thought it was just for the summer and involved just the area of his campsite. But when the chief made further claims and seemed to be ready to stay indefinitely, he realized that could be a problem."

"And how was he planning to solve that problem?"

"He had turned the matter over to our lawyer."

"Who would have taken until hell freezes over to get anything done," Rudley grumbled as Margaret winced and tried to shush him.

"So perhaps you decided the legal route wouldn't work and decided to take things into your own hands," Sherlock suggested.

"I decided to have it out with him, man to man."

"And so you did?" Sherlock raised his brows.

Margaret gave Rudley a sharp poke with her elbow. "Detective, I assure you, Rudley had nothing to do with Chief Longbow's death. Rudley is all talk. He wouldn't hurt a fly. He's never killed a single soul around here, human or otherwise. The chief wandered in here, set up his tent. We've done our best to accommodate him."

"So it seems," Sherlock murmured. He turned a page in his notebook. "Mrs. Rudley, what time did you get up this morning?"

"About six."

"And then you came downstairs?"

"Not immediately. I had my bath, helped Rudley and his cast out of bed, got him underway."

"And what time did he get underway?"

"About six-thirty. He's usually down earlier but with the cast…"

He made a note. "Go on."

"I came downstairs, got a cup of tea in the kitchen and took it to the basement office. I wanted to review last month's receipts."

Sherlock smoothed his moustache. "And was Mr. Rudley up during the night?"

"No."

He fixed her with a steady gaze. "Are you sure?"

"Detective, you may have to take my word for it, but when you share a bed with a man in a cast, you tend to notice when he gets out of it." When he didn't respond, Margaret added, "Believe me, Detective, no one here would harm the chief."

"That remains to be seen." Sherlock closed his notebook. "I've got some more poking around to do. Don't go anywhere, please. I'll want to talk to you again."

"Now he's starting to act like Brisbois," Rudley fumed as Sherlock departed.

"That's good, Rudley. You like things to be familiar."

Sherlock left the inn, noted Sheffield and Maroni taking a break by the forensics van and pulled a map from his pocket. He checked it, looking up uncertainly toward the Elm Pavilion. He decided to take a chance and knock on the door, but there was no answer. He knocked louder.

This time he heard footsteps crossing the floor. The door flung open and he found himself face to face with an imposing older woman.

"Didn't you hear me say *come in?*" the woman said.

"Sorry, I didn't." Sherlock removed his hat and introduced himself, adding, "I'd like to ask you a few questions."

"We've already been asked a few questions by Officer Vance."

"Officer Vance is filling in for Detective Brisbois," a voice called out from across the room.

The woman tilted her head toward the voice. "My sister Louise," she said. "And the one on the sofa with the movie magazine is Kate. And I'm Emma Benson." She gave him an appraising look. "Identification?"

Sherlock presented his badge. "I'm investigating the death of a man known here as Chief Longbow."

"Oh, he's not likely to be a chief," said Emma dismissively.

"You say he's dead?" Louise said in a surprised tone.

"We know he's dead, Louise," said Emma. "Officer Vance told us that."

"I thought Lloyd said he was."

Emma looked pained. "Tiffany said he was. Officer Vance confirmed the fact."

Louise clasped her hands to her bosom. "Oh, yes, I like Officer Vance. I love his moustache."

"He's bald," said Emma. She marched over to the sofa and tapped Kate on the shoulder. "Kate, put down that magazine. This man, who says he's a detective, is asking about Chief Longbow."

Kate gave Sherlock a dubious look. "How do we know you're a detective?"

"He showed me his identification," said Emma.

"It could have been forged," said Louise. "Remember the man Daddy knew who forged passports?"

"Daddy knew lots of men who forged passports," said Kate.

"He was a spy," said Louise.

"Some of them were women," said Kate.

"You aren't Detective Brisbois," said Louise.

Sherlock sighed.

"Sit down," said Emma. She hauled an occasional chair out for Sherlock. "We'll get this business straightened up."

"There's nothing..." Sherlock began and gave up. He sat down, took out his notebook and wrote: Interview with Benson sisters, Elm Pavilion. Two clearly insane, he thought. Not sure which two.

"Now," said Emma, "why would they send you out here to investigate this case? Detective Brisbois is clearly more qualified."

Sherlock mentally crossed out the word *two* and considered that all three were clearly insane. He turned a page, made a note of the time, date, place, and circumstances of the interview subjects. "So you're the Benson sisters."

"All three of us," said Kate.

"Miss, Mrs., Ms.? Sherlock asked.

"Miss," said Emma, irritated.

"Can you imagine all three of us marrying men called Benson?" Kate tittered.

"Or a man named anything," Emma murmured.

"Now, Emma," said Kate. "Not every man can be like Daddy."

"Daddy was a spy," said Louise.

"For whom?" Sherlock muttered.

The sisters looked at one another.

"It was for us, wasn't it?" said Kate. She looked wistfully at her 1940s magazine featuring Cary Grant. "Daddy was so handsome. He looked just like Cary Grant."

"I thought he looked like Ronald Coleman," said Louise.

"If you look at any of his photographs," said Emma, "you'd find he actually resembled R.B. Bennett."

"We may disagree about whom Daddy resembled," said Louise, "but we agree Chief Longbow did not look like an Algonquin."

"His facial structure was not correct," said Kate.

"And his clothing was not correct."

"Not his clothing, *per se*," said Emma. "It was the artifacts that he claimed to be particular to his situation — amulets, feathers, and so forth."

Sherlock looked up from his notebook. "So you've met the man?"

"We had him for brunch," said Kate.

"He was quite handsome," Louise added.

"He was a fraud," Emma sniffed. "Those feathers in his hat probably came from a Barred Rock chicken."

"There are farms on the road up off the lake," said Kate. "You might want to check with them."

"Or perhaps Detective Brisbois could," added Louise. "Detective Brisbois is highly intelligent."

Sherlock glowered. "Detective Brisbois is not available."

Kate snuck another look at Cary Grant. "What about Detective Creighton? He's very handsome. Rather like Ray Milland."

"I think he looks like Gregory Peck," Louise countered.

"More like Ray Milland," said Emma.

"But you're handsome too," said Louise. "Much like a young Sean Connery."

Sherlock's pen twitched. "Ladies, as much as I appreciate the comparison, I'm here seeking information about the man who called himself Chief Longbow."

"We know he was not a chief," said Emma. "He was not an Algonquin. And I doubt very much if his name was Longbow."

"Didn't Daddy know a Chief Longbow?" Louise broke in.

Emma uttered a dismissive grunt. "That was Chief Burton-Doyle in Gloucester. He lived down the street from us when we were children."

"Do you think *he* knew who your father was spying for?" Sherlock asked sarcastically.

"Oh, Chief Burton-Doyle wouldn't have known Daddy was a spy. He thought he was an economist," Kate giggled. "That's rather ironic, I suppose. Daddy couldn't balance a chequebook to save his life."

Sherlock rolled his eyes. Emma responded with a stern look and said, "I suppose you think we're a little loopy, young man."

"He's not as good at hiding that as Detectives Brisbois and Creighton," said Kate.

"Some of us may be a little muddled at times," said Emma with a surreptitious nod toward Louise. "And some of us may be inclined to fancy. But we know our indigenous North Americans."

"And we know a chicken feather when we see one," added Louise. "So there."

Sherlock forced himself to maintain a professional manner. "Did you see or hear anything that might make you suspect anyone who might have killed Chief Longbow?"

The sisters looked at one another and shook their heads.

"No one here would kill the chief," said Kate.

"Did you hear of anyone making threats to him?"

"Everyone knows Mr. Rudley was prepared to take legal action," said Emma. "Tiffany said he wasn't happy when the chief dug up his lawn."

"And he was afraid the chief would end up setting fire to the place," Louise said.

"But Mr. Rudley would never kill anyone," said Kate.

"He's put up with many people more trying than the chief," said Emma. "He has never even struck anyone."

"And Tim was getting tired of carrying things down to him, I suppose," said Kate, "but he wouldn't kill anyone either."

"He carries things down to us all the time," said Louise. "And he hasn't killed us."

"I can't think of anyone who would kill anyone," said Kate.

"I'm afraid you'll have to look further afield for a suspect," said Emma.

Sherlock folded his notebook, nodded and made his exit.

"He doesn't have very good manners," said Kate as the door closed behind him.

"I'm glad," Louise added, "we didn't offer him tea and cakes."

Chapter Nineteen

The pathologist turned from his dictation. "What did you say your name was?"

"John Sherlock."

The pathologist frowned. "I don't recall hearing about you around these parts before."

"I'm not from around here."

"Are you working with Brisbois?"

"No."

The pathologist hesitated. "Is there something wrong with Brisbois?"

Sherlock stiffened. "I don't know, and at this point, I don't especially care."

Dr. Jim shot him a hard glance. "Just surprised is all. Normally, anything to do with the Pleasant, it's Brisbois and Creighton involved."

"If it will let us get on with things, I understand they're on vacation."

"OK," Jim conceded. "Detective" — he suppressed a grin — "Sherlock. Do you ever get anyone calling you Holmes?"

"Just about everyone." Sherlock waved a hand impatiently. "Can we get on with this?"

Jim picked up the folder on his desk. "Down to business." He flipped open the folder, cranked his chair back, put his feet up on the desk and flipped through the pages. "Yes, yes, have that," he muttered.

"Noted, noted. Pending, pending." He paused. "Now what the hell is this?"

Sherlock shifted impatiently.

"Oh, yes." Jim brought his chair forward. "He had some green stuff stuck in his teeth."

"Maybe it was his breakfast. What does that have to do with anything?"

"Depends on what he ate for breakfast," Jim replied. "It's been sent for analysis. Just in case it was poisonous."

"You think someone poisoned him?"

"He could have eaten something by accident. Maybe a poisonous plant. It's not high on my list of priorities. Just being thorough."

"He claimed to be a tribal chief. Wouldn't he be more knowledgeable about plants?"

"Maybe, maybe not. Depends on whether or not he was taught." Jim shrugged. "He could have eaten something he shouldn't have, got sick, wandered into the boathouse, fell into the water and drowned.

"Drowned?"

"You did notice he was wet."

Sherlock flushed. "I didn't touch him. The coroner said he was damp. I assumed he got wet from the life preservers."

Jim suppressed a smile. "Probably the other way around. Mr. Rudley would string up anyone with the audacity to put away life preservers wet."

Sherlock pretended to be busy with his notes.

"Who's your partner on the case?" Dr. Jim asked.

"My usual partner is finishing up on another case," said Sherlock. "I'm alone for now."

"Sounds lonely. Brisbois always has Creighton."

"I assure you, I'm as good alone as Brisbois is with Creighton."

Jim smiled and threw the folder across the desk. "Well, here's the nitty-gritty. Time of death, somewhere between 1:00 a.m. and 5:00 a.m. Preliminary findings? He drowned. He has a lump on his head. Pretty minor. Probably got it when he fell in. He has green stuff between his teeth. Could be just his supper. We'll see. You'll have the usual tox screens as soon as they're complete."

"So he was murdered?"

"I think it's a pretty good bet. I don't think he got himself into that box by himself. And"—Jim sat back, smiled—"your man isn't indigenous, by the way."

Sherlock frowned.

"Bone structure's all wrong. He's Caucasian. We've taken fingerprints, of course. That may help identify him along with photographs." Dr. Jim shrugged. "Of course, people tend to look different when they're dead. Oh, yes"—he grabbed the folder back—"we took some scrapings from under his nails. There was some stuff there. Sort of stood out. His hands and nails were pretty dirty otherwise. We've sent that for DNA analysis."

"Of course," Sherlock grumbled, casting his eyes over the report. The old ladies, he thought, might not be so crazy after all.

Sherlock was exiting the building when the secretary called after him to say Dr. Jim wanted him back. The pathologist had evidently forgotten something, though Sherlock, seething, wondered if he wasn't being deliberately obtuse.

"Sorry," said Dr. Jim. "One little thing…actually two little things." He flipped through his report. "There was a bandage clip stuck in the knee of our victim's jeans."

Sherlock took out his copy of the report and made a note in the margin. "What exactly is that?"

Dr. Jim explained. "It's a little gizmo with teeth that secures the end of an elastic bandage to itself once you wrap it around."

Sherlock narrowed his eyes.

"And," said Jim, "your forensics guys got a blood stain that was on the dock. Type AB-positive. Pretty rare. There's some trace stuff as well. A bit of fabric. We're working on that. I'll let you know the minute we get anything more."

"All right." Sherlock folded his report and headed for the door.

"You're welcome," Dr. Jim called after him.

Sherlock turned and frowned.

"Detective Brisbois would have said 'Thanks, Doc.'"

"I don't care what Brisbois would have said."

"You know, we kind of like Brisbois around here."

"Headquarters hadn't informed me he'd been enshrined."

Dr. Jim shrugged. "Well, he can be a little unorthodox. We like him because he's regular folks, kind of human, willing to banter a bit."

"That's not the way I operate."

Dr. Jim peered at him over his glasses. "You've spent most of your time working in the city, I guess." When Sherlock didn't answer, he continued, "I'm just saying that because, in these parts, what you get done depends on how you strike people. They get suspicious out here if you're not being neighbourly."

Sherlock sniffed. "I don't think it's good practice to get chummy with people under investigation."

"If you say so." Jim returned to the file in front of him.

"If I have any questions, I'll call you later."

"To be sure," Jim muttered.

He sat listening to the snap of Sherlock's leather-soled shoes against the tiled corridor. Amazing, he thought, how someone could confuse folksy with country bumpkin. He himself had always been an informal guy. So had his grandfather, who'd been a provincial court judge. And his father, who was an English professor.

He turned to a large bottle on his desk, labelled *Jim*, regarded the pickled appendix within and considered that he didn't like Sherlock. He was rude and foolish. It didn't pay to be curt with people and it made the workplace less pleasant. He preferred Brisbois because he was an earnest plodder who respected other people's schedules and other people's opinions. However, he supposed Sherlock was correct about one thing: It probably wasn't wise to get chummy with people one was investigating — although he always found it useful in his own line of work.

He pushed his preserved appendix to one side, placed his elbows on the desk, and folded his hands under his chin. The murder of the chief made no sense at all, he thought. Why would someone murder an old man in a boathouse? How would anyone know he was in there?

There was, apparently, no evidence of a struggle outside the boathouse. The bump on his head suggested he had fallen against something hard rather than being hit by a blunt object. So he'd bumped his head, fell into the water and drowned. Or he'd eaten something that made him sick, got dizzy and fell in. But how did he get into the life-preserver box?

Rudley stood at the inn's doorway, which was opened a crack. He leaned on his crutches, craning to see without being seen.

Margaret, who was standing behind the desk, gestured to him. "Rudley, come away from the door."

"Now he's looking through the flower beds at the side of the house."

Margaret moved to Rudley's side, eased him away from the door and closed it. "Rudley, he'll look through the flower beds whether you watch him or not. I'll make you a nice cup of tea."

"I don't want a nice cup of tea."

Margaret reached under the desk, removed a bottle of whisky and a glass and poured in two fingers. "Bottoms up."

Rudley drained the glass. "If you're trying to get me inebriated, Margaret, with the hope I'll mellow out, it won't work."

"It's good for your nerves." She took the glass from him and set it aside. "Now, isn't that better?"

"I think Sherlock should do us the courtesy of explaining what he's doing. Brisbois would."

"Yes, Detective Brisbois always keeps us informed. I think he sees us as partners in these projects."

"I wouldn't go that far, Margaret. He keeps us informed only because he needs our help. This boob," he said, referring to Sherlock, "treats us as if we were interlopers. If he damages the flower beds, I'll sue him."

Margaret took the whisky bottle, poured an ounce and took a sip. "Rudley, I don't know how you stand this stuff." She patted her lips with a tissue. "I don't think he's harming the flower beds. I think he's being quite careful. He's probably looking for a clue."

"That makes sense, since he doesn't have one," Rudley growled. "And what's Lloyd doing with him?"

"I don't know, Rudley." Margaret sighed with exasperation. "Detective Sherlock probably just asked him to show him around."

Rudley picked up the glass and finished off the whisky. "Why is it, whenever someone is murdered around here, everyone acts as if we had something to do with it?"

"The police are inclined to be suspicious. I imagine they're trained that way."

"We've never killed anyone."

"They can't assume we wouldn't one day."

Lloyd came up the front steps and into the lobby.

"What's Sherlock doing in the flower beds?" Rudley asked, trying to appear nonchalant.

"He wanted to know if we had any flowers with poison in them."

"And what did you tell him?" Rudley demanded.

"Said no and then I said Detective Brisbois knew all the plants and never needed anybody to tell him."

Rudley smiled a lopsided smile. "And what did his nibs say about that?"

"He said he was sure Detective Brisbois knew more about peonies than investigating," Lloyd said. "Then he told me to leave."

"He could be right about that," Rudley murmured. "Did he say when he'd be finished mucking around?"

"Didn't say."

Sherlock appeared in the doorway at that moment. He walked straight to the desk and stood flipping through his notepad. Finally, he looked up. "Did you give the deceased anything from your garden?"

Margaret glanced at Rudley. "We told him he could take anything he needed," she replied to Sherlock, adding, "I did take him down a basket of greens."

"What kind of greens?"

"Mainly leaf lettuce with a little sugar and vinegar. I enjoy it that way, and he said he did too."

"And that was it?"

"We gave him various samples of cooked things, but only the lettuce from the garden."

"How generous of you."

Rudley glowered. "I won't have you being rude to my wife."

"I'm not being rude; I'm being efficient," said Sherlock. "What sort of poisonous plants do you have in your gardens?"

"We gave up on poisonous plants after several of our guests dropped dead," Rudley fumed.

"There aren't any poisonous plants," Margaret said. "We're very careful because Albert — our dog — likes to get into the garden."

Sherlock was about to cap his fountain pen and return it to his pocket when Tiffany came up the back stairs with Albert. Before anyone could intervene, Albert ran up to Sherlock, planted his paws on his chest, and gave him an emphatic push that sent him stumbling back, his fall broken only by the desk. Margaret put a hand to her mouth in horror as Albert leapt on him again and Sherlock's grip on the desk gave way. The detective landed on the floor on his back, his pen falling from his hand and bouncing across the floor. Albert snatched it in his jaws, bit down on it and squirted Sherlock with ink.

"Albert!" Tiffany ran to the dog, who was tonguing Sherlock's face vigorously, corralling him by the collar and pulling him away.

Sherlock struggled up. "This is the Albert who digs in the garden?" he asked, petting the dog.

"Yes," said Margaret. "I'm so sorry, Detective." She gave Rudley a nudge as he tried to suppress laughter.

"It's all right," he continued, "he didn't mean any harm."

"We'll replace your shirt, and" — she wrapped a piece of newspaper around the mangled pen — "your lovely fountain pen, of course."

"It's all right," he repeated. "Animals are innocent. It's people who screw things up."

"At least we can offer you a stick pen for now," said Margaret, reaching under the desk for a cloth. She turned to Rudley, who grudgingly handed Sherlock a Bic.

"No, thank you," said Sherlock. "I'll get one from my car."

"Have it your way," Rudley muttered. He hobbled out from behind the desk to examine the floor, watching Margaret as she wiped up ink before it sullied his hardwood.

Sherlock's eyes went to his leg. "That bandage on your cast seems a little loose."

Margaret glanced at the leg too. "Rudley, let me get a safety pin. If that comes loose you'll trip over it."

Sherlock smiled. "It looks as if you've lost one of your bandage clips, Mr. Rudley."

Chapter Twenty

Sherlock faced Rudley. "Now, can you recall when you last saw that clip?"

"How in hell would I remember something like that?" Rudley fumed. "It's not as if I'm sitting around all day counting the clips in this damn elastic bandage."

"So you have no idea where you lost it."

Rudley's ears turned red. "I could have lost it anywhere. I've lost dozens of them. They're always falling off."

Sherlock paused a few seconds, pretending to be examining his notebook. "What would you say if I told you we found one in the boathouse?"

"There you go," Rudley said, triumphant. "I told you I could have lost it anywhere."

"So you were in the boathouse."

Rudley crossed his eyes. "Of course I was in the boathouse. You know I was in the boathouse. I've told you a dozen times I was there."

Sherlock looked up from his notes. "So, Mr. Rudley, how did one of your bandage clips end up stuck in the knee of Chief Longbow's pants?" When Rudley stared at him in disbelief, he added, "Perhaps it happened while you were stuffing the poor man's body into your life-preserver box."

"He could have got it stuck in his pants anytime," Rudley cried. "I could have dropped one on the lawn. He was always crawling around on his hands and knees." He stopped and bit his lower lip to maintain his composure. "This is sheer poppycock."

"You seem to be the only one around with a motive," said Sherlock.

"Damn to hell," said Rudley. He slammed his fist down on the desk so hard the pen set jumped.

"And you seem to have trouble controlling your temper."

"You would, too, if you had to put up with the nonsense I do around here, including dealing with a neophyte detective who is clearly out to make his mark and doesn't have a clue about what he's doing." Rudley did a mental count to five. "I have never killed anyone in my life. I have never committed a single act of violence on anything except inanimate objects."

Sherlock was scribbling in his notebook. "What time did you get up the morning Chief Longbow was found deceased in the boathouse?"

"Around six-thirty."

"Are you sure you weren't up earlier?" Sherlock asked. "Perhaps you couldn't sleep because you were worrying about the chief's claim to your property."

Rudley seethed. "And I managed to make my way down the stairs on crutches without anyone hearing me."

Sherlock flushed. He hadn't considered that angle.

"Believe me, Detective," Margaret said. "Everyone hears him coming down the stairs on those crutches."

"But you went down to the chief's campsite," Sherlock challenged, "shortly after you got up. What would cause you to do that?"

"Because the laundryman told me the pit the chief had dug was getting bigger. I went down to talk to him about that."

"And?" Sherlock asked.

"And I couldn't talk to him because the man was dead," Rudley seethed. He paused, brightening as a thought came to him. "I know… the day before when I was at the campsite talking to the chief…I might have lost it then."

"So you think you lost the clip then?" Sherlock made a note.

"My bandage was loose," Rudley said, triumphant. "I almost tripped on it. Mr. Bole was there. He fixed it for me."

Sherlock made a few more notes, then tucked his notebook into his pocket. "I'm going to continue my interviews with your staff and guests. I would appreciate it if you made everyone available to me."

"Ask anyone you want. Interview the whole county," said Rudley. "You won't find a person who has a single bad thing to say about me."

Sherlock smiled. "We'll see, Mr. Rudley."

Sherlock returned to his car, removed his jacket and shirt, took a fresh white shirt from a cellophane wrap and put it on. He folded the soiled shirt, placed it into the wrap and put back on his jacket and tie. He was examining his notes under a pine tree when something struck his hat. He reached up to brush it off, assuming it was a leaf or a maple key, and pulled his hand away in disgust. Officer Vance, appearing on the scene at that moment, looked at Sherlock's hat and suppressed a grin.

"Get that package of wipes from my car," Sherlock ordered, trying to keep his dignity.

"Dirty bird," said a voice, startling Sherlock as he continued to examine his hat. He glanced up into the low branches of the tree. "What on earth is that?"

"That's Betty," said Vance, returned with the wipes. "She's a parrot that showed up a couple of weeks ago. They've tried to trap her but that didn't work too well. I guess she's hanging around because she's getting treated like a queen."

"Does she say anything except *dirty bird?*"

"Oh, yes. She says Tweek and Freak all the time. I don't know what that's about."

"Tweek and Freak," Betty cackled. "Sweetie's got to go."

"That's another of her favourites," said Vance.

"Sweetie's got to go. Get Sweetie."

Sherlock frowned. "I wonder who'd teach her to say things like that."

"I think they pick things up on their own," said Vance. "They hear words and phrases and repeat them, mix them up, combine them."

"You seem to know a lot about parrots."

"One of my great-uncles had one." Vance shrugged. "I don't think anything they say makes sense. It's not as if they're answering you."

"Stupid," said Betty.

"I think she disagrees with you," said Sherlock. He wiped his hands and hat with the wipes and looked around for a garbage bin.

"I'll take those," said Vance. "I'm going past a bin."

"Are you going off duty?"

"No, I just came on. I'm relieving Owens at the boathouse."

"I'll be around conducting interviews," Sherlock said. "Have me paged if you need me."

Vance went on his way, shaking his head. Sherlock didn't seem to know one officer from the other. They were just uniforms to him. He was respectful enough but impersonal. He decided he didn't care for Sherlock. Brisbois and Creighton knew each officer and a little about each one's personality, likes and dislikes. He liked working with them.

Sherlock went down the path toward the dock, sat on a nearby bench and reviewed his notes. The latest interviews with the guests hadn't yielded much worthwhile. Everyone agreed that Trevor Rudley wouldn't hurt a fly, although he was apt to fly off the handle frequently.

Interview with Mr. James Bole: Oh, Mr. Rudley yells a lot, throws things and so forth. But he would never kill anyone. Mrs. Rudley wouldn't kill anyone either. Neither would any of the staff. The guests are mostly repeats. None of them has ever killed anyone, as far as I know. I can't imagine why any of them would start now. Bandage clip? Oh, yes. Mr. Rudley's bandage was always coming loose. I don't think he secured it properly. He's impatient about that sort of thing. He came close to tripping one day, Detective. That was the day he was having it out with the chief about him digging up the lawn. Mr. Rudley has to put up with a lot.

Interview with Doreen Sawchuck: Mr. Rudley wouldn't kill anyone, Detective. You aren't taking him away, are you? We need him to keep things running properly.

Interview with Geraldine Phipps-Walker: Oh, Detective, Mr. Rudley has put up with so much nonsense around here. He blows his stack fairly often. The only one he harms is himself. He would never treat anyone shabbily no matter how vexed he was with them.

Interview with Norman Phipps-Walker: Mr. Rudley likes to shout. That's the worst thing Mr. Rudley would do.

That, Sherlock thought, remains to be seen.

Chapter Twenty-one

Frankes returned from Middleton, dumped the groceries on the kitchen counter, gestured to Luther to put them away and retreated to the veranda. He pulled a newspaper from under his shirt and handed it to Tibor, who read the story about the suspicious death at the Pleasant Inn and tossed the paper aside.

"I guess we should keep this from Leonard," said Frankes.

"What for? He didn't know the guy."

"He might figure something out," said Frankes, injured. "How do we know he didn't notice us coming or going in the middle of the night?"

"Because I added a couple of antihistamines to his cocoa."

"That was kind of risky. That could have killed him, you know. He's got heart disease. The doctor told us not to give my grandfather stuff like that."

Tibor turned on Frankes, his face ugly with anger. "I'm sick and tired of hearing about your grandfather."

"He raised me," said Frankes. "Until he died when I was fourteen."

"Bad things happen," Tibor grumbled. "But we've got to think about the here and now. And there's no way anyone can tie us to that old man." He paused. "Besides, we didn't kill him."

"We let him drown," Frankes countered. "And that's the same thing."

Tibor's hand went to the scratches on his collarbone. "He attacked me."

"He was afraid," Frankes mumbled. "We should have done something."

"So what were we supposed to do, Frankes?" Tibor asked sarcastically. "Pull him out? Call the paramedics? Get interviewed by the police? Have our picture in the paper as local heroes? Cerise'd be hightailing it back to St. Napoli so fast all you'd see was a blur."

"You said she probably didn't have any money."

Tibor grunted. "Knowing her, she'd sell her body if she had to."

"You think so?"

"She's do anything to get what she wanted." He jumped up and went to stand at the railing. "Those paintings didn't burn. There's no way that happened. Leonard was as sharp as a tack back then. He was in love with those paintings. I don't care what he's saying now. The Cartwrights exist. He was getting dotty before we left the islands. He must have made a mistake and brought another set of copies he had stashed somewhere. That means the real ones are somewhere on St. Napoli."

"OK," said Frankes. He retrieved the newspaper and turned to the sports section. "Hey, look at this, Liverpool…"

"Who cares?"

Frankes threw the paper down. "I'm getting tired of this, Tibor. I think we should just split. We're not going to get the paintings, supposing they do exist. If the old man doesn't fuck up, Cerise's going to screw us. If we stay around here, we're going to get into trouble. They'll probably be asking questions all over the lake. They'll get to us eventually, and if they start digging too deep…"

"Leave the thinking to me," Tibor growled.

"So far that's got us into a big mess," said Frankes. "I was willing to play second banana when you seemed to know what you were doing. But now you've just got us into a lot of trouble."

"If you stick with me, you'll end up set for life. If you want to go on your own, fine. But you'll end up with a fat nothing." He saw Frankes's face darken, added, "We're going to come out of this smelling like roses. As long as we don't lose our nerve." He grabbed Frankes by the shoulder as he started to turn away. "You're not losing your nerve, are you?"

Frankes hesitated, then shook his head. "No."

"Let's keep it that way."

Glancing at the Elm Pavilion as he made his way toward the lake, Sherlock reminded himself not to take anything the Benson sisters had to say lightly. If they were right about the chief not being aboriginal, they could be right about other things. The sisters were inclined to fancy. He didn't mind that. Police work brought one into contact with all kinds of people. He was also aware of the tendency of older people to feign deafness, memory loss, poor vision or eccentricity to get themselves out of trouble or simply to amuse themselves. The sisters seemed to be skilled in a number of these tactics.

He wandered out onto the dock, sat down in a folding chair, looked out over the lake, scrutinizing the shoreline and the sightlines to the boathouse. He noted a rowboat about thirty yards distant in which Norman Phipps-Walker lay dozing against a pillow, his fishing rod dipping into the water as the boat rose and fell on the swell. Sherlock narrowed his eyes, wondering if he was all right. Then Norman reached up a hand, tipped his hat forward, and eased back against the pillow.

Sherlock yawned and almost dropped his notebook in the water. No wonder, he thought ruefully, Brisbois and Creighton managed to screw things up around here. The place was so damn soporific and so damn dense, like those tiny, ancient places in the United Kingdom where history seemed to pile up layer on layer and affect the present in surprising ways. What would compel so many oddballs to collect in such a small space? Why would such a place compel so many to commit murder?

He roused himself, folded his notebook and proceeded to Chief Longbow's campsite. He reviewed the evidence. The chief had drowned. Time of death, between 1:00 a.m. and 5:00 a.m. Someone had taken him from the water and placed him in the life-preserver box. That he knew for sure. The tox screen had come back, revealing nothing more than a trace of cannabis. The chief did like the odd joint. Indeed, the pup tent had yielded little of interest beyond an envelope containing a small quantity of marijuana. The stuff between the chief's teeth was probably just the lettuce Mrs. Rudley had taken down.

Few people, he thought, were much good at living off the land, as civilization had rendered humans incredibly stupid. He knew he wasn't immune to stupidity himself, though. But he considered that his ability to recognize his flaws was an important tool in overcoming them. He realized he gave the impression he was rigid and uncompromising, but he found doing so a useful strategy. In fact, he paid close attention to what people told him. By pretending to be dismissive and uninterested, he found people were often more forthcoming.

He smiled. People hated not to be liked; they hated to believe that what they had to say was not important so, if they felt this way, they were more apt to blurt out things they never intended to say. Young women anxious to impress a dapper detective with a dangerous sullen look were the most likely to lose their inhibitions. He'd read some of Brisbois's interviews and thought he was too benign, too folksy, too solicitous of the people he interviewed, slow to be suspicious of those he took a fancy to. He didn't know Creighton. The interviews suggested he played second banana to Brisbois and did it rather well. If he were to select a partner, Sherlock thought, Creighton wouldn't be bad choice. He was an action man, confident, a guy who would have your back. He liked the idea of him being the brains and a partner like Creighton being the brawn. Not that he would let any situation come to that.

The venetian blinds were partially drawn to filter the light streaming into the den where Leonard sat staring at the blank television screen, disappointed no one had arranged to repair the satellite. With no television and no newspaper, he felt completely cut off from the world. He couldn't even find a radio around. He wondered if Frankes could pick up one in the village next time he went, which seemed to be rather often of late. He checked his watch. Even though it was early in the day, he was nicely dressed in a lightweight grey suit, yellow shirt, and mauve-and-yellow-striped tie. His socks matched the grey in the suit. The only discordant note was the shabby Romeo slippers, which he had chosen for comfort. They were a bit bigger than his shoes and with the soles not as rigid, they didn't chafe the sore growing under the metatarsal callous of his right foot.

He felt uneasy about the wound. He had kept his diabetes under control with oral medication and some concessions to diet, but since they had come to the cottage, he had been careless. He dipped into the bowl of mixed nuts. They were, of course, full of salt, but he had developed a taste for salt and sweets since they left St. Napoli. Luther was loyal but incapable of understanding his needs. He wished Cerise were here. She had always been willing to act as his nurse. The boys were useless for that sort of thing.

His memory was slipping. He knew it was. He told himself to be careful about feigning stupidity, to use the ploy carefully because he might fall too deeply into his own trap. That had been a problem even when he was a child. Isolation led him to make-believe and make-believe led him to fabrication, and, at times, he'd had trouble sorting out real from imaginary. It wasn't merely physical and intellectual isolation; the emotional isolation was worse. If he'd been willing and able to commit to Sylvia, perhaps life would have turned out differently. Perhaps she would have committed to him.

He found it hard to believe that Cerise had returned to the islands without him. He thought he was a better judge of people. Not that he doubted for one minute her tendency for larceny. He rather liked that in her. But he never imagined she would leave him to the mercies of Tibor and Frankes. She'd always told him they were capable of murder. He always believed that, if push came to shove, she would ally herself with him against the boys.

He paused, the mixed nuts in his hand. He let them fall back into the bowl. Why would Cerise leave in the middle of the night? Why wouldn't she simply leave at daylight saying she was going into town or going out for a ride on the lake?

Perhaps she had not left the area. He tugged fitfully at his tie. What if she had gone out on the lake early without a life jacket? What if she had had an accident? He knew one thing for sure: he wasn't going to leave Hiram's island until he found out what had happened to her. He reached for the phone to make an anonymous call to the police, but after holding the receiver to his ear for a moment, he returned it to the cradle. What purpose would calling the police serve now? If anything had happened to Cerise it would be too late to save her. And they couldn't afford to draw attention to themselves. Then he realized something. There had been no dial tone. He picked up the receiver again and listened. Nothing. He punched the plunger. Nothing. Nothing. Nothing.

Chapter Twenty-two

Sherlock faced Miss Miller across the desk in Rudley's office. "You are Elizabeth Miller?"

"I am."

He pored through his notes and frowned at an entry in the margin: *Miss Miller is considered the Agatha Christie of the Pleasant.* Everyone he had interviewed had advised him repeatedly of this and he was rather fed up with the idea. *If you need any help, you should ask Miss Miller. Miss Miller helps Detective Brisbois with all his cases.* He gave himself a moment to suppress his irritation lest it infect the tone of his interview. He hated civilians who solved cases by luck, leaving the lead detective looking like an idiot. For this reason, he had left his interview with her for last, lest her rash theories colour his opinions.

"And you are a guest at the inn? Room 206?"

"Yes."

"Did you know the man who was known as Chief Longbow?"

"I had occasion to speak to him twice."

"And did you form any opinion of him?"

"He was an interesting eccentric. I had some doubt that he was a chief. But I'm not an expert in North American indigenous people, therefore I couldn't assess the veracity of his claim." She leaned forward, smiled. "I didn't question his claim to be a member of the

Algonquin nation. I have since heard he was probably not. Perhaps he had a remote link and had simply latched onto that as his main identity." She shrugged. "I could claim to be descendant of the queen of some ancient Celtic clan."

He raised a weary brow. "Are you?"

"I don't know. I've never investigated the possibility. You asked me my assessment of the chief."

He tried a different tack. "Did Mr. Rudley ever speak to you about the land claim the chief had made?"

She nodded. "When Edward and I signed in, we asked about the tent on the lawn. He said the chief had made a claim for the land occupied by the tent, and that later he had extended that claim to the boathouse. I understand he had later extended that claim to the entire property. Mr. Rudley had engaged his lawyer."

"And what was Mr. Rudley's demeanour?"

"Resigned, at that point."

Sherlock looked up from his notes. "And later?"

"Mr. Rudley was rather frustrated, especially when the chief dug a large pit on his front lawn. I gather Mr. Rudley was planning to fill the hole in and seed it."

"He told you this?"

"Mr. Bole told me."

He flipped through his notes. "Oh, yes." He looked up. "And that was it? He was perfectly calm about the problem?"

Miss Miller gave him a wry look. "Of course not. You've met Mr. Rudley. He alternates between resignation and bellowing. He always has."

"And no one takes these fits of temper seriously?"

She shook her head. "Of course not. Yelling is Mr. Rudley's way of coping with the many irritations of being an innkeeper, especially the proprietor of an inn that experiences so many murders." She paused. "Surely you don't think Mr. Rudley could have killed the chief."

"The investigation is ongoing," he murmured.

"Mr. Rudley might have yelled at the chief, but he wouldn't have harmed him. I don't know of a single incident where Mr. Rudley harmed anyone." When he failed to respond, she continued, "Detective, have you considered Mr. Rudley's broken leg? The chief was a fairly substantial man. How would a man with a broken leg, on crutches, overpower anyone?"

"Stranger things have happened."

"Edward and I have been coming here for quite a few years now, and I can't think of anyone here who would have a reason or the mindset to harm the chief. I think you should be looking for suspects outside the area."

"You do?"

"Perhaps someone came into the boathouse, intending to steal one of the boats. Mr. Rudley has some fine canoes and a couple of nice motorboats. The thief startled the chief and killed him."

"I haven't ruled out anyone, Miss Miller, inside or outside." He regarded her evenly. "And I'm not ruling out anyone because they've been a model citizen to date. Where were you between one and five the morning of the incident?"

"I was in bed. Edward and I didn't come down to breakfast until almost eight."

"Did you see or hear anything suspicious?"

"No," she replied, adding, "Your *modus operandi* is somewhat different than Detective Brisbois's."

His stomach knotted at the mention of Brisbois's name. "Yes," he said calmly.

After Miss Miller left, Sherlock sat at the desk and reviewed his notes. He thought he'd handled Miss Miller rather well, but he had to admit he hadn't given much thought to Rudley's broken leg, though he was sure little effort would be needed to tip an old man into the drink. Hell, Rudley could have tripped the chief with a crutch. Getting him out of the water and into the life-preserver box would have been challenging, though, but not impossible. He sighed. His case against Rudley had rested on the bandage clip. And the volatile nature of Rudley's temper. He flipped through his notes. Mr. Bole had confirmed Rudley's story about his bandage losing a clip near the chief's campsite. Everyone agreed that Rudley had a bad temper and was apt to blow his stack whether the matters were inconsequential or not. In other words, he could fly off the handle any old time, but he never acted on any of his threats. Everyone agreed it was his way of coping — just Rudley being Rudley. Add to that Lloyd's statement that he had seen Rudley talking to an empty tent for several minutes, which implied he thought the chief was still alive.

So, Rudley wasn't a leading suspect even if he appeared to be the only one with motive.

He checked through the other interviews. There was no evidence that Mrs. Rudley had left the inn during the night. The handyman, Lloyd, had been sleeping in the tool shed. There was no evidence to confirm or deny his activities during the night. Lloyd wasn't high on his list of suspects. His blood type didn't match the specimens lifted from the floor of the boathouse. He was rather artless and frank during his questioning if — Sherlock rolled his eyes — a little obtuse. The cook was in the kitchen at four in the morning, but with half the inn stopping by to get coffee and scones for early morning fishing trips, Gregoire's opportunity to go down to the boathouse, drown an old man and load him into the box seemed limited. The surveillance camera confirmed the rest of the staff — the housekeeper, the waiter — had left the bunkhouse after six-thirty. The chief was dead by then.

He considered the guests, but found little joy there. Reconsidered Sherry Brown. She wasn't staff, but she wasn't a guest. She was a friend of Chester Creighton staying at the inn, waiting for her papers, the originals having been lost in a boating mishap. She struck him as an airhead. Her interview had given him a headache. He'd never interviewed anyone who wandered off topic as much as she did. As for Creighton's interest in her — well, there was no accounting for taste. But she too was staying in the bunkhouse and was alibied by the surveillance tape. He had to admit Miss Miller was right. No one at the inn seemed a good suspect.

He was contemplating his next move when someone knocked on the door. Tiffany entered bearing a tray with a cup of coffee and a sandwich. "Mrs. Rudley thought you probably hadn't had lunch," she said. "She wanted you to have this."

He hesitated. He made it a rule not to accept any sort of gratuity. But he was touched by Mrs. Rudley's generosity and didn't want to hurt her feelings. Nor did he want to hurt Tiffany's feelings. He found her a kind and lovely person.

"Thank you," he said at last. "We really aren't supposed to accept this sort of thing."

"Mrs. Rudley would have made you a sandwich if you were parading her off to the gallows," Tiffany said. "She'd think you would need the energy to pull the lever."

He had to smile.

"And if you don't eat it, it might go to waste." A lie, Tiffany knew, since Lloyd would demolish anything left over.

"In that case," he said, "thank you."

"You're welcome," she said.

She left. He took a sip of the coffee, which was excellent. The sandwich, a vegetable with avocado and an interesting sweet dressing, was delicious. He began to have more respect for Brisbois. These were nice people here, generous and forebearing in light of their persistent bad luck. He could understand why it was difficult to be completely clinical about them, especially after attending a slew of their misfortunes. Sherlock took a sip of coffee. And that, he thought, was a good reason for rotating the two detectives out of the area from time to time.

He smoothed his moustache with an index finger. Who was the chief? So far no fingerprint matches, suggesting no criminal background. DNA typing still pending. The police artist's sketch was circulating with no results yet. The chief had drowned. But had he fallen into the water or was he pushed? And how had he got into the life-preserver box? He hadn't done that by himself.

Sherlock tucked his notebook into his pocket, rose and exited Rudley's basement office through the back door. A patch of bright colour caught his eye when he stepped outside. The parrot was on the back porch, nibbling at a tray of fruit and seeds he assumed had been put out for her. He stopped and watched her. She ignored him at first, then hopped onto the back porch railing and peered at him.

"Hello," he said to the bird.

"Feed Betty."

"I think Betty's had enough," he said.

She cackled something he didn't catch.

"What's the matter?" he asked. "Is no one paying any attention to you?"

"Tweek and Freak."

"What's Tweek and Freak?"

"Sweetie, Sweetie, Tweek and Freak."

"You're talking nonsense."

"She's got to go."

"You've got that stuck in your head." He considered her for a moment. "You're bored, aren't you?"

She cocked her head.

"All right," he smiled, looking into her eyes, "Try this — Creepy Creighton."

She moved her beak soundlessly. He repeated the words several more times, enunciating each word carefully.

"Freaky Creety," the bird said. "Freaky Creety."

"Close." He gave her a round of applause. "We'll keep working on that."

"Feed Betty."

He shook his head at her and walked away.

Chapter Twenty-three

Tibor and Frankes were on the veranda when they saw the police boat. The navigator cut the motor as the boat approached the dock and let it drift toward a mooring. A uniformed officer jumped out and held the boat close for a neat young man in a suit and fedora.

Tibor spoke to Frankes out of the side of his mouth. "Just follow my lead. We're exactly what we are. Leonard is Leonard. I'm his nephew. Luther is the cook. And you're the general handyperson and gofer."

"What about the old man? What if he says something?"

"I'll prepare them. Come on."

Tibor left the veranda and headed down to intercept Sherlock and Owens as they started toward the cottage. Frankes followed.

"Gentlemen." Tibor held out a hand. "How can I help you?"

Sherlock showed his badge. "Are you the owner of this property?"

"No, my uncle Leonard and I are renting for the summer. I'm Tibor Gutherie. This gentleman," he said, indicating Frankes, "is Bobby Frankes. He's our caretaker."

"And your uncle?"

"Leonard Anderson. He's up at the cottage. He's got a bad foot. Diabetic."

"How long have you been here?"

"Three weeks."

"Out and about much? Do you go into town?"

"Frankes goes in for supplies every now and then." Tibor paused. "Are you looking into that murder we read about in the paper?"

Sherlock gave him an appraising look. "I am."

Tibor stuffed his hands into his pockets. "I don't know much about the area. My uncle's been here more often. I don't know if I can help you much."

"Wondering if you'd seen anything unusual."

"No," Tibor said after a moment's thought. "Nothing I can recall."

"What about you?" Sherlock turned to Frankes.

Frankes shook his head. "No."

Sherlock made a play of checking his notes. "And where were you on the night of June twentieth?"

"What day was that?"

"Last Wednesday."

Tibor ran a hand across the back of his head. "Gosh, the days all run together out here." He shrugged. "Well, I haven't been anywhere else. So I guess I was here."

"That's the night we were watching that *Mad Max* movie," said Frankes.

Tibor nodded. "Oh, yes. *Mad Max.*"

Sherlock made a note. "And the next morning?"

"What about the next morning?"

"Thursday, the twenty-first," Sherlock continued. "Where were you then?"

"Here." Tibor looked to Frankes. "I'm pretty sure no one went anywhere that morning."

Sherlock glanced toward the cottage. "Is your uncle in?"

"Yes."

"I'd like to speak to him."

"Of course." Tibor led the way up the path, opened the door and called out. "Uncle Leonard, there's someone here to see you."

"Come in," a tired voice called back from the living room.

Sherlock followed Tibor. Owens positioned himself just inside the front door.

"Uncle Leonard's had some problems lately," Tibor told Sherlock. "He's a little forgetful at times."

Leonard was staring absently at the Colville print on the far wall. The hound in *Hound in Field* reminded him of Tibor — slender, neat, and deadly. He sat up straight and was adjusting his tie when Tibor entered with the stranger. He struggled to stand but the visitor said: "Don't get up."

"Sherlock," Leonard mused after introductions. "Nice name."

Sherlock, who had been expecting the usual jokes about his name, responded, "Thank you."

Leonard gave Sherlock a smart salute, then laughed. "Sorry, I guess that's reserved for the military." He motioned to an adjacent chair. "Please. Sit." He cranked his head toward the kitchen. "Luther. Could we have some tea and cookies, please?" He turned to Sherlock. "Would you prefer coffee?"

"Tea is fine," said Sherlock, who was beginning to wonder if offering refreshments was a knee-jerk reaction to the law in this neck of the woods.

"Somebody was murdered in the area," said Tibor, grabbing a newspaper from the rack. "You remember, Uncle Leonard. I think you were reading about it."

Leonard squinted at the paper. "Oh, yes. June twenty-first." He regarded Tibor, puzzled. "Is it only the twenty-first?"

"It's an old paper, Uncle Leonard. We haven't got around to throwing any of the papers out," he added to Sherlock. "It gets so damn boring around here, we read the papers several times."

"Just in case the news has changed." Leonard laughed heartily.

"Your nephew tells me you're familiar with the area," said Sherlock.

Leonard nodded. "Oh, yes. I haven't been around much in the last few years, but I came here summers quite a lot when I was younger."

"Your nephew said you were renting the cottage."

"Yes, it belongs to a friend of my father's. He's been using the place himself the last few years but I understand he's off on the west coast for a few weeks."

"Are you familiar with the Pleasant Inn?"

Leonard frowned. "Oh, yes," he replied after a moment, "the place that used to belong to the Mafia. I imagine it's in more reputable hands these days."

"Barely," Sherlock murmured. "So do you know the current management?"

"I can't say I do."

"So, if you folks are here for the summer, where is home?"

"I really can't say." Leonard smiled. "I spend time in London, the south of France, the Caribbean. I'm back and forth. I'm in the art business."

"A buyer?"

"Not really. I advise people on what's good, what's awful but rising in value, and so on. I mainly dabble these days. I'm getting older."

"And where would your principal residence be?"

"St. Napoli, I suppose. That's home base, if you will, for all of us."

"What passport do you carry?"

"Canadian. My parents were Canadian. My entourage" — he nodded toward the others — "my nephew Tibor is Canadian. Frankes is British. Luther, our cook, is a native of the British Virgin Islands."

Luther appeared with a tray of tea and cookies. He started to leave.

"Wait a minute," Sherlock said. "I want to talk to you."

"Luther," Leonard called. He turned to Sherlock. "Luther is mute. Childhood trauma."

"Can he write? Use sign language?"

"Luther is challenged," Tibor said in a low voice. "He knows how to cook. He can clean up the kitchen. That's about it."

"All right. Maybe he can nod." Sherlock waved a hand at Luther to get his attention. "Is your name Luther?"

Luther nodded.

"Did you know a man got killed?"

A look of horror crossed Luther's face.

"I don't think you knew him."

The horror turned to confusion.

"Do you know anyone at the Pleasant Inn?"

Luther shook his head.

"You can go, Luther."

"He's been that way since he was a child," Leonard said. "He was in an orphanage. I hired him."

"Commendable," said Sherlock.

"Do you have to go door-to-door and interview everyone?" Tibor asked.

"I like to be thorough," said Sherlock. "You never know what you might turn up."

"Will you be in touch later about the paintings?" Leonard asked as Sherlock as he rose to leave.

As Sherlock flicked Leonard a quizzical glance, Tibor nudged him and pointed discreetly to his temple. "I may be in touch with you again," Sherlock said.

Tibor escorted the detective to the door and watched as he made his way back down to the dock.

"Who was that?" Leonard asked.

Tibor exhaled deeply. "Just somebody asking for directions."

"Oh," said Leonard.

Sherlock parked his unmarked vehicle outside the morgue. He and Owens had made the rounds on the lake. Most of the people were summer dwellers. Most of them were aware there had been a murder in the area. Many of them were familiar with the Pleasant Inn. Several of them had cackled the minute the words *murder* and *Pleasant Inn* were mentioned together. He had received comments such as "I never recommend the Pleasant to anyone I like" and "I'm surprised they even give the location of the crime anymore. Everyone assumes if it was murder, it happened at the Pleasant." He thought these remarks were mean-spirited. A few hadn't heard of the murder and a handful had never heard of the Pleasant. No one had anything useful to tell him. Still, it was a necessary exercise. It also gave him a chance to relax and put the incident into perspective. To look at it from the other side of the lake, as it were.

He was at the morgue because the pathologist had left a message saying that he had something more to report, but he had arrived early.

Not keen on waiting for Dr. Jim in his office, as he found the pickled appendix unappealing, he decided instead to review his notes.

Tiffany Armstrong. Nice person, he thought. She seemed genuine and rather sweet. Rather nice looking in a wholesome way. His mother, who always warned him against flashy women, would have approved of her — not that he needed his mother's advice. He was a decent-looking, respectable young man with good potential. He didn't smoke or drink. He didn't gamble or frequent what his mother called bawdy houses. He imagined that when he was ready to marry he would be able to find a suitable mate. He did like Tiffany, though. He knew she had dated several of the police officers, but he had never heard a single derogatory remark about her. At least she had never been out with Detective Creighton. That was a positive sign.

He didn't realize he had been so preoccupied until he glanced at his watch and realized he was five minutes late.

Dr. Jim was sitting at his desk when Sherlock arrived. He looked at him over his glasses, then pointedly checked his watch.

"Sorry I'm late," said Sherlock. "I dipped into my file and the time slipped away."

"Ah, yes," said Dr. Jim amiably. "Time flies when you have good reading. Like this," he added, gesturing to the file on his desk. "There was something interesting in the debris we vacuumed up. You remember the blood I mentioned earlier?"

Dr. Jim read a few lines from the report. "There was a tiny piece of fabric stuck to a nail identified as the sort that might come from a wet-suit. And there was a fleck of blood on the nail that matched those few drops on the edge of the dock. Ergo," he looked up at Sherlock, "the fabric got caught on the nail, the skin below got nicked. Enough to get a few drops of blood.

"There were also some bits of debris ground into the fabric," he continued. "Tiny amounts, which we're trying to identify."

Sherlock frowned. "Any tissue on the nail?"

Dr. Jim smiled. "A speck. We're looking into that too."

"Prints?"

"Just the usual suspects. Rudley, Lloyd, Norman Phipps-Walker, Miss Miller, Mr. Simpson. The regular guests are all over the place. They get their own boats out sometimes. Of course, someone could have been in there wearing gloves."

Sherlock nodded. "What else have you got?"

"There was other stuff in the vacuum bag, of course. Bits of vegetation, sand, the odd bird feather and droppings. There wasn't as much as you might expect. Lloyd cleans the place out regularly. Mr. Rudley is a stickler for keeping things in good order."

"Mr. Rudley is a stickler about a lot of things."

Dr. Jim smiled. "You'll get used to him over time."

Sherlock returned to his car and perused the copy of the report the pathologist had given him. He had no intention of getting used to Trevor Rudley over time. He had no intention of becoming a fixture around the Pleasant the way Brisbois and Creighton and half the detachment had. He placed the papers into his file and put the file into his briefcase. The Pleasant, he decided, was like a damn Venus flytrap. No one who went in ever came out. They just got digested.

Chapter Twenty-four

Detective Sherlock returned to the Pleasant the day after he received the trace-evidence report, keen to take another look around the boathouse, just in case something had been missed. He looked up into the rafters and let his gaze move slowly, inch by inch, over the walls and floor. He then got down on his hands and knees and inspected the cracks between the boards. He put on a pair of gloves and approached the life-preserver box, which came up to his chest. He opened the lid and noted the life preservers placed at a convenient height for easy retrieval. The bottom of the chest was divided into compartments that held extra rope, oarlocks, attachments for water skiing and the like, but these offered no clues. He straightened his back, stood in front of the box, and imagined lifting 170 pounds chest high. The task would have taken a fairly strong person to accomplish, especially without scraping the deceased's hands or face. As he recalled from the autopsy report, there was no evidence of suspicious abrasions.

Two people, he decided, definitely two people — one to fold the arms over the chest and hold them there, the other to grip the body under the hips and knees and place it neatly into the box. He paused in thought. Why would they be so careful? Because it would be quicker? Because it wouldn't make the noise bashing a body against the box would make? He thought that tended to rule out an opportunistic criminal just taking a look to see what he could get. That kind of person might not even get the body out of the water. Perhaps someone who had another purpose in mind. What would anyone have to gain by killing the chief? Apart from Rudley, whom he had pretty much ruled out as a suspect, that answer was unclear. He sighed. He would need to know the chief's identity to figure that one out. They'd had no luck on that so far.

"Edward" — Miss Miller interrupted Simpson as he was thinking about what to order for dessert — "I don't think Detective Sherlock is approaching this case from the right angle."

"I wonder if the rhubarb pie will be a full-topper or lattice crust."

"Tim will know."

"I rather like the lattice crust. It makes the pie lighter. It also has more esthetic appeal. However, Gregoire's crusts are so light and airy..."

"Why don't you try the Bavarian chocolate cake? You love Gregoire's chocolate cakes." She frowned at him. "I know what you're doing, Edward. You're trying to distract me and avoid considering my proposal. You'd be happy with the pie no matter what the crust looks like."

"I do prefer the lattice," he said. "But I have to admit I was trying to lead you away from any involvement in this case. Detective Sherlock is not as amenable to direction as Detectives Brisbois and Creighton."

"I wish they were here."

"Yes, it was most inconsiderate of them to go on vacation while a murder was taking place."

"Sarcasm, Edward."

"I apologize, Elizabeth. I think, in this case, however, you are bound to be stymied even if Detective Sherlock hangs on your every word. The word on the street, or at least at the breakfast table, is that the death of the chief was probably unpremeditated. The man was simply in the wrong place at the wrong time."

She gave him an exasperated but affectionate look. "Edward, you know it's never as simple as that."

He glanced at her over the top of the menu. "It could be."

She ignored this. "Everyone seems to believe that the chief was in the boathouse because he felt cold during the night. But why would he be warmer in the boathouse than in his tent with his sleeping bag and the extra blanket Mrs. Rudley had given him?"

"Perhaps his tent had a leak."

"It hasn't rained since we arrived here."

"Perhaps he took his sleeping bag with him to the boathouse. We don't know that he didn't."

"That shouldn't be hard to find out."

"I assume you intend to ask Sherlock that."

"I do. It seems more likely that the chief heard something in the boathouse and decided to check it out."

"That makes sense, Elizabeth, but I'm not sure if that fact advances the case in any way."

"Someone came into the boathouse to steal a boat is the theory. There's nothing else worth stealing, really. But no boat is missing."

"The murderer got scared off when he realized the chief was dead."

"Then why didn't he just leave? Why would he risk staying around to conceal the chief's body in the life-preserver box?"

Simpson frowned.

"The murderer came here for another purpose," Elizabeth continued. "He entered through the boathouse because, possibly, he came by boat and it seemed to provide cover while he scoped things out."

"That makes sense, Elizabeth. If he had come in at the front he would be completely exposed. If he came in by the road, he could be seen from the bunkhouse. If he came in from the west, he risked being seen by someone in the cottages. If he came in from over the hill, he could have been seen by someone with a room at the back of the inn or at the High Birches."

"If he came in through the boathouse, he could conceal his boat and take time to plan his next move."

"Quite right." He gave Miss Miller an approving smile. "Well thought out, Elizabeth. Now, which dessert should I choose?"

"You know my interest isn't merely theoretical," she said. "I don't think Detective Sherlock has a handle on this case. I think he needs our help."

"That's what I'm afraid of," he murmured.

She paused in thought. "I don't think his interest was in the boathouse. I think he came here for another reason."

"What would that reason be?" he asked cautiously.

"I don't know…yet." She narrowed her eyes. "I don't believe you can see the chief's tent from the water."

He considered this. "No. It's behind that little hedge."

"So whoever came into the boathouse had no way of knowing someone was camped out a few feet away."

"I suppose not." He returned to his menu, pretended to be completely absorbed in it, peeking over the top periodically to read her expression, which soon turned into a smile.

"I don't like that look," he murmured.

"Think about this, Edward. What three unusual things occurred at the same time?"

"Apart from certain Biblical events, I'm not sure, Elizabeth."

"A parrot shows up, seemingly from nowhere, Detective Creighton fishes Sherry out of the lake after she sinks her boat and loses all of her identification and the chief is murdered."

"Interesting," he said. "But Miss Brown is a personal friend of Detective Creighton. He apparently doesn't find anything suspicious about her."

"Detective Creighton is a man."

He sighed. "That's true. She's a red-headed woman. I was once led astray by a red-headed woman."

"That's not a parallel, Edward. You weren't led astray by someone with such a cockamamie story."

He considered this. "At least not the same story."

"What do you think of her?"

He handled the question like a live grenade. "She's attractive in a gamine sort of way, I suppose. She's lively. However, she's really quite a rattlebrain." He put down the menu. "I've decided on the rhubarb pie, if it has a lattice crust." He caught her expression of admonishment. "You were never a rattlebrain, Elizabeth, merely audacious and impulsive. Frankly, I don't think that young woman has an idea in her head. She's on to the next thought before the first has a chance to alight." He closed his menu, set it aside. "I've noted, Elizabeth, none of the women around here seem to like her much."

"Only men are attracted to her sort of charm," she said. "Most women can tell she lacks sincerity."

"Or perhaps she's suffering from some sort of emotional disorder."

She patted his arm. "Edward, you're such a good person."

He looked at her quizzically.

"You're always willing to give everyone the benefit of the doubt."

Sherlock finished his tour of the boathouse, then went up to the inn. Rudley was at the desk, the newspaper spread out, leaning over his crutches to read.

"How much longer in the cast, Mr. Rudley?"

"With my luck, until hell freezes over," Rudley muttered without looking up.

Sherlock hesitated for a moment before delivering the news. "I wanted to let you know that I won't be able to release the boathouse to you for another two days."

Rudley bit down on his lower lip to suppress an outburst.

"There are a few things I want to think over again."

"Damn to hell."

"The sooner I get this wrapped up, the sooner we'll be out of your hair on this."

"Out of my hair?" Rudley grabbed the sides of his hair and pulled it into two tufts. "Do you see this? This is what you and your ilk have done to me over the years."

"Sorry, Mr. Rudley." Sherlock turned to leave, tossing over his shoulder, "You might try a toupee."

Sherlock headed down the front steps, leaving Rudley spluttering in his wake. He was planning to drive to the little café near the dock in Middleton when Miss Miller and Mr. Simpson accosted him on the pathway.

"Yes?" he asked warily.

"I've been thinking about your case," Elizabeth responded.

"Fine." He continued walking.

She fell into step with him. "Why do you think Chief Longbow went into the boathouse?"

"Perhaps he thought it would be more comfortable."

"Where did you find his sleeping bag?"

He blinked.

"I understand the supposition is that the chief went into the boathouse because he thought it would be more comfortable there."

"Perhaps."

"Did he take his sleeping bag with him?" She fixed him with grey-green eyes. "Because if not, why would he think he would be more comfortable in a boathouse, which is essentially on the water with hard wooden floors?"

He opened his mouth to speak, but frowned instead.

"Now the supposition, according to our sources..."

"Your sources?"

"Tim," she replied. "According to Tim, the supposition is that the murderer entered the boathouse with theft in mind and met the chief by accident." She narrowed her eyes. "But what if he was there for some other purpose?"

"What other purpose?"

"I don't know...yet." She went on to relate the ideas in her earlier conversation with Edward. "There, you see?"

"Interesting," Sherlock said, looking past her head toward Simpson. "What do you think of your wife's theories?"

"Quite a bit, actually, Detective. She's usually right."

Sherlock sighed and said sternly, "Miss Miller, I'm not dismissing your ideas out of hand. But I don't want to find you meddling in my case. And I want to remind you, you can theorize as much as you want, but stay away from cordoned-off areas and be careful who you share your ideas with."

"I find that rather condescending, Detective."

"Curiosity killed the cat," he said. "And from what I've heard, you've come close a few times."

"She has," said Edward.

"So don't do anything risky." Sherlock turned and walked back toward the Pleasant.

"I don't think he wants my help, Edward," Elizabeth said when he was out of earshot.

"That's never stopped you before, Elizabeth."

Chapter Twenty-five

Margaret was at the desk when Sherlock entered the lobby.

"Detective," she greeted him. "I didn't realize you were still here."

"Something" — he paused — "something just occurred to me. I have a few questions." He checked his notebook while Margaret waited expectantly. "The girl who works for you but doesn't really work for you — Sherry Brown."

"She's not here at the moment."

"Where is she?"

"She said she was going to Ottawa."

"I was supposed to be notified if anyone left the jurisdiction."

"Oh dear, didn't you get the message we left with your headquarters?"

He spoke through gritted teeth. "No. Did she say when she expected to return?"

"I think she was planning to do a little shopping. And she thought she might visit an old school chum. She expected to stay overnight."

"Did she leave a phone number?"

"No. She probably didn't think anyone would be wanting to get in touch with her." She leaned toward him and whispered, "She's a sweet girl but a bit of a flibbertigibbet. She really doesn't need to be here at any special time," Margaret added. "She's more of a guest than an employee."

"Do you think she had anything to do with the deceased's death?"

She looked at him, startled at the abrupt question. "I don't see how she could. I believe the camera showed she didn't leave the bunkhouse all night. And she couldn't have gone out a window. That would have triggered the alarms. They're on the same system."

"I know. I know." Sherlock drew the palm of one hand down the side of his face. He remembered taking notes on this before. "It's amazing," he said finally. "The bunkhouse is like a fortified castle, but the main inn is as open as a church."

"Mr. Rudley wouldn't abide a security system with flashing lights and so forth. He'd forget the keypad number and be perpetually locked out. We'd have him on the front lawn, bellowing and waking the whole place. Besides, no one has been murdered in the main inn, except once." She thought for a minute. "And that wasn't on the upper floors. That one happened in the wine cellar."

Sherlock smiled. Talking to her was sometimes like a trip to Oz, but she tried so hard to be helpful. "May I run something by you?" he asked.

"Of course, Detective."

"There is some temporal consistency with the parrot arriving, Miss Brown sinking her boat, and the chief's unfortunate end. Have you given that any thought?"

She beamed. "You've been talking to Miss Miller. That's very wise of you, Detective. Miss Miller is a fountain of ideas."

Spewing all over the place, he thought with chagrin. "I wanted to know *your* opinion, Mrs. Rudley."

"I'm not sure if there is any connection, Detective," she said after a moment's thought. "Bad things happen in threes. Good things too. Of course, Betty and Sherry aren't bad things, and what happened to the chief is not a good thing." She paused. "Although I'm sure a third good thing must have happened."

Mr. Rudley breaking his leg, Sherlock thought.

"We got to meet you, Detective. That must be the third good thing."

He smiled. It was impossible to be gruff with Mrs. Rudley. "Think about it."

"Of course, Detective."

"And what does Mr. Rudley think?"

She sighed. "Mr. Rudley is suspicious of everybody."

Making his way to his car once more, he hoped no one would intercept him, as he was eager to leave. Life at the Pleasant was like the plots of *Pollyanna* and *Silence of the Lambs* mixed together. And he wanted lunch in a place where the food arrived greasy on a heavy plate and the coffee looked as if it were one step away from coating the driveway.

"Feed Betty."

He looked up, shook a finger at the bird. "If you dump another load of guano on me, you've got to go."

The bird hopped closer to him and craned her neck. "Got to go. Sweetie's got to go. Tweek and Freak."

Sherlock climbed into his car. Something was tugging at a brain cell, but try as he might, he couldn't bring it out. He scribbled down a few notes. Sherry Brown… She had told him she was from British Columbia, that she was travelling across the country, taking short-term, casual jobs to pay her way. He had her on his to-do list for background checks, but since there was no evidence to suggest she was involved in the chief's death and because she was a personal friend of Chester Creighton, he had put that task on the back burner. He tapped his pen against his notebook. Perhaps that had been a mistake.

At 3:00 a.m. Tibor woke with a start. He leapt out of bed, his heart racing, pulled on his pants and shoes and grabbed his knife. He ran to the second-floor window and looked out. Saw nothing. He darted across the hall and shook Frankes awake.

"Get up," Tibor commanded. "There's something going on outside."

"Maybe a raccoon," said Frankes. He started to roll over.

Tibor seized him by the shoulder and dug his fingers in. "It was no raccoon."

Frankes struggled up and pulled on his pants. "What's the knife for?"

"It might come in handy…if we run into a raccoon."

They crept down the stairs. Tibor stopped at Luther's door, opened it, and looked inside. "Out like a light," he reported to Frankes, moving to the next door and trying the knob.

"Locked?" Frankes asked.

"Yes."

Tibor grabbed a flashlight from a drawer in the kitchen, opened the patio door and they stepped out onto the back porch. Frankes opened his mouth to speak, but Tibor silenced him with a sharp hand gesture across his throat and motioned for him to go around one side of the cottage. He turned in the opposite direction and reached the front porch first. He faded back into the shadows and gestured to Frankes when he appeared around the other corner.

"Didn't see anything," Frankes whispered.

Tibor pointed toward the lake and whispered back. "Let's check out the shoreline."

They moved slowly toward the dock, one on either side, Tibor with knife poised, flashlight sweeping the ground.

"Look at that," Frankes giggled, as the beam of the flashlight illuminated the water. "Some idiot ran his boat into the dock."

Tibor made a sweeping gesture with his arm to shut Frankes up. He approached the end of the dock and looked over into the water.

A motorboat, its hull split, was rapidly sinking, the motor beating the air.

"I guess the motor will go off once it goes under," Frankes whispered loudly.

"Damn," Tibor rasped, staring at the sinking vessel.

"What?"

"That's our boat."

"I guess we'll have to canoe it for groceries."

Tibor gave him a furious look and marched toward the boathouse, Frankes in pursuit. They ducked inside and Tibor swung his flashlight around. "I think you're going to have to swim," he said.

"Huh?"

Tibor grabbed Frankes by the arm. "Do you see any canoes?"

Frankes looked around, puzzled.

Tibor aimed his flashlight at the water. "Because they're down there." He turned and stormed out of the boathouse.

Frankes caught up with Tibor halfway up the lawn. "What d'you think happened?"

"Probably some local yahoos thought it would be fun to wreck somebody's boats. They likely tried to get away in the motorboat and were so damn drunk they ran the thing into the dock."

"Where do you think they went?"

"Either they swam for it or drowned. That means they're either somewhere on the island or lying on the bottom of the lake."

"So what're we going to do?"

"We're going to search the island as soon as it's daylight." Tibor said. "I'm not going to risk running into some idiots in the dark. They could have guns."

Frankes figured any guns the intruders had were probably at the bottom of the lake too, but felt it was unwise to say so.

Tibor stamped off to the cottage. Frankes followed. They reached the patio door. Tibor stopped and turned to Frankes. "Did you leave this thing open?"

Frankes paused. "No, I pulled it closed."

"Well, it's open now." Tibor lowered his voice. "They must have got out of the boat and made their way up here." He pushed Frankes ahead of him into the cottage. "You go around that way. I'll have your back."

"That'll be good when someone blows a hole through my front."

The main floor was clear. Tibor motioned Frankes up the stairs.

"Nothing here," said Frankes, breathless, when they finished exploring the second floor His eyes were bright with the adrenalin rush.

They went back down the stairs. Frankes leaned against the door to Leonard's room. And fell backward, stopping himself only by grabbing the doorframe. Tibor stared past him into the room.

Had the old man vanished? Tibor flicked on the light and darted into the *en suite* bathroom. He yanked the shower curtain aside. "Where in hell did he go?"

"I guess he unlocked the door and went out."

"I locked it from the outside and took the key."

"Maybe Luther let him out somehow."

Tibor seethed. "Well, wake the damn fool up." He shoved Frankes out into the hallway.

Tibor was still standing in the room, his jaw clenched, when Frankes returned. "He's not there."

"What?"

"He must have let Leonard out and they both took off. Maybe Leonard woke up and started banging at the door. So Luther let him out. Maybe they got scared when the boat hit the dock." He shrugged. "Or maybe those guys who wrecked the boats took them out. Maybe they were kidnapped."

They went into the kitchen, but Leonard and Luther weren't there either. They fetched drinks from the refrigerator and slumped down at the table in the breakfast nook.

"What d'you think happened?" Frankes asked at last, unnerved by Tibor's silence. "Maybe that guy who came to look at the paintings just wanted to make us think they weren't the real ones," he continued. "Then he comes back, distracts us, gets rid of Luther and Leonard and takes off with the paintings."

Tibor blinked. It wasn't a completely half-baked idea. He got up and went into the living room and lifted the box where the paintings had been left after the unsuccessful transaction. His shoulders sagged. The paintings were undisturbed.

Chapter Twenty-six

"I don't know if I can go on in these slippers." Leonard stopped and grabbed onto a tree. He was short of breath.

"It's not much further, Leonard."

"Why did you anchor so far away?"

"I had to put some space between us and the boys."

Leonard sank to the ground. "I can't go any further."

Cerise turned to Luther. "You'll have to carry him."

Luther nodded, swept Leonard up and started back toward the house. Cerise grabbed him by the arm and turned him around. "We're going this way."

They reached the shore in minutes, Luther running ahead, carrying Leonard as if he were a large rag doll, Cerise scurrying to keep up with him, yelling occasionally to redirect him.

They arrived at a small sand beach. Cerise pointed out a rowboat tethered to a boulder. She jumped into the water, directed Luther to put Leonard at one end of the boat and indicated to him that he was to get in the other end. She then climbed in between them.

"Row," she commanded Luther.

Luther did as told. Leonard turned his head, squinted into the darkness. "Where are we going?"

"Just wait." She looked at Luther, who had eased up on the oars when Leonard spoke. "Keep going."

He bent his back into the task.

Luther had rowed for five minutes when Cerise called out, "Stop!" She pointed to a large craft anchored several yards away. "There."

Luther rowed closer. Cerise got up, grabbed the ladder on the side of the craft, secured the boat, then started up the ladder. She motioned to Luther to put Leonard on his back and climb aboard.

Leonard breathed a sigh of relief as Luther eased him down into a folding chair. He looked at Cerise, astonished. "How did you get here?"

"Friends in Montreal," she said.

"Are we going to Montreal?"

"Don't worry about that," she said. "We'll be out of the country before you know it."

He smiled. "I hope we're going to St. Tropez. I haven't been in St. Tropez for a long time."

She didn't answer.

"Are we going by boat?"

"Private plane."

He frowned. "Can we afford that?"

"I called in Mother's IOUs," she said.

"Sylvia?"

"The one and only."

He frowned. "How?"

"Hubby has connections," she said. "How else do you think he can keep her in the style to which she is accustomed?"

"Mafia?"

"I knew Stepdad would come in handy some day." She grimaced. "It still cost us though. I had to sell the necklace to pay for the boat and the passports."

"The one I gave you?"

"Yes." She swept the hoodie away from her face.

He stared at the blonde-haired, blue-eyed girl with the long scar down one cheek. He recoiled. "Oh, my God!"

"It's all makeup, Leonard." She patted his arm. "People will look at me, but all they'll remember is the scar." She shrugged. "Dyed hair, tinted lenses, it all works. We'll alter you a bit. Nothing dramatic. Maybe shave your head."

He ran a hand over his thick, silver hair. "Not that."

"Leonard, your hair sticks out like a sore thumb. It'll grow back."

"I suppose."

She knelt and looked him straight in the eye. "How's the other problem? The memory? Are you still having walkabouts?"

He smiled. "Walkabouts? Yes, I walk about. Not as much since my foot got sore." A troubled look crossed his face. "I feel confused at times. Sleepy."

"I think your blood sugar needs attending to," Cerise said. "I'll bet the boys haven't been looking after that very well."

"They aren't very attentive." He frowned. "I wonder if they've been slipping me something."

"We don't need to worry about them for a while." When he raised his brows, she added, "I wrecked all of the boats."

"That was very clever of you, Cerise."

"Sophie Bright. You can still call me Cerise, at least when we're alone."

"Is my name still Leonard?"

"I'll brief you on that later. Our paperwork's in order. If we can get away in the next few hours, we'll be as free as birds." She smiled. "Besides, you haven't done anything wrong. Neither has Luther. And I haven't either."

He regarded her dubiously.

"Well, not really. Nothing that will keep me out of heaven. They don't send people to the other place for ruining a few boats, do they?"

"No," he said quietly, "not for that."

"I don't think we need to worry about Tibor and Frankes. They won't be able to get off the island for a while. But I don't think they're very happy right now. You conned them about the Cartwrights, Leonard. And you are in possession of stolen art. But what can they do about it?"

More than you think, he thought. He listened to her prattle on and decided she was right. If Tibor implicated him, he would implicate

himself more. Tibor was the one who burned down the house with
Luella in it. He wouldn't go to the police with information that would
send him to prison for a long time, just out of spite. He knew Tibor
was largely self-serving. Of course, Tibor might seek some kind of
revenge in another way. But he and Cerise and Luther would be in the
south of France. Tibor had no money. Frankes would move on once he
could no longer depend on Tibor for his livelihood.

"You say your stepfather has Mafia connections?" Leonard asked
Cerise.

"Let's just say he has connections. Mother was able to talk him
into using them."

"Sylvia has her talents."

"She does."

"So she did all of this for you?"

"No, she did it for you, Leonard."

He smiled.

"We'll board a private jet in Montreal and be on our way. Before
anyone knows what has happened — if they figure it out at all — we'll
be far away."

"That will be expensive."

"We'll have enough money, Leonard. Not as much as we had
hoped for. But we won't be eating wieners and beans."

He screwed up his face. "I never liked wieners and beans."

"And if the money doesn't keep us in a style we would like to
maintain…" She smiled. "I'm quite resourceful, and" — she gave him
a playful poke in the ribs — "I know you have money squirrelled
away."

"I've never doubted that you were resourceful." He looked around.
The horizon was a shade lighter. "Who's running the boat?"

"Someone who will get the rest of his money when he delivers us
safely to Montreal."

He winked. "Smart girl."

After a long pause, she said, "So where are the Cartwrights,
Leonard?"

He sighed. "They're still on St. Napoli."

"In a safe place?

"In a safe-deposit box. They'll remain there as long as I pay the necessary fees." He frowned. "We may not be able to touch them for a while. What do you think Tibor and Frankes will do?"

She shrugged. "They'll probably flag down a passing boat or make a raft to get to the mainland." She appeared to reconsider: "I'd guess they'd make a raft. Frankes is good about that sort of thing. Then who knows? They aren't exactly good at looking after themselves."

He had to agree. He liked what she was saying. Tibor had lived off him for years; then, when he was vulnerable, bullied him. "So where have you been?"

"You don't want to know, Leonard."

"Then what have you been doing all this time?"

"Arranging things." She paused. "I'm pretty good, you know. I even managed to pull the wool over the eyes of a police detective."

"Impressive."

"He was on vacation. So he wasn't as sharp as he normally is, I suppose. Or maybe he's just a sucker for a pretty face. I play the cute act pretty well."

"You do that."

"Stick with me, Leonard, and you'll be fine."

"I'm sorry about one thing, though."

"Yes?"

"You said you wrecked all of the boats at the cottage."

"Afraid so."

"We'll have to reimburse Hiram in some way. He was a good friend to my father."

"We may not be able to. It would leave a trail." Cerise brightened. "Besides, there's always insurance."

"I suppose." Leonard moved his foot and winced. "I've got quite a bad sore."

"We'll get that looked after as soon as we get to Montreal."

"Why did you come back for Luther and me?"

"I couldn't leave Luther with those jackals." She put her arms around him. "And what would I do without you, Leonard? It'd be awfully lonely. Besides, all I would have had was the money from the necklace. You have your annuities. And your hidden stash."

He smiled. "That's my girl."

Sherlock received the report as he was about to leave the office for Dr. Jim's. According to an expert at the university, debris ground into the fabric of the wetsuit was coral. The DNA analysis showed that the tissue on the fabric did not match the tissue found under Chief Longbow's nails. Nor did either match the chief's DNA or that of anyone at the Pleasant.

"Someone didn't clean their wetsuit very well," Dr. Jim commented when Sherlock arrived. "Although I'm not sure how useful that information is to you."

"It suggests that the person the wetsuit belongs to spent time in warmer waters."

"That's true, although you would be surprised to know how many people around here have spent time in warmer waters."

"Well, it's something." Sherlock frowned.

"I know what you're thinking. You're wondering why someone who dropped in on the boathouse on the odd chance he might be able to lift a boat would be wearing a wetsuit. And you're wondering if there's a chance that piece of fabric left behind predated the murder."

"It wasn't there that long," said Sherlock. "You said the blood on it wasn't degraded."

"I did say that. And I said I know Mr. Rudley and he's absolutely a fanatic about the condition of his property. Not to mention that Lloyd the handyman is also fussy about such things."

"The fabric was left by someone who'd recently gone to the boathouse. And he was wearing a wetsuit because he didn't want to swim around in the lake at night when the water is cool. Besides, who wants to be caught in a bathing suit doing something criminal?"

Dr. Jim smiled. "I'm glad you're willing to play along with me. I don't often get a chance to play detective, not in that way.

"He was wearing something dark because he didn't want to be seen," Dr. Jim continued.

"He was being a commando."

"At least he wanted to *act* like he was being a commando."

Sherlock frowned. "The big question is what was he doing there, at the boathouse?"

Dr. Jim removed his glasses and leaned over his desk. "Normally, when such things happen, one would look for the simple answer. You know, when you hear hoofbeats think horses, not zebras. But" — he shot Sherlock a meaningful glance — "this is the Pleasant.

"When incidents of this nature have happened at the Pleasant before, sometimes it's been an inside job, or an outside job where the victim was targeted. There has almost always been a motive, and when innocent people get knocked off, it's usually because they were in the wrong place at the wrong time."

"So if history is our guide," Sherlock interjected, "the killer was after someone else." He considered this possibility. "But no one else got knocked off. I can see that he'd want to hide the body if he were planning to skulk around for a while. Why would the murderer go to all the trouble of stuffing the chief into a box if he wasn't prepared to proceed with his plan? Why didn't he just leave?"

"Maybe he was planning to proceed, but he couldn't get at the intended target. Maybe he was just scouting things out." Dr. Jim leaned back in his chair. "I don't know. But I'll bet the answer to this is right in front of your nose. That's not a criticism," Dr. Jim added amiably. "It's not easy to see things that are right in front of your nose. They're kind of blurry and often double."

Sherlock chewed at his moustache.

"Some cases just aren't that easy to crack," Dr. Jim continued. "People always think cases out here are going to be easier to solve because you don't have as many suspects. And sometimes you assume the perpetrators aren't very smart." He shrugged. "What I'm saying is, around here, it pays to lay back and keep your ears open. You'd be surprised."

Chapter Twenty-seven

Creighton walked up the front steps of the Pleasant, paused and glanced back at Sherlock. The detective was sitting on a bench halfway down the lawn staring out over the lake and appeared not to have noticed him. Creighton shrugged and went on into the lobby.

Rudley was behind the front desk, sitting on a chair, his leg balanced on the wastepaper bin. He had removed the front of his bivalved cast and was scouring his leg with a piece of loofah.

Creighton gave the bell a sharp rap.

"Jesus Christ!" Rudley's leg slid off the bin. He grabbed it before his heel crashed on the floor and glared at Creighton. "Are you trying to break my leg again?"

"Sorry," said Creighton, who really wasn't. "You're going to dig a hole in your leg going at it like that. Could set you up for an infection."

"I've never had an infection in my life."

"I'll bet you've never had a broken leg in your life, either."

Rudley slapped the top of his cast back on, wound the elastic bandage around it, grabbed a paper clip from his pocket and secured the bandage haphazardly.

"Where are the clips that came with the bandage?" Creighton asked.

"How in hell should I know? They keep falling off. Wouldn't you think the manufacturer could make something that would stay on for more than five minutes?"

"You'd think," said Creighton.

"Why are you being so damn agreeable?"

"I'm on vacation."

"Maybe you should go on vacation permanently," Rudley grumbled. When Creighton did not take the bait, he added, "Did you come here just to bother me?"

"No, that's a bonus," Creighton laughed. "Is Sherry around?"

"I don't know." Rudley ratcheted himself up off the chair, grabbing the edge of the desk for a final boost, and sifted the papers he had been sorting before the urge to scratch had intervened. "There was a note here." He shuffled the pile. "It's gone. Someone must have taken it."

"Maybe Gregoire took it. Or Tim."

"Go bother them then," said Rudley, unamused by Creighton's sarcasm. "You know where they are."

After Creighton disappeared into the kitchen, Rudley flung his crutches aside, sat back on his chair and wondered why everyone thought he should know where everyone was at all times. He couldn't understand Creighton's attraction to Sherry anyway. He found her an aggressive, insolent little twit. Wherever she was, he wasn't unhappy that she was gone.

Unfortunately, Sherlock wasn't gone. Rudley craned his neck to see out the window. Yes, there he was, just as he had been the past two hours, sitting on the bench, staring into space. The man's lost his spunk, he thought. The precise, arrogant edge had almost disappeared. He seemed morose, almost fatalistic. "He's finally getting the knack of this place," he told Albert, who was lying on the rug in front of the desk.

Albert gave him a dog smile, got up and padded behind the desk. He lifted himself on his hind legs in an attempt to see the desktop.

"Nothing for you to filch here," Rudley said. He frowned. "You've got blood on your muzzle and" — he plucked something from the corner of Albert's mouth — "two long yellow feathers between your teeth."

Albert averted his gaze.

"Unless you have avian ancestry," Rudley told the dog, "I think you're in deep trouble."

"Detective Sherlock has been sitting in the same spot all morning," Tim remarked as he entered the kitchen.

"I have been in the same place all morning as well," said Gregoire, "wondering where everyone who is supposed to be helping me has gone. Now I see they are just spying on the detective."

"What do you want me to help you with?"

"I would like you to take those leftover pieces of fruit out to the bird feeder. I am at a delicate position with my soufflés and I could hear Betty squawking all the way into my kitchen."

"Where's Lloyd?"

"He has gone into town to get some things I need."

"Where's Tiffany?"

"She is with Margaret at the High Birches. They are measuring up for new wallpaper."

"So what you really want is my company."

"I do not want your company. I want you to be ready in case there is an emergency here."

Tim laughed. "What kind of emergency could you have in the kitchen?"

"Anything could go wrong when I am making a soufflé," Gregoire responded crossly. "I like to know there is someone here."

"You're afraid you're missing out on the news," said Tim. "I heard that the morgue is ready to release the body of Chief Longbow, but no one has claimed him."

Gregoire looked up from his mixing bowl, alarmed. "Does Margaret know of this?"

"Not yet."

Gregoire tightened his grip on the spatula. "She will insist upon having the funeral here, on the land he thought was his. She will want a reception with appropriate food. There is no appropriate food for a funeral."

"How about angel food cake?"

"Angel food cake is for occasions that are light and happy. I think at a funeral one should fast. It is not a cause for celebration."

"OK, we'll have bread and water and wear sackcloth and ashes. I will have to be a pallbearer because I am one of the ones who knew him best."

"Then I will have to be, too," Gregoire sighed. "And Lloyd and Tiffany and Margaret and, perhaps, Mr. Simpson with Mr. Rudley as an honorary pallbearer."

"That fits. He's an honorary innkeeper."

"You will not want him to hear you say that."

"Hey, guys." Detective Creighton appeared in the doorway.

Gregoire held up a warning hand. "Walk softly. I have a soufflé in the oven."

"Oh." Creighton tiptoed across the floor and lowered himself slowly to a kitchen stool.

"What can we do for you, Detective?" Tim scooped up a handful of strawberries, to Gregoire's annoyance.

"I was wondering if Sherry was around."

Gregoire looked to Tim, who replied, "She said she was going to visit a friend."

Creighton frowned. "Where was she going?"

"Ottawa."

"How was she getting there?"

"I believe she said she was taking a bus."

"Did she say when she would be back?"

"I think she said in a day or so," said Gregoire.

"She said she would be staying with a friend," added Tim.

"I would have driven her up."

"She probably did not want to put you out like that," Gregoire said.

"She's never worried about that before," Creighton muttered.

Gregoire took a peek at his soufflé though the oven window. "You know women can be very strange. It is one thing one time and another thing the next."

"True," said Creighton. "Still, it seems strange she didn't ask for a ride."

Gregoire shrugged. "Maybe she thought she was depending on you for too much and thought she should be independent on this one thing."

"Did she leave a number where she could be reached?"

"No."

Creighton chuckled. "She probably figures I'd know how to reach her through osmosis." He got up off the stool. "Let me know if you hear from her."

"We will do that," said Gregoire.

Creighton left, frowning. As he passed the desk in the lobby, he waved at Rudley, who appeared to be intently studying some feathers spread out in front of him Probably something the Phipps-Walkers brought, he surmised, as he passed through the door onto the veranda. He noted Sherlock hadn't moved an inch.

He was disappointed Sherry had left without letting him know. Not that such behaviour was out of character for her. He had to admit that, as charming and refreshing as she was, she had tendencies that reminded him of some of the con artists he had had occasion to deal with over the years. He enjoyed spending time with her, particularly that she kept him off balance. She was different, a breath of fresh air. He wished the other women he had known could have been as open. He chuckled. Maybe she had no trouble being open because everything she said was a fib.

His eyes travelled across the lake. He had no reason to doubt her story, at least the bare bones of it, although he suspected she had a tendency to embellish. He had fished her out of the lake, after all, with no vessel in sight. Given her character, her story made perfect sense.

He tilted his head. Except the part about not wanting to bother him by asking him to drive her to Ottawa. The Sherry he knew would not only have accepted a ride, she wouldn't have even thanked him. In the city, she would have sent him to buy her various things — without giving him any money or suggesting she ever would. Somehow she would twist things to make it seem that he should feel privileged to answer her every need. She was very good at that.

He took a chair on the veranda and let his gaze drift from Sherlock, who had still not moved, to Mr. Bole, who was working on a finger puppet under the shade of the maples. Mr. Bole's project this time, he understood, was *The Count of Monte Cristo*. He noted the Sawchucks were puddling around near shore in a rowboat and the Phipps-Walkers, their binoculars trained intently into the trees. He thought the birds at the Pleasant should start charging an entertainment fee.

His reverie was cut short by the appearance of Miss Miller and Simpson.

"You appear to be in a brown study," Miss Miller said as she took a seat on the wicker settee opposite him. Simpson sat beside her.

"Just woolgathering," he said.

"Something's bothering you," she said.

He raised his brows. "Am I that transparent?"

"In this case," she said.

He sighed. "All right, let me run this by you."

He told them the story of his first encounter with Sherry.

"Exactly where did you find her?" Miss Miller asked when he had finished.

"She swam up to my boat in the lake."

"Where did she swim from?"

"When I first saw her, I was fifty yards offshore. She was further out."

"And she said she'd sunk her boat."

"Yes."

"When did she sink it?"

"She didn't say exactly. I assumed it was shortly before."

Miss Miller clucked her tongue. "You should never assume anything. Didn't they teach you that in detective school?"

He smiled ruefully. "They did."

"Think back, Detective, what else did you see?" When he wrinkled his brow and shook his head, she pressed him. "Any debris?"

"No."

"Any gasoline slick from the motor?"

"No." Creighton felt his face redden. "I don't know if it was a motorboat. She didn't say."

"So all you saw was a big empty lake."

"There were a couple of those little islands — you know, the kind that have one tree and not enough land to build an outhouse."

"How far away?"

"Not too far. Maybe a hundred yards from where I was. It's hard to tell on the water." He frowned. "You think she came from one of the little islands?"

"Maybe."

"But what difference does that make? Her boat sank. She swam to the nearest land and waited until she saw someone close enough to help."

"Why didn't she just keep swimming to shore?"

"Because I was there with my boat."

"How long were you there before you spotted her?"

"Maybe half an hour."

"But you didn't see her sink her boat. You didn't see any debris. She didn't tell you she'd been on the island waiting to be rescued. Although it seems she would have had plenty of time to swim all the way to the shore."

His forehead crimped.

"Did you ask her?"

He hesitated, then admitted he hadn't. "She started talking a blue streak the minute she saw me. Then she took half my lunch. Then she told me I was going to have to help her because she had lost all of her money and papers. Gave me hell for breaking her necklace."

"She distracted you with constant chatter."

She sparkled, he thought, turning to Simpson. "What do you think?"

"I think her situation sounds a little strange when you think it over," Simpson replied. "Although I'm sure stranger things have happened."

"I think we should go out and poke around those little islands," Miss Miller said. "You never know what you might find. Where are they?"

"Just on the other side of Middleton."

She clapped her hands. "Detective, I think we have some investigating to do. Are you up for that on your vacation?"

"I think you have to be," said Simpson, without adding *or you'll never hear the end of it.*

"Why not?" Creighton shrugged. "What else have I got to do?"

"We'll take a motorboat," said Miss Miller. She jumped up. "I'm just going to tell Mr. Rudley."

Miss Miller whipped into the lobby, returning a minute later. "He's in agreement!"

"Meaning he's glad to have us all out of his hair."

"More or less."

Sherlock was still in his chair when they passed, his head cocked back. He appeared to be staring at something in the trees.

"Detective Sherlock?" Miss Miller inquired.

Sherlock murmured a greeting, adding, "Betty's lost half of her tail feathers."

Chapter Twenty-eight

Tibor watched as Frankes prepared to slip into the water in the boat-house. "I don't know what you need that wetsuit for."

"It's pretty cold and slimy in there," Frankes complained.

"You should clean that thing off once in a while. You've got a kelp forest growing on it."

"I'll toss it when we're finished mucking around. It's got a hole in it anyway."

"How'd you manage that?"

"I got it caught on something."

Tibor looked at the tear without interest. "Let's just get on with this."

Frankes jumped into the water, which came up to his chin. He shuddered, pulled down the mask and disappeared below the surface. A few seconds later he popped into view and handed the end of the rope to Tibor, which he took with distaste.

"You're going to have to help here," Frankes said. "A canoe's pretty heavy when it's full of water."

After they eased up the first canoe, Frankes went back down for the second. "That's it," he said when they were finishing, pushing himself back onto the deck.

Tibor surveyed the canoes. He gave one a kick. Looked at the second one.

"The damage on that one looks high enough up," said Frankes. "I can probably fix it enough to let us get to dry land."

"Probably?"

"There's some caulk up there." Frankes motioned to the shelf above Tibor. "I can patch something over it."

"Good." Tibor gestured toward the water. "Now see if you can find the oars."

Frankes gave Tibor a nasty look and slid back into the water.

"There." Creighton pointed to the middle distance.

"Are you sure?" Miss Miller scanned the lake surface, one hand over her eyes.

"Yeah. I was parked out there in a bunch of weeds near that shoal." Creighton turned around in the boat. "That big tree was just across from me."

"I don't know if you would call those islets, Elizabeth." Edward indicated two piles of rock covered with moss and some scraggly brush.

"You might call them something to camp out on while you were waiting to be rescued," Miss Miller murmured.

"What are we waiting for?" Creighton said. "Let's check them out."

Miss Miller started the boat up and steered it carefully toward the islets. Simpson hung close to the side of the boat, watching the water.

"You'll have to bring up the motor," he called out.

"Roger that," said Miss Miller. She killed the motor and swung it out of the water. "Stand by to lasso that tree and slide in."

Creighton threw the weighted line toward the sapling. It stuck and he began to reel the boat in. Miss Miller grabbed an oar and stuck it down into the water. "It's only three feet here," she said. "We can roll up our pants and wade in."

Creighton did as instructed, but, stepping into the water, he lost his balance and came up spluttering.

"Slippery?" Miss Miller asked.

He took off his hat and poured the water out. "Not at all."

"Edward will stay with the boat in case it breaks free."

"Staying with the boat," Edward echoed.

Creighton and Miss Miller proceeded to check the islet while Simpson relaxed and fixed on a hawk circling. He was glad Elizabeth had not got too involved this time, although, from what he could gather, there wasn't much for her to sink her teeth into. He considered what she had told Detective Sherlock — three unusual things had occurred together: the arrival of Betty, the arrival of Sherry and the murder of Chief Longbow. However, as his father often told him: "Coincidences do happen, Edward. You could probably find all sorts of such triads if you looked at everything in life critically."

For example, he and Elizabeth had arrived at approximately the same time as Betty and close enough to the arrival of Sherry Brown to be part of such a triad. Still, he had to admit the possibilities were intriguing. He watched as the hawk sailed out of sight behind a tall tree. Sherry had arrived two to three weeks before, appearing out of the lake to ask Creighton for a lift to shore. She had lost all of her identification when her boat sank. Add to that the appearance of a parrot and the murder of Chief Longbow, a man stating he was aboriginal and laying claim to the Pleasant... Simpson raised his brows. Even his father would have to admit that was a rather unusual set of coincidences.

Creighton and Elizabeth returned, the latter wearing a look of disappointment.

"Nothing?" he asked her.

She shook her head.

"Lots of cormorant guano," Creighton said.

Elizabeth climbed into the boat. "You can untie and push off," she told Creighton.

"Why me?"

"Because you're already wet."

He did as told. Miss Miller used the paddle to turn the boat and head it toward the second islet twenty yards away. They tied up and once again left Edward with the boat. This islet was smaller, not more than fifteen by twenty feet, surrounded by a flat rock that tapered away into the water for several feet before dropping off precipitously.

"I should have come here to fish," said Creighton, pointing out a large bass just off the islet. "The water's so clear I could have netted something like that."

Miss Miller peered into the water.

"See anything?" Creighton asked.

She shook her head.

"Well, I guess that's that," said Creighton. "She sunk the boat. It's somewhere on the bottom. Unless I can give the inspector a good reason, he's not going to drag the lake."

"It's a big lake," he said when she made no response. "And there're probably dozens of boats down there."

"I was sure we'd find something."

"That would have been nice," he said. "But if finding something might confirm Sherry's story, finding nothing doesn't disprove it."

She sighed.

"They taught me that in detective school."

"I've got a decent patch ready," Frankes told Tibor when he'd finished his work, "but I'll have to wait for the boat to dry out before I can put it on."

Tibor took a joyless bite out of his sandwich. "How long?" he said, his mouth half full.

"Maybe tomorrow," said Frankes.

Tibor swore.

"I can put it on now, but it won't last worth shit."

"Fine," Tibor grumbled.

"Fine, you want me to put it on now, or fine, you want me to wait?"

Frankes was getting quite tired of Tibor's sour temper. Not that Tibor had ever had a sunny disposition. But at least he always exuded authority and made grand promises. Now he had lost his spunk, which made Frankes depressed and insecure. He wondered if anything good was going to happen from here on in.

"We'll wait," Tibor replied.

Frankes went to the refrigerator and looked over the slim pickings. "Did you take the last of the ham?"

"Yes."

"I wish Luther was here," said Frankes. "He can make a six-course meal out of nothing."

Tibor had many regrets, the least of which was losing Luther. He regretted helping Leonard in his scheme and assuming the bulk of the liability without much of a return, which might end up with him doing something that would put him in danger with the local authorities.

"How much money do we have?" Frankes asked.

Tibor hesitated. He knew this question would come up sooner or later. "I have about six hundred dollars."

Frankes had about a hundred in his pocket. The difference didn't seem fair. "Maybe you should give me my share of that and we should split up. That way if they're looking for..."

"They aren't looking for either of us right now. And if we're careful and don't panic and blab something we shouldn't, we can catch a bus and get over the border before they even know they should be looking for us."

"Where are we going?"

"I haven't decided," said Tibor. He didn't tell Frankes he had a couple of thousand dollars in his pocket. He'd lifted Leonard's wallet and raided Luther's moneybox, items Luther had left behind. He'd always had light fingers where these were concerned, taking a bit at a time so as not to be too noticeable. He figured Luther couldn't count that well anyway. "We'll cross into Quebec," he said. "We can lay low there for a couple of days and think things through."

"I thought we were going back to St. Napoli."

"I don't think we can, not for a long while." At least, he thought, *you* can't.

Sherlock glanced at his watch. He had been sitting for over two hours, pondering. Margaret had stopped by to see if he needed anything. He had said no, thank you. Tiffany had stopped by as she took her cart around to ask if he was all right. He had said he was, thank you. Now Tim was in front of him bearing a tray with a sandwich, a piece of pie and a small carafe of coffee. Sherlock waved it away.

Tim set the tray down nevertheless. "Mrs. Rudley noted it was well past lunch. She doesn't approve of anyone not having lunch. No one says no to Mrs. Rudley," he added as he turned to leave.

Sherlock glanced at the food. If the last time was predictive, he knew the sandwich would be delicious, with fresh, tasty ingredients complemented with just enough dressing to bring out the flavours. The coffee would be perfect. The pie would be the best he had ever eaten. He squared his shoulders.

Lloyd came along with his garden rake at that moment. "Ain't you going to eat your lunch?"

"No."

"Mrs. Rudley won't like that." Lloyd grinned. "She'll think you're sick if you don't eat and she'll take your temperature."

"I don't care if she thinks I'm sick or not," Sherlock muttered. "And she won't be taking my temperature."

"If you let her take your temperature, she'll give you a plate of brownies."

"I don't like brownies."

"Can I have your pie?"

"You can have my pie, you can have my sandwich, you can have my coffee." Sherlock picked up the tray, thrust it toward Lloyd, then returned to scanning his notebook.

"Mrs. Rudley says if you don't eat your brain don't work right," said Lloyd.

"Then you must all be fasting because nobody's brain works right in this place," Sherlock barked. "What do you do around here? Pump in halothane?"

"Just water."

Betty had been perched in the tree by the veranda. When she caught sight of Lloyd she flew to sit on the back of the bench. "Feed Betty," she chirped.

"I don't think you should let her that close when you're eating," said Sherlock. "It isn't sanitary."

"She needs extra to grow back her tail feathers." Lloyd gave Betty a piece of his bread, which she ate greedily, then began to groom the back of Lloyd's head.

"Feed Betty," the bird chirped again.

"Can't give you any more bread," said Lloyd. "Ain't good for you. I'll get you something in a minute."

"Dirty bird," said Betty. "Sweetie, Sweetie. I like Sweetie. Got to go. Sweetie's got to go."

Sherlock had to smile. "I think she believes, if she uses her phrases, you'll reward her. That's probably how she was trained."

"Feed Betty. Tweek and Freak. Freak is a freak."

"Soon as I finish the pie," said Lloyd.

Betty nibbled the side of his neck. "Leonard is stupid."

Sherlock sat up straight. "What did she say?"

"She said 'Leonard is stupid.'"

"I've never heard her say that before."

"Sometimes she says that." Lloyd fed Betty a piece of the pie crust. "Mostly she says *dirty bird* and *feed Betty*."

Sherlock flipped a page in his notebook and sat back, eyes widening.

Chapter Twenty-nine

Sherlock called in to headquarters and asked for a police boat and three officers. Within an hour, a boat appeared at the Pleasant dock with Officer Vance on board along with Officer Petrie. Officer Stubbs was at the helm. Sherlock stepped into the boat and barked orders.

Rudley and Margaret were at the desk when Lloyd returned with the lunch tray.

"Detective Sherlock said to tell you he appreciated the lunch," Lloyd said.

Rudley gave Lloyd an appraising glance "He appreciated it so much you've got crumbs all over your face."

"Said he wasn't hungry," said Lloyd. "I told him Mrs. Rudley was going to take his temperature. And he said everybody's brains was asleep and we must pump something in."

Margaret sighed. "Poor Detective Sherlock. He must be under incredible stress. It doesn't seem as if he has any leads in this case."

"So then Betty came over and I gave her some of my sandwich and he said it wasn't good for her and she kept asking for some more and all of a sudden he got on his phone and a boat came and took him off."

"That's a good reason for keeping her around," said Rudley.

"He got all excited because Betty said 'Leonard is stupid.'"

"I can't see why that would be so exciting," said Rudley. "I imagine she repeats anything she's heard more than once, especially if someone encourages her."

"He said she probably says things to get food," said Lloyd.

"I expect that's how they trained her," said Margaret. "I must say, whoever taught her could have come up with something more uplifting."

"What would you have her say?"

She pondered this. "Perhaps 'good morning,' 'lovely day,' 'may I have a cracker,' 'how do you do.'"

"It all sounds pretty boring, Margaret."

"In that case, we could have her sit beside you all day, Rudley."

Rudley smiled. "I have been known to be rather erudite at times, Margaret."

"Yes, dear." She smiled back. "You've been in such a good mood since that cast came off."

"When have I not been in a good mood, Margaret?"

She let that pass. "I would imagine you'll be in good enough shape to take part in Music Hall."

"You can count on me, Margaret." He did a little two-step behind the desk. "Not bad for a boy from Galt who just came out of a cast yesterday."

Lloyd grinned. "I guess you won't be fixing anything any more."

Tim knocked on the door of the Elm Pavilion with afternoon tea. The sisters were in the middle of a Gregory Peck marathon and it took a few minutes for Emma to come to the door. Tim entered and transferred the food from the tray to the tea trolley.

"Here you are, ladies. Watercress sandwiches and lemon meringues with Perrier, just as you requested."

"Oh, Tim," Kate said reproachfully. "Watercress?"

"Don't tease us," Louise tittered.

He smiled. "You're right. I don't know if anyone around here would recognize watercress if they fell over it. We have Gregoire's usual fine selection of salmon salad, egg salad, ham with Swiss cheese and, for the calorie conscious, peanut butter with marshmallow. All topped up with fruit tarts and maple cake. Tea, of course, and a Pepsi for Louise, who thinks she's been drinking too much tea."

"That's better," said Kate.

Emma sat down with a thump. "You know Gregoire would never send us watercress and low-calorie lemon meringues." She looked at Tim. "I noticed a police boat picking up the detective. Has he concluded his case?"

"Not by a long shot," said Tim.

"He's been sitting down there on the bench all morning," said Kate.

"We were watching him with our binoculars," said Louise.

"He's quite handsome," said Kate.

"But not much of a detective," Louise added.

"Lloyd said he got all excited when he heard Betty say 'Leonard is stupid' and got on the phone to headquarters. Lloyd heard him say something about heading for an island."

Emma frowned. "Leonard?"

"Yes. Officer Owens said he had gone to an island."

"Which island?" Kate asked.

"East of here. That's the direction the boat was headed, I think."

"He must be talking about Leonard Anderson," said Kate.

"There must be thousands of Leonards," countered Emma.

"Leonard sometimes stays on Hiram's island," Louise said, adding for Tim's benefit: "We knew Leonard when he was a young man. I don't think he's been back since his parents died."

"His father was a friend of Daddy's," said Kate.

"He was in the art business," said Emma. "I don't know where Daddy knew him from."

"Daddy was a spy," said Louise.

"He met all sorts of interesting people," said Kate.

"Many of them were spies," said Louise.

"Leonard's parents used to come to Hiram's quite often," Emma continued.

"Then they died in that awful airplane accident," said Kate.

"People were never meant to fly," said Louise.

"People have been flying for a hundred years, Louise," Emma groused.

Tim regarded the sisters with bewilderment. "Did you tell Detective Sherlock you knew Leonard?"

"He didn't ask," said Kate.

"We didn't even know he was in residence right now," said Emma.

"We really must talk to Hiram about keeping us abreast of the latest developments," said Louise.

"Leonard isn't stupid," Emma said. "In fact, he's rather clever."

"I think Leonard's father was a cultural attaché," Kate mused.

Louise tittered. "Everybody knows that's just code for *spy*."

Tibor had been sullen all day, sitting down and getting up to pace the cottage every five minutes.

"I don't know why we can't just watch a movie," Frankes said. "The canoe isn't going to dry any faster by you pacing around."

"I'm thinking," said Tibor, considering that thinking once in a while wouldn't do Frankes any harm. Still, there wasn't any point in aggravating him further. He needed Frankes — for the time being, at least. He was useful. He was good at chores, at fixing things, at carrying out orders.

In truth, he was feeling disconnected. He didn't care about Leonard, Cerise, Luther, and Frankes as people, nor did he consider them a surrogate family, but he was accustomed to having them around. And they were useful. He lived in a nice house in a nice place, had money, good food and clothing, the freedom to pursue his interests. And little was expected of him.

Except that he had set fire to a house with an old lady in it.

He ground his teeth. If it hadn't been for the goddamn paintings, if Leonard had been more receptive to Luella's romantic overtures instead of pursuing the liaison with Cerise's mother, life could have been good. Luella would have left her entire estate to Leonard. A good share of Leonard's estate would eventually be his. But no. Leonard had to consort with a courtesan, and reduce Luella's house to a pile of ashes. And now, he, Tibor, was on the hook for not one murder, but two. He especially resented the second. If that old fart hadn't been nosing around, he'd still be alive.

He was mulling over this when Frankes remarked, "There's a boat pulling up out there."

Tibor sprinted to the window and stared down at the dock. The boat was white and blue with the letters OPP written clearly on the hull. Worse, the man getting out was the same detective who had interviewed them earlier. He had three uniformed officers with him, one of them a woman.

"So they're probably just following up?" said Frankes with a yawn. "They do that, don't they?"

"Not with a posse like that," Tibor snapped. "There's three of them. No," he added as he spotted a fourth. "And it looks as if they're spreading out."

"So we'll just tell them what we told them before."

"And what are we going to tell them happened to Leonard and Luther?" Tibor hissed.

"Tell them they left for a few days. We'll say they were planning to go to Boston."

"They're going to get suspicious when they see the boats."

"Maybe they won't see them. The motorboat's sunk. We pulled the canoes out. We can say we went out on the lake and hit some rocks."

"We'll go with that." Tibor ran a hand over his scalp and waited for the knock on the door.

"How did the investigation go?" Rudley asked when Miss Miller, Creighton and Simpson appeared at the desk.

Creighton shook his head, while Miss Miller looked chagrined. "Disappointing," she replied

Rudley looked to Simpson.

"Better than usual," he said. "We weren't held at gunpoint, kidnapped or thrown into the lake."

"Except me," said Creighton.

"I've never had a case prove so frustrating," Miss Miller complained.

"I think Sherlock feels the same way," said Rudley, "although he seems to have had some inspiration. Lloyd reported that he got rather excited when Betty said something to him."

"Said something to him?" Creighton echoed.

"Something about Leonard," Rudley replied.

"Where's Lloyd?" Miss Miller asked sharply.

"He's down the hall fixing the ceiling fan." Rudley leaned over the desk and shouted, "Lloyd!"

Rudley pointed to the trio when the handyman arrived. "Tell the Three Musketeers what the parrot said. What got Sherlock so excited."

"She said 'Leonard is stupid,' 'Tweek and Freak,' 'Feed Betty' and 'Sweetie.'"

Miss Miller grimaced. "I don't see how that helps."

"Don't know," Lloyd continued. "But he got real excited and said we must pipe in something that spoils our brains. I said how about water, and then he went away and called a cruiser boat."

"I *knew* Betty was involved in this," Miss Miller said in a tone of triumph.

Creighton cleared his throat. "I think I can expand on that."

They turned to look at him.

"I think the answer might be in the jewellery shop downtown."

Chapter Thirty

Tibor answered the door when Sherlock knocked. He noted that the woman officer who had accompanied Sherlock had taken up a position slightly ahead and to the right of the door.

Sherlock nodded curtly when Tibor greeted him. "I'm here to speak to Mr. Anderson. Leonard Anderson."

"Oh," said Tibor casually, "I'm afraid he's not here."

"And where would he be?"

"He decided to spend a few days in Boston, but" — Tibor threw up his hands — "you never know with Uncle Leonard. He might decide at the last minute to go to Europe or even Australia. He has acquaintances everywhere."

Sherlock glanced around the cottage, his gaze taking in Frankes, who had retreated to the kitchen doorway and was leaning against the jamb.

Sherlock removed his notebook, rifled through it and frowned. "You let a man suffering from dementia go off on his own?"

"Luther went with him," said Tibor. "He travels with Luther quite often."

"I thought Luther was mentally challenged," Sherlock said after another glance at his notes.

"He isn't the world's greatest intellectual, but he's fine with things he's familiar with."

Sherlock held Tibor's gaze for a moment. "Do you have any pets around here?"

Tibor blinked. "No."

"A parrot turned up nearby. She had a lot to say."

"Sorry, Detective. I can't tell you anything about that."

"Hmm."

"Is that why you came here? Because of a parrot?"

Sherlock didn't answer the question. "We're going to need to take a look around," he said instead.

"I thought you had to show me a search warrant," Tibor began. "But" — he shrugged — "feel free."

"You're absolutely right. Petrie?" He addressed the officer accompanying him. Without taking his eyes off Tibor, he held out his hand as she removed a document from her pocket and handed it to him. He handed it to Tibor. "The warrant."

"Go ahead," said Tibor.

"In a minute. We're just waiting for Officer Vance. He's having a look around your boathouse."

"It takes three of you to look around?"

"When we're doing a search, yes. You never can tell what people might do."

"I suppose not."

"Why don't you make yourself comfortable. And have your friend join us."

Tibor beckoned to Frankes. "They want to look around."

"I heard," said Frankes, taking a seat.

"So, Mr. Frankes," said Sherlock. "It's just you and Mr. Gutherie here at this time?"

"Yes."

"Where did the others go?"

"They said Boston," said Frankes. He yawned. "I don't think they had bought tickets, but that's what Mr. Anderson said."

"So," Sherlock ventured, "how'd they get to town?"

There was a fraught moment of silence, then Tibor said, "They took the motorboat. We were supposed to pick it up at the dock in the village, but we ran our canoes onto the rocks. We're trying to repair the one where the damage was mostly above the water line. We aren't used to the water around here," Frankes added. "It was kind of a shock when we hit the rocks."

"Why didn't you just go in to town with them?"

Tibor paused a tick, then laughed. "Luther takes up an awful lot of a boat. And there was also luggage."

Sherlock thought this over. "We'll just wait for Officer Vance to join us then."

"I'm an excellent driver," said Creighton as Miss Miller cut a corner rather precariously.

"Elizabeth likes to drive," Edward explained as they tore down the road to Middleton. "She often says she would enjoy the opportunity to race competitively."

"I know," said Creighton, gripping the door handle. "I've seen her with Rudley's motorboats."

Creighton fell silent, pondering his idiocy. There was nothing to connect Sherry to the murder of the chief, as she had a solid alibi, but, as Miss Miller suggested, sometimes a coincidence is not just a coincidence. Sometimes the coincidence is meaningful. The parrot's appearance at the Pleasant at the same time as Sherry's sealed it, he thought.

"Is this the one?" Miss Miller asked Creighton as she pulled up in front of one of the jewellery stores.

"Oh," Creighton said, startled out of his reverie. "Yes, this is it."

"Miss Brown picked the necklace up two days ago," the saleswoman at the counter said after he'd introduced himself. "She forgot her wallet. She said you'd be in later to settle the bill."

"How much?" Creighton reached into his pocket and removed his wallet.

"A hundred and twenty-one dollars, plus tax."

"Holy Christ."

The woman regarded him gravely. "When the goldsmith got a look at it, he was quite impressed. Custom-made, twenty-four-carat gold.

And those stones were genuine diamonds and rubies. He wanted to do the job well."

"All he had to do was replace a couple of links," Creighton grumbled, handing over his credit card. "And you just gave it to her?"

"You *are* a detective. We wouldn't have had any trouble tracking you down."

"Could I speak to the goldsmith? I just want to confirm one detail."

When the goldsmith appeared he waxed enthusiastically about the necklace.

"The inscription?" Creighton prompted.

"Oh, yes," said the man. "'Happy Birthday, Sweetie.' Certainly a lovely gift."

When they returned to the car, Creighton remarked, "For a destitute little orphan, she must have had at least one rich friend."

"Of course, 'Sweetie' is rather generic," Simpson observed, aware of Creighton's embarrassment.

"Yeah," Creighton sighed. "Still, I should have checked her preposterous story out."

A silence followed. Simpson cleared his throat. "I must say, Detective, her personality was always consistent and made her story plausible. Besides, apart from having a rather fantastic story, has she done anything criminal?"

"I don't know." Creighton secured his seat belt. "I guess we'll find out when and if she comes back from Ottawa."

As he made small talk with the officers in the living room, Tibor tried to assure himself that the police would find nothing that would implicate him. He and Frankes had disposed of Leonard's things except for his watch and rings, which Tibor had simply moved to his own jewellery box. They'd taken the clothes to the other side of the island and dumped them into deep water. He doubted if they would be dredging the entire lake. At least not right away. By then, he and Frankes would be gone.

His thoughts were broken when the officer introduced to him as Vance entered the room, approached Sherlock and whispered something into his ear.

Sherlock nodded, then stood. "Gentlemen, I'm arresting you for the murder of a man known as Chief Longbow."

Rudley leaned over the desk, his brow furrowed. "Now, tell me again, Margaret, what does the necklace have to do with anything?"

"Quite a lot, it seems."

"You may extrapolate."

Margaret paused to form her thoughts. "As Miss Miller pointed out, when you have eliminated the impossible, whatever remains, however improbable, must be the truth."

"I believe Sherlock Holmes said that, Margaret."

"Miss Miller would have thought of it first had they been contemporaries." She continued. "Miss Miller was the first to point out that the arrival of Betty, the arrival of Sherry, and the murder of Chief Longbow were three unusual things that occurred at the same time."

"Margaret, we often have three unusual things happening at the same time, sometimes sequences of threes, triads multiplying like rabbits."

"Yes, we do, Rudley, but there are additional factors in this situation."

"Such as?"

"Sherry's odd behaviour, Betty's verbal clues…"

"Are the police depending on parrots now to solve cases?"

"Not as much as you may think." She gave him a stern look to warn him that he was disturbing her narrative. "But it was what Betty was saying that rang a bell for Detective Sherlock. Lloyd said the moment she mentioned certain phrases a light seemed to go on for him, and he began to backtrack through his notes."

"Now we're depending on Lloyd's acumen."

"Lloyd is a useful witness because he simply observes. His mind is a clean slate. He doesn't try to form theories. Advancing theories without adequate foundation can be a dangerous road to go down, Rudley."

"You're right about his mind being a clean slate."

"Then," she continued, "Detective Creighton, quite independently—well, in concert with Miss Miller and Mr. Simpson—realized the link between Sherry and Betty. Betty's reference to Sweetie rang a bell for him. The inscription on the necklace he inadvertently broke, was 'Happy Birthday, Sweetie.'"

Rudley's forehead rumpled. "And from these clues, the assumption is that Sherry had something to do with the death of Chief Longbow."

She swatted him on the arm. "Rudley, you'd make a terrible detective. The assumption is that Sherry has some connection to Betty and to whomever killed Chief Longbow."

"Sherry gave no indication she knew Betty." He paused. "Although, I don't know if I would be eager to admit being related to a sassy bird who eats us out of house and home and produces large quantities of guano."

"Sherry was, for some reason, not forthcoming, but that does not mean she is party to a murder."

"True. But she may be related in some way to the murderer."

Margaret considered this. "Perhaps she knew who killed Chief Longbow. Perhaps she was the victim of domestic violence by the same man. She ran away from him. He found out where she was. Perhaps he was skulking around looking for her when he encountered the chief."

"Why do you assume it was a him?"

"It usually is. But that doesn't matter for now. It is possible that she was fleeing a violent domestic situation when her boat sank. When she saw Detective Creighton on the lake, she concocted her story, hoping he could help her."

"If she wanted help, she should have told him the truth."

"She should have, Rudley, but she may not have had much faith in the police to protect her."

"I can relate to that." He knit his brows. "But where has she gone now?"

"She may have felt that she was still in danger so she's gone on the lam. Doesn't that make sense, Rudley?"

He sighed, put a arm around her shoulder. "As much as anything around here does, Margaret."

Creighton, who had been talking on his cell phone on the veranda, returned to the lobby just as Tim was entering from the kitchen with a carafe of coffee.

"Well," Rudley addressed Creighton, "did you get through to Sherlock?"

"Forget Sherlock. I spoke to Vance. They've just arrested two characters on an island east of Middleton."

Tim tilted his head. "Did you say on an island east of Middleton?"

Creighton helped himself to the coffee. "I did."

"Do you think that's Hiram's island?" Tim recounted his earlier conversation with the Benson sisters. "They thought an acquaintance of Hiram's, a man called Leonard Anderson, might be staying there this summer."

"Leonard Anderson!" Margaret turned to Rudley. "'Leonard is stupid.' That's the phrase Betty uttered that sent Detective Sherlock back to the island." She rubbed her hands together. "Oh, Rudley, isn't this exciting?"

"If you say so, Margaret."

"Vance says that the occupants of the cottage were an older man called Leonard and a manservant called Luther. They have both vanished," said Creighton.

"So," said Tim, "we have Leonard, this man Luther and Sherry disappearing all at the same time."

"Another coincidence," said Margaret with a sage nod.

Creighton turned to Tim. "You were saying the Benson sisters knew Leonard?"

"Apparently, his parents were friends of their father." Tim tittered. "According to Louise they were all spies."

Creighton frowned. "This case is getting curiouser and curiouser."

Chapter Thirty-one

Brisbois listened to Creighton's story as he sat across from him in a coffee shop along Middleton's lakeshore.

"So that's what happened," said Creighton. "The bird blabbed."

"And Sherlock made the connection."

"After everything had jiggled around in his brain for a while."

"That's the way we solve things sometimes," said Brisbois.

"The boys at the cottage had a pretty good story, but Sherlock nailed them with evidence linking them to the scene. The blood in the boathouse matched that of the guy, Frankes. Other trace evidence matched stuff on a wetsuit belonging to Frankes. He snagged the wetsuit on a nail in the boathouse at the Pleasant, left blood, tissue, and a tiny piece of his wetsuit behind. The guy, Tibor, had scratches on his neck. Tissue found under the nails of the chief matched his."

"Pretty compelling evidence, I would say."

"You'd think if a guy tore a hole in his wetsuit and nicked himself on a nail, he'd have the brains to get rid of the suit," Creighton said.

"Criminals always make the mistake of underestimating our intelligence," said Brisbois, taking a sip of his coffee. "Not to mention our persistence and deductive powers."

"Chalk up one for the good guys," Creighton said. After a long pause, he said, "I should have been more suspicious of Sherry."

"Maybe her story seemed far-fetched. But there was no reason to think she had done anything criminal" — he shrugged — "still isn't. She came across as a bit of an airhead when Mary and I met her at our barbeque. She never let down that persona — if it was a persona."

"Yes, but how many people forget the name of their employer or where they're employed, lose their identification, sink their boat...?" He squirmed, thinking how he had been bamboozled.

"Not many," Brisbois conceded. "But she would. I'd say she's a first-rate con artist."

"She's somehow connected to that parrot, and that parrot is connected to the guys on the island."

"Is Sherlock thinking the boys on the island knocked off the old guy and the servant, too?"

"Vance says he hasn't ruled anything out. They've got Interpol involved. Apparently the old man was quite a globetrotter."

"What business was he in?"

"Apparently, he was an art dealer, appraiser, and the like." Creighton chuckled. "Oh, here's an angle you'll like. The cottage the group was staying at belongs to Hiram, the Benson sisters' chauffeur."

"You've got to be kidding."

"No, I'm not. The sisters told Tim that Leonard's father was a friend of their father. Leonard's father was apparently connected to the art world too. Leonard had spent time on the island when he was younger. Anyway, Louise suggested that Leonard's parents were also spies."

"Louise thinks everybody's a spy."

"True," Creighton agreed. "In a way, Louise is sort of like Betty."

"Betty?"

"The parrot. They both pick up all sorts of things and blurt them out at the worst possible moments — for someone, at least."

"Maybe somebody should investigate those three."

"The Benson sisters?"

"Who knows? They could have been pulling the wool over our eyes for years with their harebrained act."

Creighton frowned. "Do you think it's an act?"

"No, but I could make just as good a case for them being con artists as I could for Sherry."

"I like that way of looking at it."

"That's why I'm such a good partner." Brisbois took another sip of his coffee and gave Creighton a sideways look. "I'll probably retire one of these days. Maybe you'll get to hook up with Sherlock."

Creighton rolled his eyes. "The little twit'd drive me nuts."

"He's methodical, he's thorough, he's willing to think outside the box."

"He still needed Miss Miller's help to link up a few things."

"Even the best of us need Miss Miller's help at one time or another."

Creighton shrugged. "Miss Miller is one thing. But a parrot?"

"Well, the parrot...Betty, was it? She probably expedited things. But, in the end, it was Dr. Jim's work that was critical. Without the DNA evidence, Sherlock couldn't have made a case. Dr. Jim," he mused, "now there's a man who never gets enough credit."

"So he says." Creighton drained his coffee. "So the boys — Tibor and Frankes — are still insisting they don't know where Leonard is."

"I guess they're sticking to their story he went to Boston."

"Well, if he's out there, they'll find him eventually. Leonard is well known in the art world. And his haunts are well known. He'll show up in one of them sooner or later."

"If he's alive."

"If he's alive," Creighton repeated. "They've got a team out around the island looking for him right now."

"So Sherlock isn't convinced he took off."

"Not entirely." Creighton picked up his plastic stir stick and bent it. "I wonder how many of these things they make every year."

"Probably enough to drive us all to extinction." Brisbois took a sip of his coffee. "So, no trace of Sherry?"

"Nope."

"So they think she might be with Leonard and the other guy."

"That's one theory."

Brisbois clapped him on the shoulder. "You know, Chester, I wouldn't worry too much about that girl. No matter where she is, I'm sure she's just fine."

"Probably."

Brisbois looked off over the lake. "I was thinking, we should treat ourselves tonight. I'll call Mary and ask her to meet us at the Pleasant for dinner."

Creighton smiled. "Sounds good."

The private plane headed south over the Atlantic.

"Sandwich, Leonard?"

Leonard patted his abdomen, then shrugged. "Why not? I must have lost a pound or two when you shaved my hair off."

"You look very handsome bald. Like a larger Yul Brynner."

"Hmm." He glanced out the window. "I don't get the feeling we're headed to Europe."

"How's your foot?"

"Much better. I think it'll make it now." He turned to look at her directly. "Why do I have the feeling you're keeping something from me?"

Cerise flashed him an innocent smile. "Have I ever kept anything from you?"

He smiled back. "I hope you'll be getting rid of that hideous makeup after we're settled."

"I'll keep it for a while, then I'll visit a plastic surgeon — just in case someone gets nosy."

"And I can grow my hair back."

"We'll see."

He sighed. "So I can never be Leonard Anderson again?"

"Of course not," she said, giving him an affectionate hug. You're Herr Jan Merkel. You're Austrian."

"Well, my German's good at least." He nodded. "I like that. Jan Merkel." He looked at her. "And you would be?"

"Sophie Bright. I'm just someone you picked up on your travels. I don't speak German. You're trying to teach me."

He pointed out the window. "It still doesn't look as if we're headed to Europe."

She handed him a bottled milkshake and flipped open a magazine. "Leonard?"

"Yes?"

"How do you feel about magic realism?"

"I've always rather liked the idea."

"Then you'll love Colombia."

"Colombia."

Leonard didn't ask any more questions. He'd spent a little time in Rio and Buenos Aires and always enjoyed South America. He thought he could forego London, which was damp, and St. Tropez, the social life of which wasn't what it had been in his day. He was sorry Cerise had to take risks on his behalf, consorting with criminal types to arrange forged passports, but he comforted himself with the knowledge that she hadn't done anything terribly criminal. All she had done was make a transaction with the mob to save her guardian — him! — from his avaricious nephew. She was an innocent. That thought made him laugh out loud. Cerise flicked him a glance, but he just shook his head and motioned for her to go back to her magazine.

And if the authorities caught up to him, what could they do with him? He was a senile old man, after all, being manipulated by people he couldn't resist. His moment of levity passed. He had caused Luella's death. That he could never take back. He turned to stare out the window, thinking of his house on St. Napoli, that lovely breeze off the ocean at night, his studio, his walks downtown, tea with Dreyfus.

He could never go back to St. Napoli. He would never see the Cartwrights again. That was his punishment.

"Well, Rudley," said Margaret. "It's all worked out."

"I suppose."

"At least we know who the chief really was and that his murderers have been apprehended."

"Clifton Watts, retired teacher from Manitoba," he mused. "What would possess him to become Chief Longbow? He must have had a good pension."

"His family did say he'd had a lifelong fascination with Grey Owl, Rudley."

"Not to mention he was inclined to be delusional."

"And the Phipps-Walkers are researching a good home for Betty. I'll miss her though."

"I won't."

"And Detective Sherlock has invited Tiffany to accompany him to the string quartet performance at the theatre."

"Mr. Bole invited both of them to accompany him," said Rudley.

"Mr. Bole is a romantic," said Margaret.

"I hear the boys are sticking to their story," said Rudley. "They happened by the boathouse when the chief fell in. They tried to help him, but he was already too far gone. They thought they would be blamed for his death so they stuffed him into the life-preserver box when they thought they heard someone coming."

"Every time I hear that explanation, it makes less sense."

"I suspect even a half-baked jury — the likes of which is to be found around here — would find that a little hard to swallow."

"And why were they wandering around in a boat in the middle of the night in wetsuits?"

"Not to mention the fact that the police divers found the uncle's suitcases sunk off the island. And an examination of the boats they claimed they had damaged on a rock shelf revealed they had been sabotaged."

"Officer Owens says they're still looking for the uncle, but they feel he may have met with misadventure." She paused. "I must say, Rudley, much of it doesn't make sense."

"The theory is they wanted the uncle's money. People will do anything for money."

"The murderers deny any knowledge of someone called Sherry. Perhaps she was using an alias. Perhaps she had nothing to do with them. It's all very confusing, Rudley."

"I don't think everything is supposed to make sense."

"Good thing, too, Rudley, since so little does."

He smiled. "The important thing, Margaret, is that the murder has been solved. We no longer have to put up with that snotty Sherlock or that bird-brained Sherry."

"Dirty bird," said Betty.

He made a threatening gesture toward her.

"Now, Rudley."

He did a little pirouette behind the desk. "And tomorrow night, Margaret."

She clapped her hands. "Music Hall." She paused. "Do you think the rest of the season will be uneventful?"

He sighed. "We can only hope."

About the Author

Judith Alguire's previous novels include *Pleasantly Dead*, *The Pumpkin Murders*, *A Most Unpleasant Wedding*, *Peril at the Pleasant*, and *Many Unpleasant Returns*, the first five books of the Rudley Mysteries, as well as *All Out* and *Iced*, both of which explored the complex relationships of sportswomen on and off the playing field. Her short stories, articles and essays have also appeared in such publications as *The Malahat Review* and *Harrowsmith*, and she is a past member of the editorial board of the *Kingston Whig-Standard*. A graduate of Queen's University, she has recently retired from nursing.

ISBN 978-1927426-57-9

Also available as an eBook
ISBN 978-1-927426-58-6

Everyone at the Pleasant Inn is looking forward to a very merry Christmas. Oh, irascible proprietor Trevor Rudley has his usual complaints about Mrs. Blount's non-traditional floral arrangements. And he's sure he won't like housekeeper Tiffany's new beau, Dan Thornton, who's a writer, of all things. But it's Christmas. The guests are excitedly preparing the Christmas pageant and chef Gregoire is spoiling everyone with his delightful cuisine. There's a snowstorm on the way, but Trevor and Margaret Rudley have everything under control. Surely nothing catastrophic could happen.

Bad things do happen, of course. Once the snow begins, it seems like it will never stop. Poor Margaret runs over a man lying in the road during a whiteout. Walter Sawchuck almost chokes when someone doctors his Mrs. Dash. And those disturbing little Santas begin to appear, each one representing a gruesome event in the Pleasant's past. Then a dead body is found hanged in the coach house. As the snow continues to fall, paranoia at the Pleasant mounts.

ISBN 978-1927426-26-5

Also available as an eBook
ISBN 978-1-927426-27-2

Margaret Rudley has finally persuaded her husband to take a vacation, a week-long canoeing expedition in Northern Ontario. Rudley hates the idea of leaving the Pleasant, but he is reluctant to deny her a cherished dream. They set off, with long-time guests Elizabeth Miller, Edward Simpson, and the Phipps-Walkers, and a pair of neophytes, Vern Peters and Eric Turnbull. They leave the Pleasant and a few regular guests, including the Sawchucks and their incorrigible eight-year-old grandchildren, Ned and Nora, in the capable hands of Mrs. Millotte.

But contrary to their hopes, it is chaos at the Pleasant. Ned and Nora disappear and a ransom note is received by the local paper. Tiffany encounters an intruder in the kitchen. The laundryman's truck is stolen. And a serial murderer is on the lam in the vicinity. Detectives Brisbois and Creighton are on the scene to investigate these various crimes, including the appearance of a dead body in a ditch a few miles from the Pleasant.

Meanwhile, the canoeists continue downriver, oblivious to the threat that lurks around the next bend.

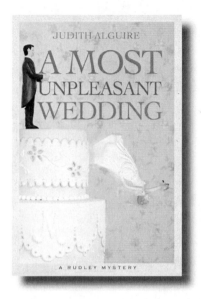

ISBN 978-18987109-99-1

Also available as an eBook
ISBN 978-1927426-07-4

Another summer, and the Pleasant Inn, nestled in beautiful Ontario cottage country, is filled to capacity. This season is especially exciting, as perennial guests Miss Miller and her long-time admirer Mr. Simpson have chosen to marry at the Inn. The guests and staff are clamouring to be involved, particularly Bonnie Lawrence, a young wife adrift while her husband is off fishing. Margaret and Trevor Rudley are delighted to host the wedding, and barring Mrs. Lawrence's obsessive interfering, everything is set to go off without a hitch.

But when a neighbour is found dead in the woods behind the inn, the possibility of a joyous occasion starts looking distinctly less likely. Detective Michel Brisbois, who is heading up the case, is back on the Pleasant Inn's doorstep. Rudley barely tolerates the presence of the police, who are once again on site interviewing the guests as possible suspects. Even though she's prenuptially preoccupied, the fearless Miss Miller refuses to be left out from solving yet another murder at the Pleasant…much to her own peril.

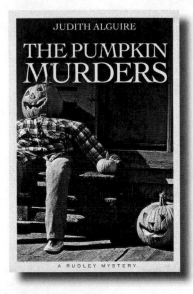

JUDITH ALGUIRE

THE PUMPKIN MURDERS

A RUDLEY MYSTERY

ISBN 978-18987109-45-8

Also available as an eBook
ISBN 978-18987109-69-4

Autumn returns to Ontario cottage country. Leaves redden. Pumpkins ripen. And Trevor and Margaret Rudley, proprietors of the Pleasant Inn, expect nothing more than a few Halloween high jinks to punctuate the mellow ambiance of their much-loved hostelry. However, the frost is barely on the pumpkin when Gerald, a female-impersonator friend of the Pleasant's esteemed cook Gregoire, turns up, dragging his very frightened friend Adolph behind. After witnessing a drug deal in Montreal, they're on the lam, hoping to blend into the Pleasant's pleasant rhythms until the heat is off. Alas, they hope in vain.

As the bodies pile up, the intrepid Elizabeth Miller jumps into the fray, fully armed with her peculiar intuition, her maddening charm, and her devoted swain, Edward Simpson, who proves a useful fellow behind the wheel of a car. Detective Michel Brisbois, in the past bested by Miss Miller in rooting out unpleasantness at the Pleasant, finds himself racing — quite literally — to keep up with his amateur challenger. But when the chips are down — as they inevitably are — it's the laziest creature on Earth who ends up saving the day for the kindly and rather eccentric folk of Ontario's most peculiar country hotel.

ISBN 978-18987109-37-3

Also available as an eBook.
ISBN 978-18987109-68-7

Trevor and Margaret Rudley have had their share of misfortunes at the Pleasant Inn, the cherished Ontario cottage-country hotel they've owned for twenty-five years. There have been boating accidents, accidental poisonings, and then there was that unfortunate ski-lift incident. But this year their hopes are high for the summer season. However, barely a week goes by before their hopes are dashed. There's a dead body making a nuisance of itself in the wine cellar, and it's nobody the Rudleys know.

The guests at the Pleasant Inn, a wealthy and eccentric lot, are dying for distraction, and one of them, Miss Miller, sets out to solve the case of the deceased, relying on wild speculation, huge leaps of logic, and the assistance of her great admirer, Edward Simpson, who is too smitten to dissuade her from her adventure in detection. Challenging her in the race to resolution is the disciplined Detective Brisbois, whose deep-rooted insecurities about his style and status are aroused by the hotel guests' careless assumption of privilege. When Brisbois stumbles into peril of his own, the intrepid Miss Miller is the only one left who can solve the crime.